In Memory of M...
Missing in Action, 25 March 1942, at the age of 23
Son of Myer Koff & Leah Rosenthal
~ Brother of Jerome

Cousin Manny, you are gone but you are not,
and never will be, forgotten

Deadly Evidence

Clea Koff

avon.

Published by AVON
A division of HarperCollins*Publishers* Ltd
1 London Bridge Street
London SE1 9GF

www.harpercollins.co.uk

HarperCollins*Publishers*
Macken House,
39/40 Mayor Street Upper,
Dublin 1
D01 C9W8, Ireland

A Paperback Original [2025]
1
Copyright © Clea Koff 2025

Clea Koff asserts the moral right to
be identified as the author of this work.

A catalogue record for this book is available from the British Library.

ISBN: 978-0-00-868779-3

This novel is entirely a work of fiction.
The names, characters and incidents portrayed in it are
the work of the author's imagination. Any resemblance to
actual persons, living or dead, events or localities is
entirely coincidental.

Set in Sabon LT Std by HarperCollins*Publishers* India

Printed and bound in the UK using 100% Renewable
Electricity at CPI Group (UK) Ltd

MIX
Paper | Supporting
responsible forestry
FSC™ C007454

This book contains FSC™ certified paper and other controlled
sources to ensure responsible forest management.

For more information visit: www.harpercollins.co.uk/green

A note for the reader

Although Agency 32/1 does not exist, it should.

It is based on the Missing Persons Identification Resource Center, a California non-profit founded by the author in 2004 to link families of missing persons with coroners holding thousands of unidentified bodies across the United States. MPID has since closed.

- The plot and characters of this book are fictional.
- The statistics on unidentified bodies are fact.
- Forensic profiles of missing persons are hope.

Prologue

It offended him to see the dirt fly into the corpse's eyes. He leaned over the body to close the eyelids. They wouldn't stay shut. He closed the zipper on the enclosing bag and resumed his task. When the bag was fully covered by soil, he applied the finishing touches of old bamboo leaves. He made it look as though they had simply fallen there from above – which they had, but long before he had chosen this spot and prepared the grave.

The bamboo grove was thick and established. No one pushed their way through the forest of smooth trunks anymore, not since the rare black bamboo specimens had been planted at the perimeter. Back here, the ground was padded with years of old leaves. It was the perfect place to dig and bury: bamboo didn't mind its roots being cut through.

He backed away from the site and looked at the ground from several angles, noting how the moonlight was filtered and diffused here. The ground looked flat. As long as no one came through in the next few weeks, the corpse would never be found. Decomposition was guaranteed thanks to a flourishing insect population. He had looked it up.

Turning his back on the grave, he walked away, his mind already on the next target he had found to kill. He was toying with using something other than the poison; he felt he had earned the right to choose his own method this time. He knew the technical terms. Blunt force trauma. Sharp force trauma. Asphyxia. But the one that kept bobbing up in his mind was 'floater', with its attendant challenges for CSIs looking for trace evidence. Not easy to find the right body of water in LA but . . . doable. He walked on, his tread silent on the springy ground but the voice in his head as loud as ever: *Stop dicking around, Junior. Finish it. Finish them all.*

2005

DAY ONE

WEDNESDAY

1

There was just a flash of something huge and dark vaulting over the intersection but it was enough to get Jayne to snap to it, almost pulling a muscle in her neck. It *was* a Chevrolet Suburban, but even as it hurtled down the cross street, she spotted the bumper label: *TCP*. A limo, not a government vehicle.

Not, specifically, an FBI vehicle driven by Special Agent Scott Houston.

Jayne wished she hadn't looked. It was a sign of weakness. She knew that Scott was in Atlanta. He would be back in Los Angeles by Friday and they would go on their first date.

But, Jayne wondered, what if he *was* back and hadn't called? The formulation of such a question due to the mere sighting of a Suburban was another sign of weakness. Jayne shook her head.

'Etch-a-Sketch,' Steelie said from the passenger side of the truck's bench seat.

Jayne glanced at her best friend. Steelie was flexing the bill of her faded pink baseball cap in the palm of her hand. The action was unnecessary because the cap already had the perfect downward curve that allowed Steelie to observe the world with her shrewd blue eyes while keeping her own expression shielded.

The traffic light turned green and Jayne pressed on the

gas to take her old Ford pick-up through the intersection with a roar of engine noise. 'Etch-a-Sketch?'

Steelie put her cap on over her short hair but the silvery-blonde wisps above her ears flared out jauntily as always. She said, 'You're like an Etch-a-Sketch toy, the way you shake your head to clear your mind.'

'Oh.'

'So. Was it Scott or Scott?'

Jayne tried not to laugh. 'You think you're so funny, don't you?'

'You're laughing.'

'I haven't progressed to full laughter. Too nervous.'

'Pshaw!' Steelie scoffed. 'You've known Scott for five years—'

'But,' Jayne interrupted, 'four point nine of those years only involved long-distance phone calls.'

Steelie waved her hand dismissively. 'And within a week of living in the same city, you locked lips. You said the kiss was a-ma-zing—'

'I didn't say that!'

'Didn't have to. Don't interrupt closing arguments, please, and get in the left lane. Where was I? Oh yeah, the kiss was a-ma-zing and then he asked you on a date by way of a gilt-edged invite – formerly entered as Exhibit A. But! You didn't reply to him, either by letter or telephonic means, so, if anyone has reason to be nervous, it's Very Special Agent Houston. I rest my case.'

'Steelie, the invite was just an inside joke between me and Scott from the day we had lunch at Cal Plaza.'

Steelie lost her self-satisfied smile. 'This is new evidence.'

Jayne spoke while watching for a traffic break so she

could turn into the top end of the UCLA campus. 'Not really. It's just . . . so silly compared to what happened when we kissed. That felt like the start of something so I didn't think I needed to actually reply to the invite.' She had the chance to make the turn and the Ford surged through the intersection, leaning on its suspension.

Steelie called out, 'Sidebar!'

Jayne rolled her eyes. 'Do I really have to pretend we're in court? You're the only one of us who's ever been a lawyer.'

Steelie's expression gave Jayne her answer so she played along, albeit reluctantly. 'What do I say again? Approach.'

'Okay, you both feel the same way about each other—'

'I thought we did but now I'm not so sure.' Jayne didn't want to spell out that what had been pleasurable anticipation of a reunion with Scott had turned, in just a few days, to continual second-guessing of their nascent relationship.

Steelie was unmoved. 'You have no evidence for that. You just need to go with the flow. What's the worst that could happen?'

'The worst?' Jayne pictured this as she slowed for a series of stop signs taking them further into the leafy campus. 'Scott and I are on the couch watching a movie. A car backfires. I hit the floor. He does not. He then leaves, never to return.'

'I'm not buying that. Scott already knows you have . . . issues.'

'Thank you for not calling it PTSD this time. But it's one thing for him to know I have issues; it's another to see them in action.'

7

'But you know he has issues himself!'

'Not like my issues.' Even Jayne heard her unreasonably stubborn tone.

'Inadmissible. You can't compare two people's post-traumatic stress disorders.'

'Mine's bigger than yours? I can't say that?' Jayne said with irony as she pointed an interrogative finger at the upcoming lane on the right.

'Hey, if you can joke about it, you're getting better. And yes, that's our turn.' Steelie sat up straighter as she looked around. 'Never been up here before.'

'There wasn't much here when we were students.'

'You mean back in the days of horse and buggy?'

'More like stone tablets. I feel ancient today.'

'You always say that but you don't look ancient. You look like you're in *lurve*.'

Jayne felt herself blushing and found that she couldn't speak.

Steelie groaned. 'I hope you're not planning to spend another five years holding hands with Scott, only on the couch instead of down a phone line. You're thirty-five. He's what? Thirty-seven? Thirty-eight? You two need to get on with it. Marriage, babies, all that stuff mainstream people do.'

'Wow,' Jayne said. 'I'm increasingly concerned that my mother is employing you as an agent of her state. You usually deconstruct marriage as a self-sacrificing cog in a capitalist wheel.'

Steelie smiled. 'I won't deny that. But that's marriage. Easily a decade or two away for you and Scott at the rate you've been going. Plenty of time for me to change my mind. In the meantime, I can keep being my little old anti-capitalist, cynical, single self. Maybe with the addition of a dog.'

Jayne pulled up near an opening in a chain-link fence surrounding a field where a man wearing jeans and a blue and gold UCLA T-shirt had begun walking toward them, his worn leather boots sending up little spurts of dust in the short, patchy grass. She said, 'A dog won't love that fakin' bacon you eat.'

'My vegetarian bacon is delicious. I just need to make sure my dog never tastes real bacon!'

'You're talking like you already have a dog.'

The man had arrived at Steelie's open window and rested his elbows on the frame in a familiar manner. 'I didn't know you had a dog.'

'She doesn't,' Jayne clarified from the driver's seat.

He said, 'Am I imagining it or do you both have bruises on your faces?'

Steelie was chipper. 'You should see the other guy.'

He looked at her appraisingly. 'And you've gone more gray since I last saw you.'

'Just more steely, Mitch.' She flicked her silver sideburns.

He laughed and opened her door. Steelie hopped down and they gave each other a bear hug.

Jayne and Steelie had liked Mitch Nelson from the moment they had met him at UCLA, when he was at graduate school studying archaeology to their anthropology. After graduation, he'd gone on to a steady field gig at an ancient site in Turkey but as soon as he and his wife had been expecting their first child, they had returned to the States.

Now he was head of cultural resource management at UCLA. He'd once called it his first 'real' job and, despite receiving occasional pressure to speedily clear construction sites for unfettered building, he remained unhurried – a man who'd seen time measured in millennia, not just minutes.

Which was why his urgent tone on the phone that morning had motivated Jayne and Steelie to collect their toolkits and make the trek to Westwood from their office in East LA.

Jayne alighted from the truck to come around and embrace Mitch.

He said, 'Thanks for coming over so fast.'

'You said it was time-sensitive.'

'Now that you're here, I can tell you why. It's still wearing its birthday suit.'

'It's fleshed?' Jayne glanced at Steelie.

Mitch nodded grimly.

'But then why isn't the LA County Coroner here? Or are they on their way?'

'They're not here because they haven't been called yet.'

Jayne said, 'But Steelie and I can't legally examine a fleshed body on the back of our agency's non-profit status, Mitch. Our remit is to profile missing persons to match them with bodies, not the other way around.'

Steelie cut in. 'And you won't just need the coroner, you'll need the LAPD too.'

Mitch held up his hand. 'Preachin' to the choir, Steelie. This wasn't my idea. Actually, calling you two *was* my idea but only after the top brass said they wanted an ultra-quiet second opinion on my first opinion that this body didn't fall under NAGPRA.'

10

Jayne could understand the brass's concern on a basal level: since the advent of the federal Native American Graves Protection and Repatriation Act, universities had been required to restore to tribal possession the archaeological 'collections' of prehistoric and historic American Indian culture – culture that could include people's skeletons.

The university brass would want this body handed over to its descendants as soon as possible and with minimal fuss. Calling in the LAPD by mistake would be fuss, maximus. Calling in two UCLA alumni who happened to be forensic anthropologists to give a back-up opinion on the down-low before calling the police could sound like a very good idea to anyone wanting to avoid such fuss.

Steelie was already putting her toolkit back into the bed of the pick-up truck. 'In that case, I'm not bringing any equipment. I say we suit up and take Polaroids so we can prove that we didn't disturb diddly.'

Mitch grimaced. 'It's already been disturbed. Backhoe tugged the body or maybe just the clothes before we realized it was there.'

'Happens all the time,' Jayne said. 'It's not like this was a planned exhumation.'

'It was a groundbreaking!' Mitch sounded exasperated. He was gesturing at a sign further along the fenceline.

Jayne looked over. *Site of the New UCLA Extensions Center – Commencement June 2005.* Now delayed, she thought.

She tried to reassure her friend. 'Either way, postmortem disturbance happens. You can't break ground with a toothpick.'

Mitch nodded but he still looked disappointed and tense.

11

Once Jayne and Steelie were in protective suits, booties and gloves, they crossed the grass together. Seeing them, the backhoe driver climbed back into his cab, apparently unsure if he'd be needed again. On approach, Jayne saw that he still wore a look of shock.

Mitch nodded to the two campus police officers chatting near the backhoe. The cops initially came closer as Jayne and Steelie approached the cut in the ground, then hung back when the sharp, tangy smell of decomposition permeated the air.

Steelie had been taking Polaroids as she walked but now lowered the camera.

She said, 'Heat, body, flies. A trifecta.'

Jayne mentally concurred. The cut in the ground showed that the backhoe had made several passes before snagging the body. It was still in situ, its right side exposed by the cut while the left side was encased in earth. The body looked like that of an adult, still clothed, and decomposing but not skeletonized; flies were buzzing with frenetic activity wherever tissue was exposed.

Despite Mitch's concern that the body had been disturbed, the backhoe driver had done remarkably well to notice any drag on the bucket because only one side of the clothing had been pulled downwards and it hadn't even been completely torn.

Steelie pointed this out to Mitch.

He nodded. 'I'll leave you to it, then.' He went to stand with the campus police officers.

Jayne glanced back at him. He was clearly discomfited by the freshness of this body compared to the many skeletons she knew he'd excavated in his career. The sooner they could wrap this up, the better. She said to Steelie, 'Are we agreed that the remains don't look juvenile?'

'Agreed.'

'I'll get a read on sex and you'll do age?'

'Works for me.' Steelie readied the camera.

Once Jayne was down in the cut, the heat built up inside her protective suit and she felt sweat start to form in her cleavage. Waving away flies, she crouched close to the body and ran her gloved fingers under the rim of the eye socket while her thumb traveled above the opening.

She called up to Steelie. 'Well-developed supraorbital torus and smooth supraorbital rim.' Then she palpated both the outside and inside of the mandible through the remaining tissue. 'I think I'm feeling a flaring gonial angle. So, that indicates male and post-pubescent. Your turn.'

Steelie gave Jayne a hand to climb out of the cut, handed over the Polaroid camera and said, 'Don't forget to take a drink of water. You look overheated already.'

Jayne removed a layer of gloves and reached for the water that they'd brought with them. The first sip was warm, tasted of bottle, and gave her immediate déjà vu.

She was back in Kosovo, at an exhumation of a clandestine grave one July years before. Their UN war crimes investigation team had been waiting for a military escort and drinking bottled water that was actually hot from the sun. The wait had allowed time to contemplate the break in the surface of the earth that had exposed not just soil and grubs and roots, but whole bones, hanks of hair, loosened teeth, scraps of cloth. Human leavings.

There had been countless other quiet moments like that, before or between digging, and they had always felt the same regardless of the country, the graves transcending geography and borders because the dead speak only one language around the world.

Jayne shook her head and then thought, *Etch-a-Sketch*. She'd never noticed until Steelie had pointed it out that she shook her head physically to clear her mind. Or maybe it was a new thing.

She focused on documenting Steelie, who was carefully pulling the shirtsleeve up by an inch on the body's arm. Flies disturbed from their exploration of the corpse lifted off in phalanxes.

'I've got a good look at the radius and a so-so one of the ulna but they're both fused. Like you said, he's an adult.' Steelie peered closely at the bone that was circular at the end. 'Jayne.'

Jayne lowered the camera. 'Why are you whispering?'

Steelie flicked her eyes over Jayne's shoulder.

Jayne followed her gaze and saw the campus police officers, but they were too far away to hear Steelie. Mitch was even further away, greeting several people arriving on a golf cart. But Steelie was still gesturing for her to come closer.

Jayne climbed back down into the cut and crouched, knees popping, until she was close enough to see what Steelie had seen. 'Oh.'

Steelie continued in her confidential tone. 'You saw the line of fusion? That makes him an adult but young. Young enough to be in the right age range for that missing UCLA student.'

'I know.' Jayne knew exactly who Steelie was talking about, could picture his serious smile on the missing person poster a year or so ago. Her heart started to pound as her eyes traveled over the body, wondering if it was him. Why hadn't this occurred to her the minute Mitch had called that morning? When he hadn't given details, she'd imagined he needed a consult on unusual trauma on an ancient skeleton. When he'd later informed them that the remains were still in their 'birthday suit', she'd imagined some off-campus fight where the victor had made use of a quiet corner of campus to do a body dump. The one thing she hadn't imagined was that it would be the body of a student. Did she have blinders on?

Steelie had been watching her. 'Well, what do you think we should do?'

'What we were already going to do: tell them to call the police.'

'But this could be him.'

Jayne found herself arguing. 'You don't know enough about him to say this is him.'

'I know his name is Jared Stilson. And he went missing over a year ago.'

'Fine, but he's not ours. We don't have an agency profile on him. If we were to tell them it might be him, who knows what they'd do. They could announce it. They could call his folks. And then it could turn out to not be him. Just because we're at UCLA doesn't make this the body of a UCLA student. Anyway, look at the hair.'

'I noticed it.'

'The missing person poster for Jared Stilson identified him as white – and I don't remember his photo sparking any discussion between us – but this hair is more like mine.'

'Wavy-curly.'

'Because I'm mixed, not because I'm handy with a curling iron.'

'Those posters aren't always accurate,' Steelie grumbled.

'Which is my point. We can't be accurate either because we aren't getting a proper look at the body and we don't have identifying information on him from his family. Now, if I could just . . .?' Jayne gestured with the camera.

Steelie moved out of the way and Jayne leaned forward in her crouch with some effort. Her lower back was the main reason she felt ancient, thanks to time spent exhuming mass graves without enough space to bend the knees when lifting heavy corpses and even heavier grave dirt.

Mitch walked up. He eyed the body. 'Burial at about three feet?'

Steelie nodded. 'Your usual lazy perp. Can't even be bothered to dig the whole six.'

'Ready to tell them what I tried to tell them earlier today?' He nodded his head toward the men from the golf cart. 'We've got two deans and a vice-provost who came in person to make sure I was doing my job correctly.'

Jayne and Steelie climbed out of the cut, de-suited and followed Mitch.

'Gentlemen,' Mitch said once they reached the administrators, who'd been standing well away from the cut with its stench. 'These are the two Bruins I told you about from Agency 32/1. They're forensic anthropologists with extensive experience of both modern and historic exhumations.'

He made the introductions.

One of the deans smoothed a hand over his wavy white hair. He looked under strain. 'Thank you for coming at such short notice. What would you recommend as the next step?'

Jayne said, 'We've examined the remains without exposing them further but it is already clear that this is a matter for the coroner's office and probably the Los Angeles Police Department.'

The dean exchanged a worried glance with his colleagues. 'You're absolutely sure it's not Native American? The police would be an unnecessary complication.'

Steelie frowned lightly. 'Um, Native Americans still live and die in the present day, not just thousands of years ago.'

The dean's eyebrows came together. 'I don't follow . . .?'

Jayne thought Mitch looked gratified by Steelie's pedantic interjection. He would have already tried telling the dean that 'Native American' was not a synonym for 'prehistoric'. But Jayne didn't think it was the best time for Steelie to pontificate.

Jayne got in before Steelie's rejoinder. 'We are confident that NAGPRA will not apply to these remains.'

He nodded, relieved, and thereby confirmed her read on him: he was worried that the body could be ancient despite the fact that it was still decomposing. If the body found today did turn out to be a couple thousand years old, then it wasn't a body, it was a hot potato.

The other administrators also seemed to accept this conclusion, having heard it first from Mitch and now from them, and had moved on to the new worry that this was likely a modern homicide. They thanked the scientists and turned away into a huddle, already talking about calling the LAPD. Mitch indicated for Jayne and Steelie to follow him back to where they'd parked outside the chain-link fence.

But Steelie slowed her pace and gripped Jayne's forearm. 'I've just realized that if the body in that grave is Jared Stilson's, then odds are that this is a case of "student missing from campus, killed on campus, dumped on campus". And what are the odds on who would do that?'

Jayne answered, 'Someone else on campus.'

Steelie tilted her head southwards toward the buildings. There was now a small crowd watching them from beyond the chain-link fence. Some people were using cell phones; others were holding backpacks or books. Most looked curious, some worried, some were talking to each other. A couple of people were standing alone.

Looked at through Steelie's filter, these ones weren't alone; they were loners.

Jayne almost came to a halt. The only reason she didn't smack herself on the forehead was that she'd just been in close proximity to biohazard. She'd learned not to touch her face in those conditions long ago. But she had clearly not learned another lesson – one only a few weeks old: don't put yourself in a killer's crosshairs by waltzing into crime scenes.

2

When Special Agents Scott Houston and Eric Ramos rounded the corner in the FBI's LA headquarters, they saw their boss leaning against the doorway to their office as he talked to Lance, their administrator. On seeing the agents, Lance sagged – only slightly, but Scott caught it and he knew why. Supervisory Special Agent Craig Turner would have been holding Lance by the throat until he provided a suitable explanation for why Scott and Eric weren't already in their office, given that they were only coming in that morning from a domestic terminal at LAX.

Turner's chokeholds were hands-free but they were still chokeholds.

'SSA Turner,' Scott said once they reached him.

'Sir,' Eric added for his part.

Lance crept away when Turner shifted his focus onto the agents. 'Welcome back, gentlemen. Did you enjoy the week in your old stomping grounds?'

Eric briefly tracked Lance's departure. 'It felt good to close that case.'

Turner used a long-fingered hand to usher them into their own office. He stayed just inside the doorway, legs spread, arms crossed over his lean chest.

'Did you see SSA Franks get hauled in by OPR?'

The FBI's Office of Professional Responsibility was like any internal affairs department: it wasn't talked about with

19

enthusiasm. Turner certainly didn't betray any. Not that his voice ever betrayed enthusiasm. That was as legendary as his stare, his unblinking blue eyes rarely revealing his thoughts. Bureau agents who had trained under him called him the Iron Curtain because 'you never know what's going on back there'. But in just two months of being posted to his unit, Scott and Eric had discovered that the evolution of Turner's nickname from the acronym IC to 'Ice' was more apropos because the man actually had a melting point.

He had trusted their methods and instincts as they had pursued a serial killer who had evaded them at their previous posting in Atlanta. Turner had also run interference with their old boss, Supervisory Special Agent Franks, when Franks' personal vendetta against Scott had almost derailed the successful completion of that investigation. Despite the Ice Man's show of faith, the atmosphere in his presence remained frosty.

Scott spoke cautiously. 'We never actually saw SSA Franks because we were primarily at the hospital, on the King interrogation.'

'And here you are, back two days early. You did finish your reports before leaving?'

'Yes, sir,' Eric said. 'They're with the prosecutors now.'

'What's their take on us using Agency 32/1 for direct gathering of missing person data on King's other victims?'

Scott immediately felt a frisson of electricity sparked by the thought of seeing Jayne again. 'They're good with it as long as we have an MOU with the Agency.'

'You have the draft for me?'

Scott opened his briefcase and pulled out the folder that

held the Memorandum of Understanding he and Eric had worked on during the past week.

Turner took the folder and opened it. 'I need Legal to go over this. Have you taken the temperature over at Thirty-Two One?'

Scott cleared his throat. 'We don't have an indication from them yet.'

'You did reassure them, as I requested, that they wouldn't again be physically assaulted while working on our behalf?'

Scott flinched. He didn't need a reminder that he'd had to lift a semi-conscious Jayne up from a blood-soaked floor with Steelie looking on, her own face red and swollen from a punch thrown by a deranged suspect.

Turner was scanning the document and didn't wait for a response. 'I'll let the scientists know how seriously we're taking their safety when they arrive.'

'Jayne's coming here? And Steelie?' Scott cringed inwardly; Turner would have caught the late addition.

Turner looked up from the document, eyes narrowed. 'I've asked them to brief me on their methods. I want to see where else we can use them.' He closed the folder. 'And if I want you in the meeting, I'll call you, so stay in the building.' He left the room, his swift movements as economical as usual.

Scott dropped into his chair.

Eric began unpacking his briefcase. 'Hoo boy, am I gonna enjoy watching this.'

'Maybe he won't notice.'

'The Ice Man not notice that you're in a room with the

21

chick you've dug for five – count them, five – years when you're only days away from your first date? No way. Especially not now you shit your pants right in front of him at the mention of her name. Why'd you squeak it out like that? *Jayne, sir? Coming here, sir?*' He chuckled.

Scott groaned. He sat watching Eric unpack. 'This'll torpedo the MOU. You know how Turner is about conflicts of interest – even a whiff of 'em.'

'But you told me you don't want Thirty-Two One to sign the MOU.'

'That's only because I don't want them getting targeted by the perps we go after.'

'Then if Turner kills the MOU, you get what you want.' Eric sat down at his desk.

Scott paused in thought. Then he said, 'But I also wonder how we would have cracked the King case without them.'

'Then it's either the MOU or hangin' with Jayne. It's a clear choice, partner.'

Scott gave an expressive shrug.

'Oh, no,' Eric cautioned. 'I know that look. You think you can have it all, don't you? For a guy whose knees were shivering from the cold a couple of minutes ago, you're getting pretty cocky.'

'I'm thinking that Turner doesn't need to know about the potential conflict of interest.'

'No, Scott. You don't know where he's got his eyes and ears. LA is his town, not ours – not yet.'

'We'd just have to keep it between us. We know how to do that.'

'Your job could be on the line.'

'Not with Thirty-Two One helping us close cases.'

'They're not superheroes,' Eric groused. 'Although Steelie *is* a hundred and ten pounds of whoop-ass.'

'So, you've got my back on this?'

Eric sighed. 'Do you have to ask?'

Scott grinned.

3

Jayne sat on the dropped tailgate of her Ford F-150, watching Mitch and the campus police officers. The officers had asked the anthropologists to hand their Polaroid photographs directly to the LAPD to avoid an extra step in chain of custody, so they were stuck waiting on their arrival.

But her gaze repeatedly slid off Mitch to linger on the crowd in the distance. It was too late to hide the license plate on her truck or mask their identities. They would already have been photographed by the camera Jayne had decided Jared Stilson's killer would be carrying. Unless the body wasn't Jared Stilson but John Doe and the murderer had only been on campus once, to dump the body, thereafter hightailing it to . . . Canada.

She tried this theory out on Steelie.

Steelie raised her sunglasses and searched Jayne's face. 'You taking some happy pills I don't know about?'

'Just trying to be optimistic.'

'Optimism isn't as useful as a good weapon in situations like this.'

They turned around at the sound of tires displacing gravel behind them. A mushroom-colored sedan with a CA EXEMPT license plate pulled up and a man and woman emerged from it. Without their suit jackets on, the LAPD badges on their belts were visible, glinting in the sunlight.

A white van had followed them with the word CORONER emblazoned on the side and was now disgorging jump-suited personnel.

Mitch went over to meet the group, and then pointed out Steelie and Jayne by the truck. Jayne recognized Jenny Sweetzer, who gave them a wave before bending her head to catch whatever Mitch was explaining. Sweetzer was one of two forensic anthropologists on call to the LA County Coroner's Office.

Mitch led the newcomers through the fence to the grave without stopping to speak to Jayne and Steelie, but within minutes, the two detectives were backtracking across the weedy scrubland, heading straight for them. They both looked to be in their early forties, but where the woman had the trim muscularity of a Secret Service agent, the man looked as though he'd paired a loose shirt with a beautiful tie to camouflage a recently discovered beer belly. They had the decency to lift their dark sunglasses when they arrived but that didn't make it any easier to read their expressions.

'Detective Matt West,' the man said by way of introduction. 'My partner, Detective Theresa Sanchez. LAPD Homicide Special Section.'

Steelie introduced herself and Jayne.

Sanchez was flipping to a page in a small notepad. 'You're the ones who approached the body?'

'Yep,' Steelie said. 'Here are our Polaroids. The only photos we took.'

West took the stack and glanced through it casually. 'We understand you made some conclusions?'

'Not conclusions,' Jayne said. 'Just observations.'

Sanchez frowned as she read her notes. 'But you told the

25

dean it was the body of an adult male.'

Jayne felt like this was already getting out of control. She didn't want to end up being on a witness stand defending herself against whatever was in the detective's notes. 'No.'

Sanchez looked up at Jayne's firm tone. 'No?'

'We said probable male.'

Sanchez's pen hovered over the page. 'Does that mean probably male?'

Steelie intervened and her tone was almost breezy compared to Jayne's. 'It means we had a quick look at a body where only some of what we needed for an assessment was available. What we could observe, or touch actually, had male characteristics. Who knows what the rest of the body has to say.'

Sanchez nodded. 'Got it: you couldn't be sure it was male.'

As Jayne watched Sanchez make another note, she realized the detective hadn't been trying to nail them down to future testimony. She was trying to ensure she understood and could therefore use their observations.

Sanchez looked back over at Steelie. 'Now, the dean raised the outside possibility that this isn't a criminal matter but an ancient body that's been dressed in modern clothes. What are your thoughts on that?'

'Sounds like a crime to me,' Steelie said lightly.

West chuckled at Steelie's joke but Sanchez looked like she was still expecting a serious answer.

Somehow, that made Jayne feel expansive toward her. She supplied, 'The body is dressed in pants with stretch in them but that wasn't the only reason we thought it was buried within the past five years. It's also still decomposing

26

and we didn't see any sign of fly larval activity, so that could mean it was buried fresh. The coroner's team might find some evidence to the contrary, of course.'

Steelie held up a finger. 'Um, are you two over here asking for our very limited observations because Sweetzer just told you to get the hell out of her crime scene?'

Sanchez finally smiled – slightly – as she said, 'She wasn't even that polite.'

Steelie let out a short bark of laughter. 'You've worked with her before, then.'

Sanchez pointed a thumb at her partner. 'She calls him the Hovercraft.'

'Aha,' Steelie said, looking at West. 'Her name for detectives who hang around the scene while forensic folks are trying to work.'

He was quietly defensive. 'I'm not going to apologize for liking to know what's going on at my scenes.' He focused on Jayne. 'Back to these observations, as you called them. What did you observe, exactly? In more everyday language, if possible.'

Jayne said, 'A young adult, possibly male, probably between sixteen and, say, twenty.'

Sanchez looked up from where she was again taking notes. 'Race?'

'We won't go out on a limb on ancestry based on what little of the skeleton we could see.'

'Height?'

Jayne smiled. 'We can do this all day, Detective. It's not that we don't know what information you'd want; it's that we can't give it to you.'

Sanchez finally pocketed her notepad. 'So, nothing

27

jumped out at you on cause of death?'

Steelie said, 'No, but since you're from Homicide, you're obviously keeping an open mind on that?'

West nodded. 'The fact that the body didn't bury itself is the one thing we're clear on.'

Steelie almost snorted. 'Only because Sweetzer didn't have to tell you that herself.'

He pointed at her as though she'd found the right answer and then said, 'We may have more questions in the next couple of days, so if we can have your contact information?'

Jayne and Steelie gave their business cards in exchange and turned away.

As soon as they were out of earshot, Steelie said to Jayne, 'I can't believe they didn't ask if we thought it was the body of a student.'

'I'm relieved they didn't,' Jayne said. She looked over at the now-diminishing crowd of onlookers. Anyone still watching the activity at this stage would be showing an unhealthy interest in work only performed by personnel from the coroner's office. *Unless they're budding forensic scientists*, she thought.

Steelie said, 'But if the body is Stilson and the detectives aren't even thinking about him—'

'They've got to be thinking about him, Steelie. There are two students missing from UCLA and one of them is female. That leaves Jared Stilson.' Jayne went around the pick-up to get in the driver's side.

Steelie hopped in. 'But if they're not, we should, y'know, tell them.'

'It's too soon.'

'The sooner the better.'

Jayne started the truck. 'Think of Stilson's parents, Steelie.'

'Who else do you think I'm thinking of? Just because we don't want it to be him doesn't magically make it someone else.'

Jayne knew Steelie was right. She put the truck into reverse and looked over her shoulder.

*

Junior leaned slightly to the left and watched the pick-up truck reverse on the gravel, then pull away, taking the two women with it. The unmarked police car was still there and the pair who went with the vehicle, detectives he assumed, were walking back to where the boiler-suited crime scene type people were cordoning off the ground with yellow caution tape and erecting a tent. None of the people still present concerned him. They were employees of whoever issued their badges and, in his experience, their motivation only extended as far as their paychecks.

His problem was the two in the truck. They were true believers. Their motivation came from inside, whether from guilt or intense drive or maybe they just didn't have enough to do. Not married, either of them, he remembered that. No children. Now they never would. Just like him. Never, never – or 'never/ever', like the surveys said. No wedding outfits. No happy snaps. No bulging bellies.

Just him.

4

Craig Turner came around the desk to meet Jayne and Steelie when they were sent into his office by his assistant. Jayne immediately saw why Scott had described his boss as 'formidable'. He was tall and sinewy, had a piercing gaze and moved like he owned the place.

But Scott had also conveyed the impression that Turner was less a hard-ass than a by the book, old-school agent who had simply moved into management without losing his bootcamp mores. Jayne thought that explained why his glass-topped mahogany desk didn't face the window in a corner office whose views took in West LA rooftops and a promise of Pacific coastline. Instead, the desk faced the door like he wanted to see what was coming.

After the introductions, Turner indicated that they should sit at the conference table. He glanced down at the women's dusty boots as they crossed the room. 'Been in the field today?'

Jayne answered in the affirmative.

His lips retracted into something like a smile. 'I appreciate that you could make the time to come down here.'

He gestured toward a tray of bottled water and sandstone coasters sitting in the center of the table as he took the seat at the end. 'Help yourselves.'

He continued after Steelie and Jayne had settled

themselves, notebooks in front of them. 'I'd like to thank you myself for the assistance you gave us on the King case. It appears that the injury you sustained is healing up nicely, Ms. Lander.'

Steelie nodded in acknowledgment.

'It's partly that injury that led me to call this meeting,' he said. 'You've been informed of my interest in having your agency enter into a Memorandum of Understanding with this office of the Bureau. I have the draft document here.'

He lifted the folder in front of him. 'Now, I would understand if the threats you endured on the King case produced concerns about an MOU. I'd like to give you my assurance that the Bureau would mitigate or eradicate any similar threats by building various safeguards into the proposed agreement.'

Jayne liked the sound of safeguards and made a note to show that she felt this was important as Turner barreled on with his opening spiel.

He was saying, 'To do that, I need a better understanding of what you do and how you do it so we can make use of your services without involving you in parts of our cases that could expose you, as civilians, to danger.'

Steelie said, 'Works for me.'

Turner looked at her. 'Now, on the King case, you primarily assisted us by examining human remains. But I've been informed that your agency is actually focused on missing persons?'

'With a view to improving the chances of identifying them if found dead,' Steelie confirmed.

'Interesting.' Turner consulted his sheet. 'I have it here that you make up something called a "forensic profile".

I assume this profile differs in some way from a police missing person report?'

Jayne nodded. 'Our profiles focus on what's intrinsic to a body – features that can survive significant decomposition or even skeletonization.'

Steelie supplied, 'For example, where a missing person report gets the fact of a scar, we take steps with a misper's family to establish what caused the scar, then we determine whether it could have left a mark on bone.'

'And then you chase X-rays?' Turner asked.

'We do, and we also focus on dental.'

Turner's eyes narrowed. 'Internal reviews show that there's a logjam getting cops to put dental into the National Crime Information Center database. They can't or won't or just don't translate dental X-rays into the necessary codes.'

'Yeah,' Steelie grinned. 'External reviews show that too. That's why we do NCIC coding for them.'

Turner raised an eyebrow. 'Save them a step.'

As Jayne watched him make a note, she felt proud of the fact that she and Steelie had designed the agency to address the fundamental issues contributing to the backlog of unidentified bodies.

Turner looked very interested now. 'And you don't need to see bodies to do any of this?'

'No,' Jayne said. 'Bodies – fleshed bodies – are handled well by coroners' offices. The problem is that missing person reports are in law enforcement language, with law enforcement goals put first, while coroners' reports are in forensic language with no interest in law enforcement goals.'

Steelie added, 'Plus, we're interested in John and Jane

Does that have long since been cremated to make space in coroners' freezers for . . . y'know, new bodies.'

'Why the focus on the backlog in particular?' Turner was looking at both of them.

Steelie pulled herself closer to the table as though she was really getting stuck in. 'Because those are missings who have already been found. It's just a matching job, not a hunt-and-find job – which is and should be in law enforcement's wheelhouse, since you've got investigative powers.'

Turner leaned back in his chair and crossed one leg over the other, his knee jutting up just above the height of the table. 'So, you've operationalized John and Jane Does as formerly missing people.'

Jayne suddenly liked Craig Turner, very much. 'Exactly.'

He looked thoughtful. 'What's the count on unidentified bodies, nationwide?'

Jayne answered, 'Forty thousand, give or take.'

He frowned. 'That many? What's the figure on DNA for those cases?'

'No one knows.'

Steelie said, 'A lot of Jane and John Does were cremated before DNA sampling was de rigueur. But even if you could get DNA from all the bodies, no one seems to want to front the money to get DNA from the families of the hundred thousand known missing persons where you might get a match. We take samples for DNA if a family will let us but we don't make that the basis of our profiles. No point. Not for the long-term unidentified.'

Turner looked at the sheet in front of him and then closed his folder. 'At the request of Agent Houston or Agent

Ramos, you've gone to scenes for this office but what I'm hearing from you here is that you don't need to see bodies in order to bring your expertise to bear.'

Steelie spread her hands. 'Look, you guys have the whole Quantico lab at your disposal to deal with crime scenes.'

'Judging from the reports I've received about the King case, I think my agents would beg to differ with you, Ms. Lander. That includes the entire Critical Stabilization and Recovery team.'

'The Critters?' She smiled. 'They appreciate anyone who thinks what they do is normal.'

Turner stood, the folder in his hand. 'I want to pinpoint that a little more. Walk with me.'

They had to walk fast to keep up with him. As they went down the hallway, Jayne expected him to stop at the elevator so they could go to Critter Central on the tenth floor, but he didn't. It looked like they were about to pass Scott's office.

Jayne braced herself to see his empty chair. But Turner was stopping at Scott's door, and there was Scott sitting in his chair – Eric was at his desk, too.

Turner cleared his throat. The agents got to their feet and said, 'Sir' before stepping forward, hands extended to the two women.

Even as Jayne registered Scott's familiar features – the dark blond hair she knew was soft to the touch, the green eyes whose flecks of hazel were discernible at close range, the mouth whose lips were warm – she was confused by his neutral expression. He barely touched her hand before he switched to Steelie. Eric at least gave her a smile, his brown eyes warm under dark hair that shone along its side part.

34

Turner had begun speaking. 'I was just reminded that these scientists have done a lot of recovery work – including in Kosovo. Correct, Ms. Hall?'

'That's right. For the UN.'

'Like you, SA Houston.'

'Yes, sir,' Scott said.

'So, you've both had experience with mass graves.'

Jayne didn't know how to respond to this, given that it was delivered the same way a cop might say, 'So you both have criminal records.' Too much of her brain had been delegated to Scott's presence.

Steelie stepped into the breach, reeling off a list. 'Mass, multiples, singles. Depended on where we were. In Rwanda, there were a lot of surface bodies.'

'You're saying you've been to enough scenes to last a lifetime,' Turner concluded.

'Well, you're not going to see us working for the coroner.'

'Indeed. I can only hope the Bureau will be able to take advantage of the professional freedom your current position affords you. I'm going to add a couple of clauses to the MOU. Then our legal people will review it before it gets sent to your office. You'll be free to negotiate adjustments, of course, but I'm confident that we'll present you with an amenable agreement.'

Jayne exchanged a glance with Steelie and could see that her friend was impressed by SSA Turner's no-nonsense, tell-it-like-it-is communication style.

Turner was saying, 'Ms. Lander, Ms. Hall – thank you for your time. I'll have someone escort you downstairs.'

Scott took Jayne's hand again, briefly. 'Good to see you,'

he murmured.

Her mouth had dried out. 'Likewise.' She turned to follow the others to the elevator.

Turner pressed a button on the BlackBerry holstered on his waist and then pressed the elevator button. 'When were you in Kosovo, Ms. Hall?'

She tried to get a grip. 'In 2000.'

'And that's where you met Agent Houston?'

'No, I understand he was there in '99.'

'I see.'

Jayne was relieved that Turner's assistant arrived at the same moment that the elevator doors opened. She turned to shake hands with Scott's boss but Steelie was ahead of her.

'Good to meet you, SSA Turner.'

He nodded as he shook Steelie's hand. 'My office will be in touch. Thank you for your time.'

Jayne tried to return the firm grip Turner gave her. 'Thank *you*,' she said and gratefully stepped into the elevator where the assistant was holding the doors open.

After turning in their visitor badges, Jayne and Steelie crossed the hot parking lot in silence. As often as Jayne knew what Steelie was going to say, Steelie knew what Jayne was thinking and this time, she must have gauged that Jayne wouldn't welcome her usual jokes about Scott Houston, Very Special Agent.

They opened the Ford's windows to release some heat while the air conditioning ramped up and Jayne got them moving east on Wilshire Boulevard. She felt preoccupied, and not about the MOU. She was feeling doubtful about – and doubting – Scott. Did he still want to go on a date on Friday? Had he been neutral toward her because she'd never responded to his invitation? But surely he'd been neutral because his boss had been right there? That thought brought the MOU to the front of her mind and with it, a mixture of relief and excitement. The meeting of the minds she'd felt with Turner was unexpected and she saw how someone like him could produce an MOU tailored to her and Steelie's professional skills as well as personal security. 'Personal security'. She wouldn't mind having Scott in her life doing some very personal security. Was that just a fantasy?

Hearing a chirp that could have been her cell phone buried in her bag, she said to Steelie, 'Can you—' Her throat sounded constricted. She started again. 'Can you see if that's Carol?'

Steelie dug around in the bag and pulled out the phone. 'Let's see,' she said. 'You got a text and . . . yeah. That's not from Carol.'

Jayne sighed as she changed lanes to get around a bus still getting up to speed on the upslope of the hill. 'What's it say?'

'It says, quote, just flew in today, don't think I can wait until Friday, how about tonight, I can be with you in a couple of hours, end quote. So, I'm guessing that's from Scott? Why don't you have him programmed into your contacts?'

Jayne stared over at the phone.

Steelie whistled. 'Oh, you do *not* have a poker face. I'll text back that "yes", shall I? All caps should do it. You just concentrate on staying in your lane. Precious cargo here, sheesh.'

5

As though in tune with Jayne's anticipation for the evening, the City of Angels unfurled a path clear of traffic all the way back to the Agency. Their small premises sat in a no-man's land east of Griffith Park, facing a narrow valley carved by the Los Angeles River but laced with rail track and ten lanes of Golden State freeway. The valley's westward backstop was the line of low hills that camel-backed their way to Dodger Stadium. Jayne thought of the open flatland before the hills as the Agency's front yard. It made up for the fact that their actual frontage was a diminutive concrete parking lot.

Jayne pulled her truck in next to Steelie's dark green Jeep Wrangler, its soft top down like an invitation to play hooky, and they went inside. Carol, the retired grief counselor who was now their volunteer receptionist, was standing on the other side of the room in her usual pedal pushers and tunic top, watering Fitzgerald, the office plant.

'Hey, Carol. Hi, Fitz,' Steelie said.

They stopped at the counter in front of Carol's desk to look through the mail.

Carol came over with the watering can. 'How'd it go at UCLA?'

'It turned out to be a police matter,' Steelie said.

'It was a recent death?'

'A decomposing body, but buried.'

38

'Probably homicide, then.' Carol moved behind her desk but then looked suddenly stricken. 'Not one of the missing students?!'

Jayne said, 'We don't know.'

Carol came out of her thoughts. 'It's sad, regardless of who it is.'

'Either way, we're leaving it to the LAPD.'

Steelie raised an eyebrow. 'For now.'

Carol sounded curious. 'Homicide detectives arrived while you were still there?'

'Mitch asked us to wait for them.'

'That makes sense,' Carol replied, starting to get her bag together. 'Did the detectives prevent you getting to your meeting with Supervisory Special Agent Turner?'

'No, we made it in time for a very interesting *set* of meetings.' Steelie looked pointedly at Jayne.

Jayne added quickly, 'Not that interesting. The MOU is definitely on the table; we'll have a proposal from the Bureau soon.' She indicated Carol's bag. 'Can I drive you somewhere? I was only here to drop off Steelie.'

Carol glanced at her watch in surprise.

Steelie explained, 'She's got a date.'

'I thought that wasn't until Friday,' Carol said but then her hand flew to her mouth. 'Oh! Forgive me for thinking you only have one date this week.'

Steelie deadpanned, 'This week? More like this *year*.'

Jayne waited with a smile. 'Got that out of your system?'

Steelie beamed, unabashed.

After Jayne dropped Carol off at her small cottage clinging to a bit of canyon wall on Division Street, she hooked up her cell phone to the Ford's speaker system, dialed Gingergrass, her favorite restaurant near her apartment in Silver Lake, and placed an order for two dishes of Shaking Beef plus a couple of their special basil-lime elixirs. Using the 2 Freeway for the short hop to the bridge that spanned the LA River, Jayne arrived at the restaurant before the food was ready.

She waited on the bench outside the door, enjoying the warmth of the early evening and feeling relaxed because she'd have time to shower before Scott arrived. Then the reality of Scott arriving at her apartment hit her.

The sensation of nerves made her sit up and put a hand to her stomach. She wondered if Steelie was right about Scott being nervous as well. It seemed impossible to her that he could be. He was handsome, athletic, at one with his job and emotionally well-balanced despite having worked in a war zone while the bombs were still dropping. Meanwhile, she was – or at least had been until recently – weighed down to the point that it didn't matter if anyone else thought she was attractive or interesting because she kept seeing herself – her survival – in relation to Benni.

Benni. She'd been only feet from him when he'd triggered the antipersonnel mine in northern Kosovo. It had shattered his legs and he'd bled to death while she'd had to stay away from him, under orders from the de-miners who were screaming that *NOBODY MOVE!* She'd kept calling out through chattering teeth, *Je suis içi, Benni! I'm here! I'm here.* Even when she saw his flak jacket was no longer moving up and down with his life force, she didn't – couldn't – stop talking to him. *Je suis içi—*

Benni! For all the dead bodies she'd handled, she'd never seen anyone die before, let alone someone she knew.

And she'd never forgotten that it could have been her. That path had been de-mined just hours earlier; they could have been there without an escort walking point ahead of them. Benni could have been on a perimeter somewhere else. But someone had wanted to stop the forensic team from investigating the alleged grave on the other side of that field. Instead, they'd stopped a twenty-year-old French peacekeeper in his tracks, forever. Jayne felt like a part of her had stopped with him, gone with him.

Him: Benni. It was only when Jayne had been locked in the kiss with Scott just over a week ago that she'd fractured off from the part of her past that was bound up with Benni's death. Since then, she'd felt like an iceberg that had caught a current, being drawn to warmer waters and thawing as she went, her edges softening, her core melting, her shape changing. She no longer felt frozen in time with Benni.

Benni, who'd never even called her by her first name. She'd been 'Mademoiselle 'All' to him, every time they'd conversed in a mixture of French and English during downtimes at grave sites – Benni having a smoke, one forearm resting casually on his M16; Jayne drinking that water that tasted of bottle. She smiled again at the memory of the time she'd said to him, 'In English, it sounds like you're calling me Miss All.' He'd replied, with a mischievous grin, '*Mais bien sûr*, Miss All *That*.' They'd both burst out laughing, water almost coming out of Jayne's nose while smoke shot out of Benni's mouth around his nicotine-laced, very French, very young teeth.

'Your order's ready,' said a voice behind her.

She turned, startled into the present.

The maître d' was holding the door open for her. 'Everything okay?'

Jayne rose, wiping the tear that had come with the smiles of remembrance. 'Everything's okay. Thanks.'

*

Scott wiped the shower steam off the bathroom mirror. As much as he liked his loft apartment in Downtown LA, it was going to take some time to get used to this internal bathroom ventilated by an extractor fan instead of a window, like he'd had at his place in Atlanta. He looked at the reflection of his face, framed in the clearing, and decided that he would shave again since he was hoping to spend many hours of the night close to Jayne. He had no idea how sensitive her skin might be but he knew it looked supple as well as soft, a golden landscape he'd only been able to explore in his mind since they'd kissed on the side of a road a week ago.

As he shaved, Scott thought back to that kiss. He'd recalled it many times but, this time, he was only focused on who had started it. He was almost sure it had been Jayne. She'd been trying to comfort him about the Alston case, kissing his forehead or his hair or something, but when her lips had landed on his, they'd connected, like puzzle pieces interlocking, their tongues searching and intertwining— *Shit!* Scott inspected his jawline. Yeah, he'd nicked himself.

He held a tissue to the small wound and then waited a minute for it to stop bleeding, his mind already back on that kiss. It had been long and intense, almost desperate. He remembered feeling Jayne's whole body against his as he'd pulled her to him – and she'd pulled him to her as well, he would swear to that. The fit of their bodies had been so good, as he'd always imagined it would be, from the first time he saw her across the room in Quantico five years ago.

He could remember it like it was yesterday. He hadn't just stared at her from afar; they'd sat and talked for multiple nights, about his Bureau experience and her charity work and NCIC 2000. She'd been so switched on, so full of ideas. Academic, sure, but also sensitive and curious, like no one he'd ever met. Talking with her had taken the physical attraction and cranked it all the way up, off the charts. At the time, the holistic nature of the attraction had almost scared him. Now, he felt ready to take a chance, to allow for a connection that deep, beyond the superficial bond that sex usually created for him. A connection that he thought was going to take him to a place where he'd feel like maybe, just maybe, he couldn't live without her.

This was why, he told himself, it mattered whether Jayne liked him in the same way. She might not be looking for a deep connection; maybe she just wanted to date casually. They hadn't had a chance to talk since the kiss because of what went down in Atlanta. The wait had been excruciating – well, his days had been full with the interrogations and report-writing and drafting the MOU, but the nights . . . Jesus Christ, the nights in the hotel room had been long and he'd fallen asleep to the memory of Jayne's mouth on his and the thought of kissing that beauty mark at the base of her throat and running his tongue down her body. Scott closed his eyes and flattened his hands onto the bathroom's granite counter, feeling the cool surface pull the heat out of his palms. He was so turned on at the thought of being with Jayne but he was also nervous:

43

a combination of sensations that he hadn't felt since he was . . . well, a lot younger.

The nervous arousal was why he hadn't wanted to break the spell by calling her or having some mundane interaction over at her office or his. Having to see her this afternoon with Turner standing there like a freaking human lie detector was so far the opposite of what he'd wanted that he'd been almost unable to talk. He'd wanted to go from the kiss on the side of the road back into Jayne's arms like nothing had happened in between.

He looked in the mirror one last time. His body was as fit as his job required but his face looked tired, like he'd started his day in an earlier time zone, which he had. He patted aftershave onto his face and then ran a hand over his chin and jaw. Smooth. At least he had that going for him besides being clean. He left the bathroom and looked in his bedroom closet. Most of his casual clothes were FBI logo T-shirts and shorts that weren't appropriate for going out to dinner. Then again, he didn't want to leave Jayne's apartment to get dinner once he'd arrived. *That's what delivery is for, right? Those guys have to make money too.* He reached for one of the well-fitted polo shirts that he had multiples of in shades of gray, blue and mushroom. The drape of the fabric made his pecs and shoulders look good while the slight pull over his biceps gave definition right where he wanted it. He could only hope that Jayne would find him irresistible in the same way he found her.

*

By the time Jayne had showered and was turning on the stereo at her apartment, the outside staircase was reverberating noisily.

She knew it had to be Scott, but to open the door and find him actually standing there – something she had thought just a few hours ago would never happen – made her feel light-headed.

Scott's lips curved into that self-amused half-grin that she found so sexy. He said, 'Finally.'

She laughed and only found his word in reply. 'Finally.'

They stepped into each other's arms and Jayne turned her face into his neck where summery warmth and the scent of aftershave emanated in a faint sheen of perspiration. Then they were kissing as though taking up from where their last kiss had left off, moving blindly into the apartment as one.

When Jayne took Scott to her bed, she felt what was left of the iceberg she'd been trapped in with Benni ride a strong current out to open water, where it finally gave way, falling into the deep as dancing points of light.

Later, much later, lying against Scott's chest as he slept, a phrase entered her mind unbidden: 'Gone but not forgotten.' It encompassed and remembered all the POWs, MIAs and KIAs, from all the wars and all the conflicts, and her eyes brimmed with silent tears of relief and guilt. The iceberg was gone. Gone but not forgotten.

DAY TWO

THURSDAY

6

Junior woke with a start. There was a loud noise coming up behind him. He straightened up and looked in his sideview mirror. It was a street-sweeping vehicle, almost upon him. His heart rate shot up as he tried to get his seatback upright to reach the ignition while watching the huge truck approach in his rearview. His was the last car on this side of the street.

He couldn't believe he'd fallen asleep, and on the wrong side! He didn't even need the voice to tell him he'd been stupid. He knew. He could have been given a ticket and then there would have been a trace. Evidence. His Highlander's engine started just in time and he got it moving faster than its usual sluggish start. But his haste didn't stop him looking over at the driveway one last time. The woman's pick-up truck was still there, all but blocked in by the Suburban that was parked next to it, half on the driveway and half on the grass. He slammed his hand against the steering wheel and only then took in that he was still wearing the gloves. He shimmied them off, holding the steering wheel between his knees as he braked to a halt at the red light.

In a belated, new panic, he felt around his neck. The mask was still there. He took a steadying breath and felt under his seat. The syringe packet was still taped securely, the false insulin label smooth under his shaky fingers. Everything was in place but everything was wrong. He wasn't on the path provided by the master plan for Operation Concentration and had almost ruined everything. He watched the few cars cross in front of him as they navigated the narrow curves coming down from Silver Lake's hilly back lanes. He didn't understand the Suburban or the man who'd emerged from it to run upstairs and clearly stay all night. She'd said she wasn't married. He was positive about that. So, she was either a liar or she was a . . . he couldn't bring himself to use the word.

Whore!

The voice was loud inside his head. He squeezed his eyes shut like that would stop it, even though that had never worked.

You can't even say it, can you? Whore! Whore! Son of a whore! Man up! Grow a pair! Pfft!

Junior wiped his face automatically and then looked at his hand. There was no spittle, no trail of that warm, jellified, stench-filled mucus.

There was no one in the car but him.

*

Jayne's cell phone rang while she was brewing coffee and musing on the fact that this quotidian task felt completely different because she was brewing for both her and Scott. It was early for a call and she didn't recognize the number, so assumed it was a client call on the after-hours line, which was forwarded to her that week.

'Ms. Hall, it's Matt West, Homicide Specials.'

Jayne was surprised and crossed to the living room away from the noise of the automatic coffee machine. 'Yes?'

'Sorry, did I call too early?'

Before Jayne could explain that she was surprised to be hearing from him at all, he continued.

'I always forget when I'm on this shift. Usually, my partner's here to warn me.'

Jayne found it interesting that he was explaining himself and was now curious about the reason for his call. 'It's no problem, Detective. What do you need?'

'So, we got good dental information from the body at UCLA. Ran it through NCIC.'

Jayne sank down on the couch. With good postmortem dental data, the National Crime Information Center system should have identified Jared Stilson, the missing UCLA student.

She mentally skipped ahead to what she'd have to do: first, she'd have to tell Steelie that she was right about them possibly being watched yesterday by whoever murdered Jared Stilson; second . . . But then she realized West hadn't spoken again.

She prompted, 'And you got an ID.'

'Nope.'

'Oh! So it's not—' Jayne managed to stop herself from saying, 'Jared Stilson'.

'It's not what?'

'Sorry. Nothing.' She hurried on. 'Can I ask, when you say "good dental", was it like a couple of extractions or was it more like a gold cap way up front where it could be seen in a smile?'

'I don't know what good dental is. I'm just repeating what Sweetzer said.'

'Oh . . . hm, then that should have produced an ID. That probably means your body is either someone who hasn't been reported missing, or has but doesn't have dental records in NCIC.'

'That's exactly what Sweetzer said.'

'Hey, great minds think alike,' Jayne said cheerily, aware that she was taking this call as some kind of confirmation that the body wasn't that of Jared Stilson. She swung her legs up onto the couch and sat back more comfortably, further cheered at the sight of Scott walking over with two cups of coffee.

Scott raised an interrogatory eyebrow at her as he placed her cup on the table and then sat next to her, lifting her legs to rest them across his lap.

West was saying, 'My partner and I are wondering if maybe they don't think alike, though. Is there anything else that you or Ms. Lander observed on the body that might help us out here? I got the sense that maybe there was something else.'

'I think we told you everything.' Jayne had to suppress a gasp as Scott began massaging one of her feet.

'I mean, maybe some little nuance?' West said. '*Are* there nuances on bodies? I don't even understand what you people do.' He sighed. 'Can you give us anything here?'

'The thing is, Detective—'

'You can call me Matt.'

Jayne put her hand over Scott's to stop him caressing her all the way up her thigh. 'Matt, the only anthropologist who's actually examined the body is Jenny Sweetzer and she's a good FA.'

'Hey, I'd be the last person to suggest otherwise about Sweetzer – I wouldn't care to think what she'd do to me. It's just . . . we're grasping at straws here.'

Jayne took in West's tone and tried to make sense of why a homicide detective was so discomfited by the inability of NCIC to identify the victim in his case. Every detective would have encountered this in their careers before. She said, 'Don't take this the wrong way, but a half-skeletonized John Doe doesn't usually get this much attention. Why is this one so special?'

The detective exhaled audibly. 'Well, Ms. Hall, we've got an unusual cause of death: poisoning. In fact, we're reliably informed that this one wouldn't have been pretty. Muscle paralysis but functioning sensory awareness, feeling your own lungs shutting down. Basically, it would have been torture, like a death penalty dose gone bad. So, me and Sanchez are sitting on our asses here, thinking about what kind of perp wants to do that to an eighteen-year-old and I'm about ready to give my left nut to get this kid ID'd so we can get this case off the freakin' ground. Pardon my French.'

'No apology necessary.' Jayne now understood that West hadn't been questioning the coroner's anthropologist when he'd called her this morning. He was marshalling forces for what he correctly perceived could be a battle to identify a John Doe after NCIC hadn't produced an answer. And if unusual poisoning was involved, she could imagine that the detectives were motivated to pull out all the stops to find the killer.

She noticed that Scott was watching her intently.

She said, 'Well, Matt, why don't you get the body's NCIC record to the Agency and we'll review it in light of our observations.'

'Can't do that.'

'Just a print-out.'

'Can't. But you guys could come down here and go through it with us.'

Jayne knew Steelie would welcome the chance to get behind the thin blue line at the Los Angeles Police Department, as though her ex-criminal defense lawyer aura was enough to blur that line. Jayne agreed to the meeting on behalf of herself and Steelie and hung up.

Scott immediately asked, 'What was that about?'

He was holding out her cup of coffee.

After Jayne swallowed her first sip, she told him about the discovery at UCLA the previous day. She was hoping Scott would now return to caressing her legs but he was sitting up straighter.

'You went to a crime scene? I thought you and Steelie had been to enough of those to last a lifetime.'

'It was your boss who said that, not us.'

'But Turner wasn't far off the mark, was he?'

'Maybe it depends on whose scene it is,' she teased.

'Oh, really?' He smirked and put his cup on the table. 'So, you'll sign the MOU with us?'

'That's different.'

'Why?' Scott glanced at Jayne's phone and frowned as he moved her legs off his lap. 'Who is this guy you were talking to? Matt what?'

Jayne smiled at what she thought was a jealous tone.

Scott, however, did not look amused as he pressed, 'How long have you known him?'

Jayne was still amused. 'Since . . . let's see. Yesterday.'

'Okay but was that the first time you've done this for the LAPD?'

Jayne cocked her head. 'What do you mean by "this"?'

'What you've done for us.'

'And there I was thinking it was *me* you wanted to keep to yourself, but it's just the Agency.' She smiled.

He smiled back. 'Maybe.' But he didn't drop it. 'You didn't say what the detective wanted, exactly.'

Her coffee finished, Jayne crossed back to the kitchen. 'We're just going to look at some NCIC stuff for them,' she said.

'What division is he in?'

'Homicide Special Section.'

'Homicide Specials?' Scott turned to look at her. 'Then what's the COD? You said you didn't see anything obvious on the body.'

'We hardly got to see the body but we wouldn't have been able to discern cause of death because it was poison.'

'So, what you were actually doing yesterday was poking around the body of a homicide victim who was poisoned? A vic who's probably going to turn out to be a student killed on campus?'

She tried for a light tone as she rinsed out her coffee cup. 'Well, no one knew then—'

'That's not the point.' Scott came over to face her across the kitchen counter. 'Did it occur to you or your friend at UCLA or this *detective* that maybe your proximity to the body would put you in danger? Poisoning's a specialist thing. It's used by perps who do premeditation and by people who like to watch. If this is a crime that took place on campus, the perpetrator could have been there. Was anyone watching you?'

Jayne bit her lip.

'So, people *were* watching.' Scott started pacing. 'A nice big crowd or just a few looky-loos? Anyone catch your eye?'

'We were sort of busy with the body . . .'

'Great. That's just great, Jayne. Jesus, after Atlanta, I don't need to tell you—'

'No, you don't.' She took his coffee cup and started rinsing that one as well.

He stopped pacing, came closer and spoke more softly. 'Sorry. Of course I don't. Look, what kind of poison was it?'

'I don't know, something that paralyzes you but you can still see what's going on.' The two cups went into the dishwasher.

'Wait, the death penalty cocktail?'

'The detective just mentioned something about that. How'd you know?'

Scott shook his head impatiently. 'I want you to be careful today. You can talk to this guy, Matt whatever his name is—'

'Scott!' Jayne felt her blood pressure rising and raised her voice with it. She knew she was arguing about something she actually agreed with him about, but she didn't know how to stop. 'You don't get to tell me – you're not – this isn't – this doesn't have anything to do with you!'

'You're right.' Scott pulled out his phone. 'It doesn't have anything to do with me *yet*.'

7

Jayne and Steelie drove with the radio tuned to 98.7, coming in on the middle of a commercial-free stretch of The Killers, which meant volume up and windows down, no discussion required.

A fence protected the squat LAPD parking lot but the guard's gatehouse wasn't occupied. Jayne parked in the first available space and pulled the truck in as far as she could to keep its long bed from jutting into the passageway. She would have preferred to reverse into the space, keeping to the principle of being prepared for a quick getaway – a habit left over from driving with NATO troops in Bosnia. A few years back, Steelie had pointed out that what Jayne called a 'habit' could also count as a symptom of PTSD, given that quick getaways weren't needed, let alone welcomed, in the congested parking lots of Los Angeles.

Like clockwork, Steelie remarked on her parking. 'Nose-in. Progress.'

'Actually, I was afraid I would hit one of the cars next to us if I reversed in.'

Steelie waited until they were out of the truck to reply. 'Ya know, you could have left me thinking you were "fixed". But no, you didn't want me to labor under a misapprehension. Thanks for looking out for me like that.'

'Okay! You made your point,' Jayne said as they used the pedestrian crosswalk to approach the rear of Parker

Center, which was a wider building than was suggested by the verticality of its front entrance. The officer at the guard post asked them to wait. He made a call. Eventually, Detective West emerged from the building.

Jayne noticed that West's cell phone, badge and gun were clustered on a belt whose orangey-brown leather matched his shoes. As he came closer, she saw how the blue of his shirt nicely set off his light brown hair and brown eyes. He was clearly fashionable. As he approached them with an affable expression, Jayne suddenly wondered why she'd been so quick to dismiss him the previous day as someone using loud ties to hide a nascent beer belly. And even if he had been hiding something, how did that compare to her using a phone line to hide trauma symptoms from Scott – for five years, no less?

She just avoided doing the Etch-a-Sketch shake; she was in no position to judge anyone.

West was saying, 'Good of you guys to come down,' as he shook their hands.

'Glad to assist, if we can,' Steelie said.

He smiled at her. 'Sanchez is waiting inside.'

They walked past rows of parked black-and-whites and ascended a ramp to enter the building. This brought them into a hallway that could have been in any American high school: gleaming linoleum flooring, wooden doors at regular intervals, glass trophy cases holding photos of LAPD officers receiving commendations over the years, and wall-mounted drinking fountains. They went upstairs, where they traversed a large space divided by an internal wall fitted with a clerestory of windows. According to a posted sign, the other side of the wall housed the elite Robbery-Homicide Division. West led them in.

The room had a hum of noise from telephone conversations and keyboards and printers in use. Jayne spotted Detective Sanchez. She was wearing a charcoal-gray suit. Her highlighted brown hair fell in waves to her shoulders and she was wearing very sensible black shoes with a low but distinguishable heel. She had the same humorless manner she'd had at UCLA but shook hands politely with the visitors.

'Welcome to Homicide,' she said as she indicated that Jayne and Steelie could take the rather decrepit fabric and wood chairs across from where Detective West was settling at his desk, turned to the side as he unlocked his computer monitor.

Steelie's chair creaked noisily as she took a seat. 'Nice office, but what's the time since death on these chairs?'

West chuckled as he one-finger typed on the keyboard.

Sanchez did not laugh but perched herself on the edge of the desk. 'Needless to say, anything seen or discussed in here . . .' She made a zipping motion across her lips.

'Theresa,' West said. 'They know.' Then he swiveled his computer monitor on its axis so everyone could read it. 'Okay, here's the NCIC record.'

The code fields of the NCIC system made the page instantly recognizable. It still evoked computer language from 1983, when the unidentified person system was created by CJIS, the Department of Justice's Criminal Justice Information Services Division.

Jayne was reminded, as always, that the legacy of the

59

law enforcement – not scientific – founders of this system was still with them. She scanned the relevant line of the record, decoding it swiftly as she did so.

M.B.1983-1988.20030901.20050607.507-511.
160-175.UNK.BRO.

She said, 'Sweetzer's estimated he was born in the mid to late '80s, so if she's right that he died less than two years ago, then she's given you a similar age range to what we estimated. Late teens to early twenties.'

Steelie pointed at the screen. 'Height Jayne and I can't speak to, but she gave you race as black?'

Sanchez pounced. 'Why? Was that wrong?'

'Not wrong . . . but maybe not quite right.'

Sanchez shifted on the edge of the desk. 'Isn't it either wrong or right? There's not really any gray area, is there?'

'Well, to me—' Steelie nodded toward Jayne. 'To us, he looked like he could have been mixed. Maybe white and black. Could have been black and Asian. So, I guess that would be like what you were calling the gray area.'

West, who had been leaning back against the wall, brought his chair thudding down to the floor. 'Wait a minute. Mixed-race? How could Sweetzer make a mistake like that?'

'It wasn't a mistake,' Steelie clarified. 'She probably noted mixed ancestry but had to make a guess on what single race to give you. It's your form's monoracial categories that wouldn't have allowed her to describe things accurately.'

'She didn't say anything.'

Steelie arched an eyebrow. 'Maybe you were hovering over her too much during the autopsy.'

West looked at her for a beat. 'As it happens, we didn't attend the autopsy. Had to go to a scene for another case. But what did you mean about our form being the problem?'

'Sweetzer wouldn't have been able to give you a mixed-race designation since you wanted to put this body's details into NCIC.' Steelie gestured at the computer monitor. 'NCIC doesn't accept multiple race entries for a single individual, though it will take a record as Unknown Race. I'm obviously leaving aside the possibility that Sweetzer estimated race as black after she was able to do a full exam. Which she might have been able to do.' Steelie shrugged, as if to say, *Take it or leave it*.

Sanchez swiveled around to face her partner, effectively blocking out Jayne and Steelie. 'The race designation doesn't matter, Matt. We had good dental and still didn't get a match, so this Doe's not in the system yet, like we already figured out.'

Jayne leaned forward. 'Detectives? If I could just add something? Dental isn't the threshold you have to meet to get a match in NCIC. It's race.'

They looked at her blankly.

She continued, 'NCIC is set up in a hierarchy, with race at the top of the pile when it comes to matching mispers with bodies. If race doesn't match, dental's not even getting a look-in. Especially if one record is coded "white" and the other "black". I think the system might be able to compare every other race but not those two.'

West leaned his chair back toward the wall again, this time using his feet to rock up and down. 'You're saying we could have a perfect match on dental records in NCIC but the system won't flag it for us if Sweetzer guessed the wrong race for this kid who's actually of mixed race.'

'Not just that,' Steelie added. 'If you want to get a match, you've also got to estimate the race selected by whoever put in the misper report. Let's say this kid was in fact mixed. His mom reports him missing and she's faced with the same problem as Sweetzer when the cops tell her to pick one race. What does Mom pick? You'd have to be a mind reader to work that out. And what if his teacher reported him missing and didn't even know he was mixed and thought he was white – though with that hair . . .'

West stopped rocking his chair. 'This is like throwing Jell-O against the wall.'

Jayne glanced at Steelie and then did a double take. Steelie was grinning at West. Steelie never grinned at cops. Jayne looked at West, who now had a classic look of frustration, so she adjusted her interpretation of Steelie's grin: she was enjoying West's pain.

Sanchez had folded her arms. 'What can we do to fix this? Can we re-run the record with the vic as white? Then as Asian?'

West snapped to attention and started typing at the keyboard, looking at the computer monitor intently. 'Yeah, let's update the record. Get the system to re-run it with all the same details but make the vic white. Then we do it again and make him Asian. Work around all this stuff about who put in the misper report and what they knew and yada.'

'Good luck with that,' Jayne said. Clearly, these detectives were end-users of NCIC but didn't know some of its architecture for handling data on people. They were like so many other law enforcement officers she and Steelie had met but, after today, they would join the ranks of cops who knew that human identification could still require hands-on intervention.

West grimaced. 'What don't I know here?'

Steelie said, 'The system won't let you re-run a record as white that was first coded as black. Or vice versa.'

He stared at her for a moment. 'You're shitting me.'

'Nope. This is what the detectives in Missing Persons are dealing with all the time. You can ask them.'

He reached for his desk phone, started dialing then put his finger over the cradle and cut the call. He looked up at Sanchez. 'Prevo is 5136?'

Sanchez nodded and he resumed dialing, saying to Steelie and Jayne in explanation: 'Our NCIC instructor.'

Steelie said, 'Five bucks he says the same thing we did.'

Digging in his wallet as he cradled the receiver in his shoulder, West slapped a five-dollar bill on the desk almost simultaneously with Steelie. Then he was speaking into his phone. 'Lieutenant, it's Matt West here from Homicide. How are you, sir? I'm glad to hear it. Thank you, we're doing just fine. I've got a John Doe NCIC question for you, and let me warn you, I have money riding on this. Is it big money?' He raised his gaze from the bills to Steelie's face. 'Yes, sir, it is big money.'

West put his question, listened for about a minute and then thanked Prevo. He hung up and pushed the bills toward Steelie.

She scooped the money off the table like she was at a Vegas high rollers' table. 'A pleasure doing business with you, sir.'

Sanchez said impatiently, 'What'd he say?'

West replied, 'We get to run a search for him as Asian. But we don't get to see if he's white.' He was rummaging in a drawer. 'Where's my freakin' codebook?'

After a moment, he brought out a thin three-ring binder that was marked *NCIC Codes*. A second label had bigger font highlighted in yellow: *West – RHD HSS – Do Not Remove*. He put his finger under one of the tabs protruding from the outer edge and opened to a section, flipped over another page and then held his finger on a line before transferring the information to his keyboard, taking his time to get the codes right.

While West was typing, Steelie poked Jayne on the shoulder.

Jayne knew why and looked up at Sanchez. 'Can I just ask if you guys are aware of the missing student at UCLA? The male undergrad?'

'Stilson?' Sanchez said.

'So, you know about him. Isn't he your first thought for the matching process? The age range is right.'

'No point. Stilson's white.'

Steelie said, 'Yeah, but you gotta stop thinking that the body you have is black. Why don't you get the ME to do the comparison with Stilson's records by hand?'

West cut in. 'By hand? What the hell is NCIC supposed to be for then? All this great technology?' He jabbed at a key and pointed at his screen. 'It's about to run it with the John Doe as Asian.'

They waited in silence. After a while, the system reported that there were no matches among the missing Asian males in the correct age and height ranges who were not already excluded through identifiable scars, marks, tattoos, surgical devices or other characteristics. West crossed his arms in an aggressive pose as he stared at the computer screen.

After a moment, he looked at Steelie. 'So. You recommended that we call the coroner's office and ask for a what?'

She replied, 'A straightforward antemortem-postmortem comparison between Jared Stilson and this body. It'll probably only take one call to Missings and then a call to Jenny Sweetzer. Although it sounds like you'll need your partner to call if you want a hope of getting that kind of favor.'

Sanchez said, 'I'll be doing it anyway; Sweetzer won't even answer her phone if she sees it's him calling.' She glanced at her watch. 'Thanks for coming in. I'll see you two out.'

In contrast to his partner's brusque manner, West was giving Steelie a warm smile while shaking her hand, like he was enjoying being the butt of the joke as long as it was Steelie doing the joking. Jayne couldn't see Steelie's expression but was inwardly amused. West had no idea that his occupation put him at a singular disadvantage with Steelie. But as Steelie turned away, Jayne saw that her friend was looking about as pleased as West. *That* was a surprise.

For her part, Sanchez looked as if she couldn't wait for them to leave.

*

Once she and Steelie were outside of the building, Jayne said, 'What was that all about?'

'All what about?'

Jayne waited for a uniformed officer coming toward them to pass. 'With Detective West.'

'What do you mean?'

'You tell me. I can't remember the last time you smiled at a cop of your own volition.'

Steelie snorted. 'I can. It was in 2002, before I dealt with that cop who got the prosecutor to suppress evidence that exculpated my client. I smiled at a lot of cops before him.'

'My point exactly.' Jayne pressed the button for the pedestrian crossing. 'What makes West so different?'

Steelie shrugged. 'He got mad at NCIC. I liked that.'

They crossed the road.

'And that's why you were teasing him, too?' Jayne said.

'I tease everyone.'

'I know. But you won't deny that you . . .' Jayne searched her mind for the right phrase as she unlocked her Ford.

'I won't deny that,' Steelie said with a slight grin as she hopped into the pick-up.

Jayne's grin was much larger. This was momentous, but before she could probe further, Steelie said, 'Do you think they'll actually go through with asking the coroner's office to specifically check the body against Jared Stilson's records?'

Jayne navigated out of the parking lot before answering. 'My sense is that they're motivated to get an ID because not having one is making it harder to find the person who did the poisoning in the first place . . .' She paused for a typical Steelie interjection along the lines of, 'God forbid that cops should have to work hard!' but nothing came, which was yet another surprise.

Jayne continued, 'One good thing is that they won't look at the NCIC Unidentified Persons file the same way again.'

'For today, anyway,' Steelie said. 'Maybe a month. Then they'll forget.'

'That's pretty cynical.'

'You know me.'

Jayne decided to be bold. 'You could always give Detective West a personal refresher sometime.'

Steelie only said, 'Maybe,' but Jayne saw her smiling.

8

Scott checked his watch once he'd showered and changed clothes at his apartment. He decided he could spare five minutes before leaving for the office, to stack the moving boxes he hadn't yet dealt with into the hallway closet. Task completed, he looked around. The place looked better. Anyone – Jayne, just as an example – who came into the apartment would now focus on the spectacular view of Downtown LA through the floor-to-ceiling windows, not the bare bookshelves or the kitchen, which had more dishes on the counter than in the cupboards.

Well, Jayne might notice, Scott realized. Everything was in its place in her apartment. Not, he told himself, that he was intending to have her over that night *per se*; he just knew he wanted to see her again, and soon.

When he pulled out of his building's underground parking in the Bureau Suburban, he turned west on 2nd Street.

As he drove, he pictured Jayne, recalling the glow of her skin, the unruliness of her dark hair, the beauty mark in the center of her neck. Now, he had a night's worth of other images. *So much for taking things slow*. Scott suddenly realized he was curving around the on-ramp to the 110 Freeway with no recollection of getting there. He sat up and concentrated on getting to the office with minimal risk.

By the time he was in the elevator at his office building in Westwood, he still hadn't had a reply from Eric to the voicemail message he'd left earlier about where else the death penalty drug cocktail had been used outside of a state execution room. He figured Eric would either remember the case or would track it down. He was more patient than Scott when it came to research. But as soon as Scott opened his office door and saw Eric's face, he knew he wasn't going to be able to just sit down and talk case histories, which he desperately needed because it was proving impossible to get his mind off of the sudden leap forward he and Jayne had made in their relationship.

He said, 'Can I at least get a cup of coffee?'

Eric grinned. 'No time for breakfast, partner?'

Scott just smiled and went to fill his mug at the coffee machine down the hallway, said good morning to Lance, and returned to the office, closing the door behind him.

Eric looked at the closed door expressively. 'Must have been a good night.'

Scott took a sip of coffee. 'I didn't leave until this morning.'

'Then congratulations are in order.'

'Congratulations?'

'Because you've finally graduated from daydreaming about Jayne while dating other women. How many were there in the end? Five? Eight?'

'Two. Two girlfriends and one rebound . . . thing. Jayne is completely different.'

'Glad you waited all this time?'

'Kicking myself, man.'

''Cause five years ago you would have had more stamina.'

'Okay, we're done with this subject. Did you get my message?'

Eric twisted to pick up some papers. 'Yeah, the homicide case you were thinking of where the death penalty cocktail was used was the Bailey brothers. They presented it in our class on problems of evidence.'

Scott snapped his fingers in recognition. 'At the Academy. I knew it.'

'Why were you asking?'

'It was a closed case, right?'

'Yeah. Rural Tennessee. Red Bailey used the drugs on his brother Treat who had brutalized him after their parents died.'

'Where did the Feds think he got the drugs?'

'I seem to recall they never figured it out and Bailey's since died in prison. Three different companies make the components and sell them to our Corrections departments, so any of them can spring a leak, plus all the pharmacists who sell the separate ingredients to hospitals or vets.' Eric shrugged. 'I guess that's why they're on our watch list if they show up in the commission of a crime.'

'Each of these drugs is on the federal watch list?'

Eric nodded. 'I'm still waiting on the answer as to why you're interested.'

Scott pulled himself closer to his desk and reached for the phone. 'Those drugs or something like them have turned up in an LA homicide, and I have a feeling the LAPD hasn't shared their news with us.'

'Before you call them, check with Lance. The PD may have reported it but we just haven't heard about it.'

'Oh, ye of little faith,' Scott said before speaking into the phone. 'Yeah, Lance, I need you to run a check on something.'

*

While he was waiting for Lance to get back to him, Scott took the material Eric had printed out on the Bailey case, divided it into two batches and handed one to his partner.

Seeing Eric's expression, he said, 'Humor me. See what avenues they were looking at for how those specific drugs got into Bailey's hands. I'll do the same.'

Scott spent some time taking a highlighter to his batch, and then he said, 'Did the Bureau make a psych profile for the perp who would use those drugs?'

'Yeah.' Eric shuffled the pages in his stack until he found the one he wanted. 'It's what you'd expect. Someone after the ultimate control, possibly abused in his own life, probably used it against an abuser. The paralysis before death allows the perp to exact some revenge the victim will actually know about, or the perp can tell them something while the victim's powerless, etcetera, etcetera.'

'Is that profile watertight?'

'It's a profile. A start.'

Scott used his thumb to point over his shoulder at the papers on his own desk. 'This guy Bailey, he didn't confess right off the bat.'

'Let me see?'

Scott handed it over. 'The evidence against him was circumstantial but enough to convince the jury.'

Eric looked up at him. 'What are you thinking?'

'Not thinking; just noticing. Some very particular drugs used in a homicide in rural Tennessee might have turned up out here in another homicide . . . could the cases be related?'

'Well, what is the case out here? You still haven't said.'

'Something Thirty-Two One was called in on. At UCLA. I'm going to call Jayne to find out who caught it at the PD.'

'And we want to be involved because . . .?'

Scott's voice took on a punchy note. 'Because LA is our turf now, Ramos. Gotta be proactive, take care of our city.'

Eric raised his eyebrows but he was smiling slightly. 'Is that what they're calling it these days?'

*

As Jayne pulled the truck into the Agency parking lot, Carol came out the front door. She held a hand above her eyes to block the sun as she called out, 'Jayne, Scott Houston just called. I saw you pulling in so I asked him to hold.'

Steelie made a teasing noise like, 'Oooo.'

Jayne trotted ahead without so much as a backward glance. Steelie hadn't yet asked outright about her date with Scott, no doubt hoping Jayne would talk about it first, but Jayne didn't trust herself to characterize it just yet. She went into her office, closing the door from reception behind her.

'Scott?'

'Hey.'

'Hey, yourself.' Her answer came automatically; they had greeted each other like this for five years over the phone but everything was different now.

Scott said, 'How'd it go down at Parker Center?'

'Parker—?' In her mind, she was still in bed with Scott and had assumed that was where his mind was, too. 'Riiight, Parker Center. That went fine.'

'Did it seem like the detective needed more help?'

'You don't have to counsel me against this anymore. We're not involved.'

'I meant, did it seem like he could use some federal assistance?'

'You'd have to ask him that.'

'You're absolutely right. Why didn't I think of that? Who's lead again? Matthew something?'

She could practically hear his half-grin. 'West. Matt West. Happy now?'

'Very.' After a moment, he resumed more softly, as though he didn't want someone to overhear him. 'I've been thinking a lot about last night.'

That took Jayne's breath away. 'Me, too.'

'Good.'

9

Steelie sat on a stool in the Agency's lab at the back of the building, taking notes while she was on the telephone.

T/C fr D West – John Doe – UCLA – Dental work-up – 'by hand' – Positive ID – Jared Stilson – DOB 8/12/1985.

She underlined the name Stilson, her mind jumping over to his parents and the grief they must be feeling at that very moment, and then tried to focus again on West, who was still talking.

'We've got the vic's parents coming into town tomorrow and they want to meet everyone involved in his recovery. That includes you and Ms. Hall. As far as we're concerned, if you guys hadn't helped us out on this, it might have been weeks before we made the ID. We're going to take them over to the burial site tomorrow morning. Can you be there?'

Steelie didn't need to check with Jayne on this one. She would want to be there as much as Steelie did. 'Absolutely.'

'Thank you. Okay, let's see, dut-da-da.' It sounded like West was flipping through some papers. 'The chancellor's going to meet them first so he can express the university's condolences and then we'll drive them over to the site, where Mitch Nelson will meet us.'

'Is the chancellor coming?'

'No, keeping it small, but we've been told he's sending over flowers or a wreath of some kind. Not at the site. By

74

the perimeter fence.'

'Good.'

'After you guys talk to the NOK, I figure we can let them do what they need to do. Just stand back until they're done. They won't be taking in too much after they see the burial site anyway.'

Steelie nodded in agreement even though West couldn't see her. Next-of-kin couldn't be expected to keep it together when their kin had been murdered. 'Um, Detective West, I don't suppose you could tell me if you've got any leads on who did this?'

'Why, do you know something?' His tone was sharp and hopeful at once, which surprised Steelie.

'No!'

'Oh, well, all I can tell you is this: we're keeping the Stilson ID out of the media for now. It's need-to-know only and if anyone shows special interest in who was buried out there, we're gonna take a real close look at them. And, as you'd expect, campus security is being beefed up.'

'I see.' Steelie asked for the details for the logistics of the next morning, then hung up and went to Jayne's office.

When Steelie told Jayne that the body they'd examined at UCLA was indeed Jared Stilson and that they'd be meeting his parents, Jayne sighed.

'So you were right to move quickly on pushing them to check on him.'

'In all fairness to Detective West,' Steelie said, 'he did call us first.'

Jayne put her elbows on her desk and rested her head in her hands. 'Did he say that we needed to be concerned about our safety?'

'No. Look, we're way out of this case.' Steelie was aware that she was also trying to reassure herself. Going back to the scene of the crime wasn't top on her list of destinations right now but West's reference to 'beefed up' campus security had helped, even if she was a vegetarian.

Jayne was looking at her in disbelief. 'Except for meeting his parents tomorrow right at the grave site!'

'I know, but we kind of have to go because of our previous involvement. Plus, safety in numbers, right? Now . . .' Steelie settled her backside on the edge of the desk. She was going to change the subject, big time, because Jayne's mother Marie had tasked her with getting at least a top line if not details of Jayne's date with Scott Houston. Steelie usually just parried when Marie queried her as to whether Jayne was dating anyone seriously, which, it seemed to Steelie, was Marie's primary concern at this point in her life. Nonetheless, this base-touching about Jayne had become a feature of Marie and Steelie's relationship, which had verged on mother-daughter since Steelie had been in college. And as much as Marie was the polar opposite of Steelie in style and sensibility, they shared a real desire to see Jayne out of the shadows of the PTSD symptoms that had kept her hermetic and jumpy for so long. If Scott was going to help bring her out into the light, Steelie wanted to know.

She went for Jayne's buy-in first. 'You have to admit I've been really good all day.'

Jayne sat back. 'Your restraint was noted.'

'This was more than restraint! I sprouted, like, two more gray hairs, I was concentrating so hard on being good. So, where'd you and Scott go for dinner? Was it fun or, like, magical or what? When's your next date – the weekend?'

Jayne hesitated.

Steelie stared. 'Oh, no. You didn't bail on the date, did you?'

'No, not at all. It was very . . . nice.'

After a moment of waiting expectantly, Steelie deflated. 'You're really not going to say more than that?'

'Concerned that the mastermind behind this Q&A will be unhappy with you?'

'Mastermind?' Steelie said weakly.

'Also known as my mother.'

'Marie hasn't—'

'Oh, stop now before you get struck down.'

'Okay, so she's asked me.'

Jayne made a noise of exasperation. 'I never understand this. Why doesn't she just ask me?'

'Because you never tell her anything!'

'Only to stop her announcing my re-entry into the world of Dating Singles on her radio show.'

'Aha! So, you do consider yourself to be dating.'

Jayne flourished her hand. 'Yes, look at that – a little crumb to take back to Marie.'

Steelie slid off the desk and began walking out. 'This ain't over.'

'You can talk tough, Steelie, but it won't help. I know better than you that when it comes to my mother, this is just the beginning.'

*

Scott sat at his desk to read the fax of the LA County Coroner's preliminary report on the body at UCLA, now identified as Jared Alun Stilson. The name meant nothing to him. Eric had already run it through the federal system. Stilson wasn't known to government or law enforcement but his parents were: both had served in the military until their mid-forties. But Scott wasn't going to use the victim's name to convince his boss that the FBI should buck protocol and insert itself into the case before the local police department had requested federal help.

He was going to use the cause of death.

He turned to Eric. 'If the coroner's further tests confirm it, then this will be the first time the same combination of sodium pentothal, pancuronium bromide and potassium chloride has surfaced outside a state penitentiary since the Bailey brothers' case, right?'

'As far as we can tell, yes, but the LAPD can get on with their investigation alone for now.'

'Not if there's crucial evidence inside a federal file they don't have access to.'

'What crucial evidence?'

'An accomplice who was never caught.'

Eric frowned at the files on Scott's desk. 'Since when?'

'Hear me out. The Bailey brothers' crime scene, 1980. Workers from the local water company doing a survey of residential septic systems arrive at a rural hideaway about halfway between Nashville and Knoxville and find the body of Treat Bailey who had lived there in near seclusion. He was propped up in a sitting position against a tree and had been dead for a day or two, with evidence of a shotgun wound from a gun fired at some distance. His brother, Red, was nowhere to be found but wasn't immediately suspected, as the wooded area where they lived was frequented by hunters during the season and accidents happen.'

Eric nodded. 'Then it turned out it wasn't the gunshot that killed him but the drugs sometime earlier.'

'Right. Begging the question, why would someone take aim and fire at a corpse? When the local PD eventually tracks down Red Bailey at an encampment used by transients, Bailey purports shock to hear that his brother is dead and blames hunters. No surprises there. He only confesses to killing his brother after prolonged questioning by investigators and without a lawyer. He's later convicted despite no one locating the shotgun he admitted to discarding or determining how he sourced the poison. The only things that fit about this guy were that he said he'd killed his brother to get out from under his abusive thumb and that before the fatal effects of the drugs had kicked in, he'd quote, unquote, given that SOB a piece of my mind.'

'You think that Bailey took the rap for someone else?'

'No. I'd go for participation . . . guilt, too. But he doesn't seem resourceful and yet he's supposed to have acquired a shotgun—'

'The brothers may already have owned the shotgun. The file didn't say.'

'The file didn't say a lotta things. But even if they owned this one, he still had to discard it somewhere between his place and the camp in the woods.'

'Everything's in the woods out there,' Eric said.

'How does he discard a shotgun so thoroughly that the local cops can't find it?'

'Someone could have found it and kept it. A shotgun's a useful thing to have around, especially in the woods.'

'True. Okay, so he discards it. What about the poison? How does he get it? How does he pay for it?'

'Yeah, that part was questionable,' Eric said, 'given that he lacked a criminal record and therefore lacked criminal contacts and, y'know, lived in the woods. This all happened before the internet became an emporium to order anything you want.'

'If he did it, he had a contact as well as some serious money under the mattress. Yet the file says that this is a guy who never worked for a salary and spent a lot of time locked in a shed by his bully of a brother after they returned from 'Nam.'

'Alright, so I can see how you think there's an accomplice,' Eric said. 'It could be someone who didn't want payment for the drugs as much as a chance to observe them being used in a murder, as well as have a convenient fall guy in the form of Red Bailey if the cops did figure out how the murder went down.'

'Yeah. Someone really fucked in the head, who just wants to torture people or see 'em get tortured.' Scott thought for a moment. 'He and Red Bailey meet. Bailey's talking about his asshole brother and the contact sees a good opportunity. Sells him the drugs for peanuts but wants to watch. Doesn't care if Bailey gets picked up for it later because he won't have even given Bailey his real name.'

'Just walks away,' Eric said. 'Hmph. I see room for that when I think back to the original report. But that could just be a poorly written report. There could be more to it than what they wrote up at the time.'

'If there's more, why not put it in the report? You're being too generous, Eric. You know how it works.'

'Sure, but sometimes a lazy report doesn't mean there was a lazy investigation.'

'You know as well as I do that a good investigator doesn't write a lazy report. No way. They want it to show that they crossed all the t's and dotted all the i's.' Scott picked up the original print-outs of the file and waved them. 'This ain't that report.'

'Okay, fine. There's room for an accomplice.'

'And that accomplice was not picked up with Bailey.'

Eric blew out his cheeks. 'It's all pretty speculative.'

'But if instead of Bailey's defense lawyer having him plead guilty, he'd put this argument to a jury . . .?'

'A jury-jury or a Southern, woodsy jury?'

'Come on. Drop the woods bullshit.'

Eric smiled.

Scott rejoined, 'Any jury would've seen reasonable doubt. Bailey might not have been convicted.'

Eric eyed his partner. 'You're not trying to bring in some miscarriage of justice stuff, are you?'

'No. Not necessarily.'

Eric intensified his gaze.

'Okay!' Scott held up his hands. 'Right now, I'm just saying that a killer who struck in Tennessee may have escaped justice and could've gone on to kill a college kid in California. Whether he's doing murder for hire or he's just a psychopath dancing to the beat of his own drummer, we don't know yet. But he could be good for this murder at UCLA and we're within our rights to take over that part of the LAPD case.'

'Enjoy it while it lasts.'

'What do you mean?'

'Did you forget about Turner? He's the tall guy with the icy stare that signs your time card. We're not taking over a local PD's case – that they won't want to give us – until he gives us the go-ahead.'

Scott stood up and began to gather the files together. 'Then let's see if he wants to take home a little light reading tonight.'

DAY THREE

FRIDAY

10

From where she was leaning against the construction site's perimeter fence, Steelie watched Mitch Nelson bat at a patch of dust on his cargo pants. He did that a few times, then held the material taut and examined it.

He batted at it again. 'Dammit.'

Steelie guessed he was concerned about Jared Stilson's parents thinking he didn't look presentable. 'They're not going to notice. Or care.'

Mitch straightened up, still looking uncomfortable. 'I've never had to do this before.'

'Didn't you meet the descendants for the Gabrielino-Tongva site near Downtown back in the day?'

'They asked us to do that dig.'

'Only because of impending construction on what is actually their ancestral land,' Steelie reminded him. 'It wasn't elective.'

'But that was ancestors. This is someone's kid.'

Jayne, who had been listening but not joining in up until now, said, 'Exhuming ancestors produces all kinds of emotional disturbance. But why am I telling you? You know.'

They fell back into silence. Steelie had noticed that Jayne had been preoccupied since they'd arrived. She seemed to have been watching the area around the construction site to see if anyone was watching them. No one had passed by since they'd arrived but Steelie felt somewhat responsible for potentially triggering Jayne's hypervigilance. She decided to join in the scanning, letting her eyes run all the way along the chain-link fence to the nearest building. That was when she saw something moving. She squinted toward the building, wondering if it was a bush or a person.

'Hey.' Steelie glanced briefly at Mitch. 'Is that one of your people lurking by the building?'

Mitch looked. 'I can't see anyone. Anyway, my people don't lurk.'

Jayne tilted her head to the side. 'I can see someone. Maybe someone tall, depending on how tall that bush is.' She reached into her bag and handed Steelie a pair of binoculars.

Steelie located the corner of the building, traced the wall down, found the bushes, saw dark hair and then she was looking directly into another pair of binoculars.

'What the—'

'What?' Jayne reached for the binoculars but stopped because a car pulled up behind them. It was an unmarked Ford Crown Victoria used by the detectives.

West and Sanchez stepped out of the car and held open the rear doors. A pair of shiny penny loafers settled into the dusty ground on the side where Sanchez was standing sentry. The rest of the person emerged as he gripped the door for support: a somewhat stocky man of medium height whose creamy skin looked pallid, as though a tan was fading. His salt-and-pepper hair was cut short along the back and sides and he was wearing a pale yellow golf shirt over dark suit pants.

He walked around the back of the car to join the person being given a hand by West. Again, the shoes were visible first – loafers similar to the man's but with a slight heel. When the woman stood, she was taller than the man but not taller than West, who moved to close the door. Now Steelie could see a dark skirt hitting just below the knee and a crushed silk top in the same pale yellow as her husband wore but the color was more flattering against her brown skin. As the group advanced, Steelie wondered if the Stilsons had dressed alike on purpose. It made them look united.

West said in introduction, 'Mr. and Mrs. Stilson, this is Mitchell Nelson, the head of UCLA's Cultural Resource Management Division. His role is to monitor all construction excavation on campus. He moved swiftly to ensure your son was recovered with care and dignity.'

Steelie liked the phraseology West had chosen. He had managed to convey that finding Jared was the only thing that mattered and that procedures were followed.

Mr. Stilson seemed composed until he spoke. 'You saw Jared first? His body, that is?' He sounded tentative, out of his depth.

Mitch cleared his throat. 'Yes, that's correct.'

'We've been told that your quick response helped to prevent him – his body . . . from being damaged further. Thank you.'

'I would also like to say thank you.' Mrs. Stilson put a hand out toward Mitch.

West then gestured toward Jayne and Steelie. 'These are the scientists who we relied on for key assistance in identifying your son.'

The Stilsons continued their formal statements of gratitude as they were introduced by name.

Mr. Stilson held his wife's hand. 'We were at the coroner's office earlier today. They explained that you could show us where Jared was?'

'Of course,' Jayne said.

They filed through the gate, Mitch leading the way. Jayne and Steelie walked to the front as they approached the cut itself. It looked different now that the coroner's Special Operations Response Team had been there. SORT had created a larger and deeper hole that had straight sides. There were some scraps of white flagging and fluorescent twine left from the grid lines they must have placed over the area for their maps.

Steelie joined Jayne in stepping down into the hole and they quietly consulted with each other as to where Jared's body had been within this much larger cavity. They canvassed Mitch's opinion too before speaking to the Stilsons.

'Jared was here,' Steelie said. 'He was on his back, stretched out with his head at this end and his feet about here.'

Steelie was watching to see if the Stilsons had followed. They had. Their newfound knowledge brought them closer to each other, now merged almost into one body thanks to the matching clothing. Their arms were around each other and where Mrs. Stilson's eyes had closed as she put her head against her husband's, his eyes were wide and unblinking as he looked toward the ground, the muscles of his jaw working.

It was time to leave the parents alone by the grave for a few minutes. Steelie and Jayne walked away with Mitch and the detectives, almost shoulder-to-shoulder in a line. But when an anguished cry pierced the air from behind them, their line went slightly ragged, each of them faltering to a different degree. A second unmarked LAPD car was pulling up to the fence.

Sanchez said, 'We're going to send the parents back to their hotel. Can you stay a bit longer?'

Jayne and Steelie nodded simultaneously but Mitch pointed at his own chest. 'Are you going to need me?'

West responded that they wouldn't and thanked Mitch, who gave his old friends a grim nod before walking away.

When the Stilsons eventually began walking back to the fence, they looked lost. They weren't even heading for the open gate. West and Sanchez hurried back and re-routed them. They put them into the unmarked car, which progressed slowly over the uneven construction track and then accelerated sedately away when it gained the tarmac.

Sanchez nodded toward the departing car. 'So, we were interested to have confirmation that Jared Stilson was mixed-race, given that his missing person report has him down as white. When we spoke to the Stilsons, we learned they didn't put in the misper report. The informant was actually Jared's Residential Advisor here on campus because it was the school that reported him missing.'

West said, 'We're about to go talk to the RA to flush out if this was done on purpose to delay identification. Just need to rule that in or out. Thought you might be interested in joining us.'

Steelie was so ready to join them that she almost forgot

to check with Jayne before speaking. They exchanged a glance. Jayne shrugged, so Steelie agreed on their behalf.

*

Jayne sat next to Steelie in the back of the detective vehicle as West drove them over to the east side of the UCLA campus. He parked in a space reserved for UCLA employees near one of the student unions. The four of them wended their way past large dumpsters to come along the backside of the union into a courtyard dotted with umbrellas shading café tables. The place was busy with summer session students and staff.

Sanchez murmured, 'There he is. Green shirt, table by the wall.'

Jayne wondered how the detectives knew what the student looked like just as the young man noticed them. He stood up uncertainly. He had the broad-shouldered frame of a swimmer but stared out at the world like an owl from behind black-framed glasses with a heavy prescription.

Sanchez gave him an encouraging smile. 'Owen Reid?'

'Yeah, that's me.'

'Theresa Sanchez. We spoke earlier. This is my partner, Detective Matthew West, and these are two scientists assisting us. Can we join you?'

Owen nodded vaguely but sat back down. Jayne and Steelie sat a little further away from the group but Jayne could see that the textbook open on the table was heavily lined and highlighted. The pencil and highlighter were sitting next to the book, along with a flip cell phone. She couldn't see the spine of the book to read its title but the pages had as many bar graphs as text.

West opened a small notebook while Sanchez talked.

'As I told you, we have a couple of questions about how the missing person report on Jared Stilson came about.'

'Okay. I'll do the best I can.'

'Was it you who determined he was missing?'

Owen put his hands out in a distancing gesture. 'No, not at all. It was his roommate. But his roommate came to me and I called campus police.'

'And did campus police come and interview you?'

'Yeah, they came to the building, looked in Jared's room, which he shared with Kit. Kit Kaneo. Then they asked me a bunch of questions.'

'What kind of questions?'

Owen thought for a moment. 'Like what was he wearing, what did he look like, where did I think he might have gone. Stuff like that.'

'So, were you the one who made the list of what he was wearing?'

'Well, I told the campus cops but I got the list from his roommate. It was his best guess anyway.'

'The details for the missing person report . . . did you fill out a form or did campus police ask you questions?'

Owen shook his head. 'I never filled anything out. Just answered their questions.'

'And did you provide them with a photograph of Jared?'

'Yeah. It was the photograph from the freshman board in our dorm. The one he would have sent in when he was accepted to UCLA, so he was maybe a couple months older than that?'

'Okay. And when did you call his parents?'

'Right after I called campus police. I thought they'd

appreciate that the cops were already looking into it.'

'Had you ever met his parents before?'

'No, because I wasn't the RA from the start of the quarter; that was Steve Jones. I took over when he had to stop being RA because of his class load. I hadn't met any parents at orientation like he had.'

'I see,' Sanchez said. 'But you met the Stilsons eventually?'

'Yeah, they flew in the day after I called them.'

'You met both Mr. and Mrs. Stilson?'

'Yeah.'

'Now, on Jared's missing person report, you gave his race as white.'

'Uh-huh.'

Sanchez glanced at Jayne and Steelie before putting her next question. 'But you did see that one of his parents is white and the other is black? When you met them.'

'I saw that his mom was black, yeah, but I figured she was his stepmom.' He now looked to Jayne and Steelie as though *this* was the reason they'd accompanied the detectives. 'Did I do something wrong?'

Jayne tried to make her expression reassuring but Sanchez was already drawing Owen's attention back to her by saying his name firmly. 'Owen. You didn't think to ask if she was his stepmom or his mom?'

He compressed his lips and started to blush, an almost maroon tint blossoming across his throat, and then he barked, 'You have no idea what it was like!' He blinked. 'Or maybe you do since . . . you guys are cops and you do this, like, all the time.'

He gestured at Sanchez. 'Look, the guy's parents had just

92

arrived, having heard from me that he's gone missing. His mother was totally upset and his dad looked like he was trying to find heads that could roll. I had already done the missing person report. I never knew or thought or *suspected* Jared wasn't white and I sure as hell wasn't going to say to one of his parents, while they're, like, packing up his stuff in his room and, like, crying: "Um, excuse me but are you really Jared's mother?" I mean, dude!' He appealed to West.

West used a hand to pat the air, apparently trying to calm Owen down.

But Owen wasn't calming down. 'Do you know what it's like to be an RA?' he squeaked. 'I mean, I was basically in charge of those kids and I had to call one of their parents and say that their kid's gone. *Gone*. He was only a freshman.' He shook his head. 'And this week's brought it all back. It's him, isn't it? The body they found?' He looked back to Sanchez, his neck now blotchy with red and white patches.

She nodded.

Owen's face contorted and he looked away. After a moment, he said, 'What happened to him?'

'We're still investigating that,' West said.

Owen finally met Sanchez's eyes again. 'And did I mess things up when I did the missing person report or something? I mean, is his mom, y'know . . . his mom?'

Sanchez said, 'You didn't mess anything up. Someone had to take responsibility for reporting Jared missing. You took on that responsibility and his parents will have been appreciative. We certainly are.'

Owen took off his glasses and wiped his eyes with the

back of his wrist before putting his glasses back on. 'We got training on lots of stuff as RAs. CPR and stuff. We were told to call campus police the minute there were any problems like that, so I was just doing what I'd been told to do.'

He looked composed again but now his eyes seemed vulnerable behind his glasses.

Sanchez nodded. 'We're not going to take up any more of your time, Owen. Thank you for meeting us.'

They all got up and Steelie and Jayne shook hands with Owen as well before they left him to his open book.

West was the first to speak as they walked back to the car. 'So, there you have it. Student reported missing by someone who barely knows him. He thinks the kid is white so reports him as a missing white person. Eventually meets parents and dismisses mom as mom because she's black.'

Steelie cut in. 'I don't think this kid connected the contents of the missing person report with the parents. I mean, they happened separately; he processed them separately.'

'But it wasn't more than twenty-four hours later,' West pointed out.

Jayne said, 'It may as well have been a year later given the emotional impact of meeting the parents, leading them into their son's room . . .' She trailed off. They'd arrived at the car.

Sanchez shook her head. 'That kid shouldn't have had to face the parents.'

Steelie looked at her. 'I noticed you decided to try to make him feel better in the end, Detective Sanchez.'

Sanchez shrugged her shoulders. 'Seemed like the right

thing to do. We got the vic ID'd.'

West held open the rear passenger door. 'It's obvious it wasn't done to delay ID. It was just a mistake.'

Steelie said, 'I keep trying to tell you, it isn't a "mistake" to call Jared white. He was as white as he was black, from an anthropological perspective.'

West gestured for her to get in the car. 'Don't start.'

Steelie said, 'Fine. So, you've got your victim ID'd now. What's next?'

Sanchez was quick with her answer. 'We've got a homicide investigation to run.' She let Jayne into the backseat on her side and closed the door firmly behind her.

*

Junior chanced a look around the Podocarpus hedge that screened the back of the student union from the parking area. It had been a shock to see the two women in the very place he'd gone for lunch. His throat had closed around the mouthful of food he'd just swallowed and he'd almost choked. The worst part was that they were so close but he couldn't do anything to them. He couldn't have even made them choke on their own food somehow, because they didn't order any. And then there were the cops. Always there. He was confused by what was going on. In the café, the two women had seemed to be observing, as opposed to helping the cops. Which would be a good thing. But just now he'd seen the cops put them in the back of the sedan like they did with people who they'd arrested. He felt a thrill at the outlandish idea of the women being incarcerated. That would be perfect. He took a chance to step out to see more.

The cop car was pulling away. It had been parked in an area reserved for staff. The arrogance. It bothered him. They wore their power on their sleeves, these cops. They didn't look behind them, didn't look around. He'd been right there, right in the same space, and they'd been chasing their tails with that boy-child Owen Reid. They had no idea how close they'd been to him, the real doer. It made him feel powerful – like his invisibility was an asset, not a flaw. But he wasn't so invisible that he could get close to the two women without them noticing. They were trained observers. The blonde was small but she was watchful. The brunette was sure-footed and well-prepared. He hadn't expected her to have brought binoculars to the construction site. She liked to see things coming; that was obvious. He'd have to take her by stealth, no question. The blonde, though . . . an idea was forming, a picture developing in his mind of how he could get past her defenses, right into her inner sanctum, with his needle readied. A tiny but insistent beep started up. He looked at his digital watch. Breaktime was over.

11

SSA Turner appeared in the doorway to Scott and Eric's office. 'I'm on my way over to that dog-and-pony show at City Hall.' He held up a file folder. 'Your plea for the case over at UCLA? I'll buy it for a dollar.'

Scott felt immediate relief but didn't say, *Thank you* aloud. That would have made Turner suspicious. He went with, 'Sir.'

Turner proffered the folder. 'Made a couple of calls to get you started. You're good to go on setting up a mutual aid agreement with the LAPD. I've had a talk with the chief over there and we conferenced in the coroner; the final tox report will be sent here first.'

Scott was stunned. He hadn't expected SSA Turner to grease the wheels like that. It made him want to build on it and fast. He looked at his watch. 'Given that we've still got the afternoon, would you have a problem with us talking to the detectives before the paperwork's signed by everyone?'

'I have no objection to that, but get the paperwork on Lance's desk before you leave.' Turner continued to speak even as he walked away, raising his voice so it would carry: 'You're still up next on the roster if a Bureau assignment comes in, regardless of this UCLA stuff.'

Scott turned back into the office. 'Eric—'

'Let me guess,' Eric said. 'I'm going to do the paperwork while you call the detectives?'

When Scott and Eric arrived at LAPD headquarters several hours later, a uniformed officer escorted them to a conference room. Detectives Sanchez and West arrived shortly afterwards, and where they were slightly wary, Scott was exceedingly matter of fact. He spread out a few pages from a leather folder across the table in front of him.

'This is in regards to 050233, the Stilson case,' Scott said.

'You mentioned on the phone,' West said.

'You've got a COD of poisoning. Specifically, sodium pentothal, pancuronium bromide and potassium chloride.'

'Actually,' West said, 'we're waiting on further tox testing.'

'That report will be copied to you when our office gets it.'

'Your office?'

'These drugs are on a federal watch list, so we're mandated to lead the investigation into how the drugs were acquired, who acquired them and where, when they were acquired and how they were used. We're also authorized to be copied on all your files relevant to the case, in so far as any aspect could assist us with our investigation into the drugs.'

Sanchez spoke into the silence that followed. 'Is this a wind-up?'

Scott looked at her. 'Does this sound like a wind-up, Detective?'

She crossed her arms. 'Don't you need to do a mutual aid agreement?'

Eric said, 'The LE agreement is in the works but we thought you'd appreciate getting a heads-up before someone came over and started copying your files.'

'Are you expecting our notes, too?'

Eric shook his head. 'Just copies of the files. But we'd appreciate being briefed right now from your notes. This isn't going beyond the four of us until a report needs to be written.'

Silence prevailed again for a few seconds.

Sanchez said, 'Are you going to brief us on your findings on the drugs?'

'Of course,' Eric said.

'We're all on the same side here,' Scott added.

Sanchez looked at him. 'Right.'

'Think of this as some assistance on one aspect of your case.'

West said, 'We didn't need any assistance. And we didn't ask for any, either.'

'Then think of it as some medicine that you're going to have to take,' Scott said. 'You might not like it but that doesn't mean it's bad for you.'

West looked over at his partner with widened eyes. 'Interesting analogy.'

Eric leaned forward. 'Federal intervention in crimes involving these drugs has been on the cards since before you guys caught this case. It's not personal and it's not a reflection on your capabilities. Maybe "assistance" is a bad word here at the LAPD but it's what we do at the federal level. We can look across state lines, access material from other cases, we can get more testing done and we can get it done at our lab. If we can bring forward a break on the case, that's good for us and it's good for you.' He opened his hands. 'Can we move on as a team here?'

Sanchez said, 'Doesn't sound like we have much choice about it.' She glanced at her partner.

West gave an almost imperceptible nod.

Eric took the win. 'Thank you. Now, could you start by bringing us up to speed on any leads you have regarding the victim and the possible perp in relation to the poisoning? We already have the prelim coroner's report.'

West straightened up in his chair. 'You have that, do you? Well, I guess you have access to everything since you're the feds.' He made a huffing noise but continued. 'You know we don't have the full toxicology results yet. I can tell you we also don't yet know how the drugs were administered. The victim disappeared in October 2003, so he was in his very first quarter at UCLA, which means we're looking at his contacts from his hometown since he hadn't had time to make a lot of contacts in college. He's from Pleasanton, some suburb inland of San Francisco. No suggestion so far of any long-standing feuds with anyone, let alone issues on campus. According to the detectives in Missings, no one saw anything suspicious on the day he disappeared, which was October 20th—'

'He disappeared from campus?' Scott had looked up from the notes he had been taking.

'Yep. Disappeared there and was found there. We don't think he was transported anywhere in between. No physical or other evidence for transport found so far.'

'Are you thinking the perp's someone from the campus?' Eric asked.

'Not necessarily. It's an open campus; anyone can get on it. It could have been someone he knew and trusted from back home.'

Sanchez said, 'We figure not just anyone can walk up to our vic and give him these particular drugs.'

'Plus, do it unseen,' West said. 'It's not impossible but we think it's too many unknowns for a perp like this to feel safe enough to act.'

'A perp like this,' Scott repeated, making air quotes with his fingers. 'You've worked up some kind of profile?'

West looked at him.

Scott elaborated. 'We'd be interested in hearing it, if you're willing to share? Maybe we can add to it.'

West took that in then said, 'Poisoning is unusual even without this particular drug combo. Burying a body more than a foot down isn't common. Even killing an eighteen-year-old in LA outside of, say, a gang context or a robbery is just . . . It's not run of the mill.'

Scott nodded. 'Do you have any evidence for the person who administered the drugs being the same as the one who did the burial?'

'That's our working theory at this stage.'

'Any thoughts on the burial site? Is it significant?'

West frowned. 'I thought you were restricting yourself to the poisoning side of this.'

'You just said yourself that your working theory is that the person who did the poisoning did the burial. So, any thoughts on the burial site as it relates to the perp?'

Sanchez said, 'We've picked up a piece of information that suggests the burial wasn't done by someone from the victim's past, unless he or she also knew the campus.'

'Go on,' Scott said.

She looked at West uneasily. 'Well, at the estimated time of burial, the site was on land earmarked for construction.

There wasn't a set date for groundbreaking but there was an administrative memorandum that it would take place in 2008. It was brought forward to 2005 when the university got some grant money specifically for the new building.'

Scott tapped his pen against his pad. 'You're telling me the vic's body was buried where it should have remained undiscovered for another three years? And that would have brought time underground to a total of four to five years?'

'We've been thinking that,' she said.

'Like, enough time that it would just be a bunch of dry bones and no trace of the drugs?'

West said, 'Maybe. We'll need some experts for that.'

Scott looked at Eric, then made a line out from the notes on his pad and wrote *32/1* next to it. 'Any leads on who was in the know about the original construction date?'

Sanchez said, 'A shitload of university staff, none of whom look like good leads.'

'Yet,' West added.

His addition amused Scott but he tried to hide that. 'Interviewed any?'

'Still making up the shortlist.'

'Keep us posted on that?' Scott stood up.

'And you're keeping us posted on what, exactly?'

'The results of our investigation into the origin of the drugs.'

As the two men eyed each other, Eric stood and extended his hand to Sanchez. This broke the impasse between Scott and West, who shook hands stiffly.

In the car, Scott slung his folder onto the dashboard in a discontented fashion.

Eric said, 'Don't act like you don't enjoy playing the

heavy. You didn't expect West to lie down just because we're from the Bureau? You wouldn't have respected him for that.'

'True.' Scott tugged his seatbelt forward. 'He and Sanchez are thinking in the right way about the case because the vic has lots of associations but not necessarily close associations. There's a huge field of potential contacts out there but they're narrowing the field by focusing on who knew about the dumping site *and* knew it wasn't meant to be dug up anytime soon.' He started the engine. 'It's good thinking.'

'It's logic,' Eric said.

Scott pulled out of the parking lot. 'Yeah, and how many cops – hell, how many agents – do you know who employ logic, especially in a challenging case like this one?'

'Do I hear a note of respect?'

Scott accelerated through the yellow light at the corner. 'If you can hear that, I'd better do something about it.' He turned right on Main.

Eric craned his neck behind him, looking at the route back to the office that they should have been on and were fast leaving behind. 'You got somewhere you need to be, Houston?'

'I figured that while we were down here, we could get Jayne and Steelie's take on the burial site.' Scott kept his eyes forward but when Eric didn't speak, he looked over at him. 'I'm thinking maybe they need to draw us some kind of diagram and walk us through it. Our boss would go for that.'

Eric assumed a deeper and flatter tone of voice. 'And what would this diagram depict, SA Houston?'

'Wow, you sound just like him.'

Eric resumed his normal voice. 'Just work on answering the question for when our boss *does* ask you.'

Scott lifted his hand from the steering wheel and opened his mouth as though starting a speech, then closed it.

Eric scoffed. 'You can't even answer the question.'

'You're my partner. Help me.'

'Nice try. Seriously, though, *partner*,' Eric turned toward him, 'I figured you were trying to get between Jayne and this business over at UCLA, not get her more involved.'

Scott pulled the Suburban left onto Pasadena Avenue without using his indicator, garnering an indignant honk from a car on the opposite side of the intersection that was forced to brake to avoid them.

He said, 'We own part of this case now and we could use their help.'

'Scott, we've turned it into a federal investigation into poisoning. That kind of heat can make a perp . . . unpredictable.'

Scott agreed but he'd felt driven to put this train in motion when Jayne had talked about the case that morning. His only thought had been, *I need to be with her*. He didn't trust anyone except maybe Eric to watch out for her. Most of all, he didn't want a repeat of Atlanta.

Scott tried to keep the note of concern out of his voice. 'Which is why we need to maximize our resources.'

'I notice it's always "we" when it's your idea.'

Scott grinned. 'Hey, if you ever *had* any ideas, I'd get on board.'

Eric chuckled but he didn't offer a rebuttal.

12

When Jayne and Steelie came up to the Agency reception area to see what the sudden hubbub was, they found Scott introducing Eric to their receptionist. Carol was blushing under the concentrated force of Scott's charm, just as she'd done the last time they'd met. Scott was partway through showing off that he remembered every detail of what he'd learned about how the young Carol had been in the passenger seat of her mother's wood-paneled Suburban when she drove the Alaska Highway in the 1940s. Eric was looking suitably impressed – with both Carol and Scott.

Steelie said, 'There's more to Carol than that Alaskan adventure, Houston.'

He replied, 'You mean, like how she was an LE grief counselor?'

Steelie started. 'How'd you know Carol worked for law enforcement?'

Jayne was wondering the same thing.

Scott smiled at Carol. 'We've had a few chats, haven't we?'

The proud grin on their receptionist's face made Jayne feel very warm toward Scott.

Carol said, 'I'm enjoying renewing our acquaintance, Scott, but you said you were hoping for a consult with Jayne and Steelie?'

Jayne had just begun to speculate about why the agents

had come over in person. She was intrigued about the consultation. 'We'll take Eric on a tour and you can catch up with us, Scott.'

In Jayne's office through the glass doors from reception, Eric took in the wall of filing cabinets that Jayne explained were only partly filled with agency case files on missing and found persons.

He jutted his chin out toward the cabinets. 'Have you ever made a match with a living person?'

'Not yet.'

'But how would you do that? I mean, you don't go on the road looking for mispers, do you?' He looked around.

'No, we don't,' Jayne said. 'We leave that to the police. But we search hospitals and hospices caring for people who've lost their identity, whether through trauma or amnesia or dementia. Or institutions fostering juveniles who are so young, they can't identify themselves. So our search parameters remain rooted in physical description, medical X-rays, dental, etcetera.'

Eric had started nodding with understanding halfway through. 'Of course! I forgot about living Does. How do you reach hospitals? Are they part of some kind of network?'

Jayne shook her head. 'Nope. No network for that yet. We approach directly when we have a case where it's possible that this was the outcome.'

Steelie added, 'You gotta keep in mind that the hospitals should have already entered someone like an amnesiac into the NCIC Unidentified Persons file. Medical institutions are pretty good about reporting to law enforcement, actually. The issue is getting law enforcement to work with the quirks of NCIC.' She gestured for him to go out the other set of doors that led to the hallway.

They stopped by the kitchen-break room – Eric accepted a bottle of cold water – and trooped into the laboratory at the back of the building.

'This is Steelie's domain,' Jayne said.

Eric took up a stool and Steelie showed him the various stations for examining X-rays, taking measurements, storing equipment, and the all-important computer for the All Coroners Bulletin.

Steelie patted the monitor. 'We use this baby to notify coroners of particularly identifiable characteristics on missing persons that couldn't have been included on a missing persons report.'

'Is this how the LAPD got you involved on the Stilson case over at UCLA?' Eric was pointing at the computer.

Jayne cut in. 'You know about that case?'

He smiled. 'My partner has talked of nothing else.'

Jayne felt herself blushing and then Scott was in the doorway.

Scott looked around the group. 'What is it that I'm talking about?'

Eric said, 'The case we just picked up.'

Catching Scott's eye, Jayne said, 'The LAPD requested federal involvement?'

Eric gave a short snort of mirth.

Scott said, 'We've taken over the investigation into the drugs.'

Jayne frowned. 'Have you talked to Detective West?'

Eric nodded. 'We just came from there.'

But Jayne's eyes hadn't left Scott's face. 'He didn't ask

how you'd heard about it?'

Scott's mouth twitched with the hint of a smile. 'Locals don't get to ask Federals. They just get told.'

Jayne persisted. 'You didn't say you heard about it from me, did you?'

Steelie interjected, 'How could Scott have heard about it from you?'

'I . . .' Jayne felt helpless on how to answer Steelie without revealing that she and Scott had woken up in the same bed. Meanwhile, Eric was clearly trying to cover his amusement again so she figured he already knew this factoid. That made her strangely happy as well as weirdly embarrassed. How would Scott have characterized their first date to Eric of all people?

Scott put his hands out as if to have the final word on the topic. 'Listen, the drugs are on a federal watch list so our office would have been notified any day now. We just sped things up. *And* we wanted to pick your brains a little on that very case. Is that okay?'

Steelie said, 'Fine by me.'

Jayne nodded.

Scott continued. 'Can we talk about the condition of the body you saw—' He stopped himself. 'This is still sub judice, capiche?'

Steelie barked out a laugh. 'We were on this case before it was a twinkle in your eye, Houston. Get on with it.'

Eric chuckled.

Scott remained focused. 'Okay. If the body hadn't been discovered for another couple of years, would it have been just bones?'

Jayne answered with her eyes on Steelie's. 'Fully

skeletonized in four or five years total? Sure, that's possible. Right?'

Steelie waggled her hand. 'He wasn't buried very deep but we don't know anything about that soil. Like if it was acidic or something. That could affect rate of decomposition.'

Scott asked, 'Would there be hair still?'

'Definitely,' Jayne answered. 'And those pants would be present, and shoes if there were any. Anything man-made should still be around after only five years underground if the soil isn't particularly acidic or if a chemical agent wasn't added to make everything disintegrate.'

Eric said, 'But if the body was basically bones, that would make it tough to do a tox test, right?'

Steelie shook her head. 'You've always got the hair. Depending on when a drug . . . I assume that's what you're getting at? Depending on when it was ingested, you can always try testing the hair. The results are limited by other factors beyond simple ingestion or introduction to the bloodstream. But you should ask a forensic biologist or even a pathologist.'

The lab telephone beeped with an intercom call. It was Carol, calling from the front of the office. Steelie activated the speaker. 'Yeah, Carol?'

'There are two LAPD officers here to see you. A Detective West and a Detective Sanchez, regarding the matter at UCLA.'

Scott reached out and muted the intercom. 'Stall them, Steelie.'

'This isn't your office, Houston.' Steelie unmuted the intercom and told Carol to send the detectives back to the lab. Then she rubbed her hands together. 'This should be fun. Anyone got popcorn?'

Scott groaned and stood just as the detectives appeared.

West was in front. He stopped short then recovered, shot his cuffs and glanced at Steelie and Jayne. 'Ms. Lander. Ms. Hall.'

Smiling broadly, Steelie gestured toward Eric and Scott. 'Introductions not necessary, I take it?'

'We know each other,' Sanchez said, coming around her partner with a slight frown.

West looked discomfited.

Jayne decided to call time on Steelie's enjoyment of seeing four law enforcement officers looking uncomfortable all at the same time. 'Everyone's here about Jared Stilson. If you think Steelie and I can assist, we're all ears.'

After a moment of silence, Sanchez said, 'The groundbreaking ceremony that revealed the body was way ahead of schedule. We're looking at the possibility that the body was buried at that location to prevent discovery until the scheduled groundbreaking.'

'*They're* looking at that possibility,' Scott clarified. 'But what *we're* working on is whether the choice of site was about more than just delaying discovery. Like maybe the perp thought that when the ground was eventually dug up, there'd be no trace of drugs. No one would be able to figure out how the vic died.'

Eric crossed his arms. 'A thought. Why bury the vic where people are sure to find him, even if discovery is four years down the track?'

'The perp wanted him to be found . . .?' Scott let the question hang.

110

'Or,' West said, 'a delay of four years is great because if he'd dumped the body in an alley in West LA, it would have been found in about four hours.'

Jayne said, 'Don't forget that body dump sites have their own lexicon. A lot of it is about convenience for the person doing the dumping, right? It's about locations that are good because they don't require a lot of digging to successfully hide something. They're usually pre-existing holes or depressions or bushes, and they're usually within ten miles of the perpetrator's home or maybe their business – less, if someone has to transport a body without a vehicle.'

Scott said, 'We're trying to narrow the field, Jayne, not make it bigger.'

She felt her cheeks flush. 'You came here for our input, right?'

West was gesturing at the door while giving Scott a fixed stare. 'Feel free to leave.'

Scott gave Jayne a look that she read as either embarrassed or apologetic or maybe both. He said, 'Yes, we came here for your input. Which we consider valuable. Go on.'

Jayne accepted this with a nod. 'All I was trying to say was there are some known body-dumping MOs, and a piece of land like the one on campus that no one's going to touch for a few years fits nicely. It fits even without a plan to obscure the cause of death.'

Scott looked interested and then looked around the room. 'You got any maps here?'

Sanchez stepped out of the way as Steelie crossed to the cupboard by the door. She pulled several poster rolls from the top shelf. Twirling each to find its label, she put them

111

all back but one and unfurled it. She brought it to the wall-mounted lightboard above the counter and used pieces of masking tape to hold the poster in place.

She said, 'A map of west Los Angeles that includes the UCLA campus. And with the distance marker, we can see . . .' She pulled down her tortoiseshell-framed glasses from where they'd been holding her bangs back from her forehead and peered at the corner of the map. Then she took a ruler and pencil and drew lines out like spokes from a small dot she'd put in. 'Ten miles out in every direction from where the body was found.'

She drew a circle along the outer ends of the lines, and then stood back so the others could look more closely. She said, 'You're looking at Brentwood, some of Santa Monica, the hills above Sunset, the areas flanking the 405.'

Sanchez said, 'At least you can rule out the huge swathe of land that's the VA cemetery.'

'But not the people who work there.'

'Good point,' Sanchez reflected.

West said, 'Someone who works in a cemetery could just tip a body into a hole they've already got open.'

'Detective Sanchez,' Jayne said, thoughtfully, 'you hit on something when you remarked on the size of the land.' She pointed at the Veterans Administration cemetery on the map. 'You've got both the VA land as well as the freeway alongside it and it's a wide one – what, eight or ten lanes across?'

'Ten,' supplied Eric.

Jayne gave him a nod of thanks. 'Together, the two features almost form a geographical barrier. I would focus on anything east of that barrier but within your radius

112

closer to the campus.'

West had been studying the map and spoke like he'd forgotten he was in the room with other people. He tapped the map firmly. 'I want to compare the home addresses of everyone on campus who knew about the construction dates with this map. See who overlaps, if anyone. I bet not that many people who work at UCLA live within ten miles of campus.'

Scott said quickly, 'Do you have that list with you?'

'It's back at headquarters,' Sanchez said.

West suddenly seemed to register the room. 'How about we work on our stuff and you just work on your stuff?'

Scott gave a single nod.

Eric pointed at his partner. 'You don't want to ask Thirty-Two One about a diagram?'

'I was just thinking that this counts as a diagram.' Scott indicated the map.

Eric raised his hands in capitulation. 'It's your funeral.'

Scott turned to Steelie. 'Can I borrow this?'

'Sure.' She started to remove the tape securing the poster.

West put a hand against the map. 'We need that.'

Jayne stepped in before things escalated. 'Folks, we can make copies.'

West removed his hand.

'Hang on,' Scott said. 'Could you mark the body location a little darker?'

'Well, if I'm going to do that,' Steelie said, 'let me make it a little more accurate, too.'

'No, this is fine where it is.'

Steelie shrugged and darkened the point from which the

113

spokes radiated. Then she pulled the map down, copied it on the large format copier and swiftly shimmied the original between her fingers to produce a tight roll. She smoothed a piece of tape over the center of the roll and held it out toward Scott.

'Good luck with whatever it is you're doing with this,' she said.

He took it with a grin.

She raised an eyebrow. 'Probably best I don't know.'

Scott tapped her on the shoulder with the poster. 'Spoken like a true criminal defense lawyer.'

When Steelie gave West his copy, he said, 'I thought you were a youth crime lawyer.'

'Can't think why. Anyway, it's past tense,' Steelie clarified as she led the rest of the group into the hallway. 'Was a lawyer, now an anthropologist.'

'Is there any past tense to being a lawyer?' West asked.

'You think it's like AA? Once a lawyer, always a lawyer?'

'Something like that.'

Steelie glanced at him. 'You in need of legal representation, Detective?'

Everyone laughed and West dropped it.

Jayne was at the back of the group and Scott held her arm so she'd stop in the hallway. He spoke softly.

'About earlier, when I made that comment about you making the field bigger?'

Jayne just waited. She liked that he was circling back to this.

'I didn't mean to sound like I was trying to shut you down – or actually, I sounded like that because I hadn't expected you to . . . expand beyond talking about the body. It just made me think about the danger you might've been in at the crime scene the other day. The reminder that the perp could very well have been there, watching you.'

Jayne was enjoying the sensation of someone wanting to protect her. 'Thank you for explaining. And for the record, I don't want to be in danger.'

'Glad to hear it. So no driving around Westwood, trying to add to or improve on your anthropological insights on this killer.'

Scott looked down the hallway, which was empty, the rest of the group talking together in reception. He took Jayne's hand and squeezed it. 'Stay safe, okay?'

She nodded and squeezed his hand back.

TWO DAYS LATER

DAY FIVE

SUNDAY

13

Steelie sipped her beer and surveyed the wasteland in front of her. After two years of home ownership, she still didn't know what she wanted to do with her backyard. The front yard had been successfully transformed into a low-water paradise with the help of Jayne's mother, but that had yet to inspire her to transform the back. That modest rectangle was still the weedscape it had been when she'd bought the property. And they were some weeds. Steelie was amazed that the two-punch of heat and drought hadn't been enough to keep them down this summer.

She took a last swig from the bottle and set it down on the table. She tied the laces on her boots, labored over her gloves and took both sides in a debate about starting by the patio or the back fence. She decided on the patio because it was closer to the beer. Finally, she couldn't procrastinate any longer.

Once the pile of yanked weeds grew, Steelie found she enjoyed the chore. She was sitting back to survey progress when she heard her doorbell ring. Going down the side of the house so she didn't have to take off her boots, she found Jayne's mother standing on the front porch, her back to the door as she surveyed the front yard.

'Marie? Hi!'

'The garden's looking wonderful, Steelie.'

'If you do say so yourself, right?'

119

Steelie walked through the pea gravel Marie had chosen to complement the drought-tolerant succulents in their shades of gray and green.

'It was a joint effort as I recall.' Marie gave Steelie an air-kiss near the cheek.

Steelie focused on keeping her dirty gloves away from the full skirt of Marie's very white dress. The woman even had a white silk scarf tied at her throat, the knot off to one side, which combined with the bright sunshine to form an up-light under her chin. Her caramel-colored skin looked radiant. The white hoop earrings she wore were straight out of the Eighties and they fitted well with her blow-dried, backswept *Charlie's Angels* coiffure. Between her looks and the transcontinental-tinged British accent she'd acquired when immersed in British schooling in Caracas as a child, Marie was unique, even in LA.

Steelie said, 'Do you want to come around back? I was just weeding.'

Marie followed her. 'Still deciding what you want to plant?'

'I'm thinking about getting a dog, so maybe grass? But not the kind of grass you have to mow. I don't know what that stuff's called but I've seen it.'

'Blue Fescue or Japanese Mondo Grass perhaps? Mondo does grow happily in our climate though it would be happier with some shade. With a dog, however, you have to think about the hit of nitrogen a lawn will get if you let him relieve himself on it.' Marie stood on the back patio and tilted her head as she took the measure of the space. 'You might need different zones within the garden to address that. And good training for the dog.'

'As much as I would love to get your professional advice,' Steelie said, 'I bet you didn't come here to discuss my yard. Can I get you a drink?'

Marie eyed the beer bottle doubtfully.

Steelie put her gloves down and retrieved the bottle. 'I'll make us some tea. That stuff you gave me for my birthday. Tottenham and Hotspurs, was it?'

'Fortnum and Mason's,' Marie corrected before she caught Steelie's grin. 'Oh, you got me – again!'

'It's just so easy, I can't help it.' Steelie indicated the bench. 'Take a load off. No, wait, let me get you something to sit on.'

Marie protested that she was fine and Steelie went in to make the tea. By the time they'd had a cup and discussed the yard some more, the bench was in the shade of the house and the afternoon temperature had cooled to perfection.

'Have you heard from Jayne at all this weekend?' Marie said.

Here we go, thought Steelie. 'I take it you haven't?'

'No. So, you don't know any more about her date with the legendary Scott Houston?'

Steelie shook her head and looked into her cup. Marie had never stopped by to interrogate her in person before. It had to be because the man in question was Scott: the one Jayne had always referred to as an example of a 'better man' whenever a relationship of hers had ended.

Marie was still calculating. 'This was meant to be the second time they were seeing each other this week and she hasn't called you? Do you think everything's alright?'

Steelie made a face. This was almost as bad as talking to her own mother about sex when she was in high school. She assumed Jayne was lounging, in bed, with Scott. The last thing she needed was for her mother to bring her sky-blue Mercedes coupe screeching to a halt at the curb outside in order to celebrate this happy occurrence. Steelie grabbed her gloves and went back to weeding.

'Ohhhh!' Marie said with understanding. 'You think everything's *very* alright, don't you? So, what's led you to believe they've spent the weekend together?'

Steelie was considering how to put this into words when her cell phone rang. Thanking a god she wasn't sure she believed in for the full 365 days of the year, she held up a finger toward Marie while she answered.

The voice said, 'Ms. Lander, it's Detective West.'

'Working on a Sunday?'

'It's shift work.'

Steelie chided herself. She knew cops worked shifts, plus, she was a staunch advocate for the separation of church and state. Her implication of a Day of Rest was ridiculous but she couldn't stop herself from teasing this guy. Trying to get serious, she said, 'Right. So, what can I do for you?'

'I'm calling with an ask. We've got a link between Jared Stilson and the other missing UCLA student.'

Steelie felt the hairs on her arms stand up. 'Regan Hart?'

'That's the one. She's classified as voluntary missing as of now.'

Steelie was already picturing Regan Hart's body being found like Jared's if indeed there was a link between the two students. 'I'm aware of her status.'

West's tone was curious. 'Her parents are clients of yours?'

'No, but Jayne and I . . . take note of a lot of missings. Follow any updates in the news. So Regan and Jared knew each other?'

'Well, they'd met.'

Steelie felt immediate relief. Two students at the same university meeting didn't constitute a link in her mind. 'A bit of a leap to expect you're going to find Regan Hart deceased too. That's what you're thinking, isn't it?'

'I'm hoping for a different outcome, obviously, but I'm a homicide detective. My days usually start at a crime scene and end at the morgue. I skew dead.'

Steelie gave a rueful smile. She knew what he meant. It wasn't too different from what forensic scientists were known to say: *Our day begins when your day ends.*

West was still talking. 'But it's not just that these students met. It's where they met. We've got a student from Jared's dorm who knew both of them separately saying he saw them talking in front of a stand for a campus club. Apparently, there's a day when students sign up for these?'

'That's right.'

'I thought the name of the club would interest you: Mix it Up.'

Steelie's mind drew a blank. A club for people who switched between voting Republican and Democrat every election? 'That name's not saying much to me.'

'I'm surprised. You who like to pontificate about mixed-race people.'

Steelie rolled her eyes. She should have thought of that, given how West had trailered it. 'Mix it Up could've meant anything,' she said defensively.

'You just can't admit that you weren't fast enough to catch this one.'

Steelie grinned. He was right, he knew he was right and now he was the one teasing her. Then she noticed that Marie was inside, watching her from the kitchen window above the sink, where she was no doubt washing up everything in sight, including Steelie's breakfast dishes and maybe even the window itself.

After a faint chuckle, West continued. 'So this Mix it Up is the only crossover between these two students that we've found so far. We're right now working on a theory that the club exposed them both to the same predator and that, yes, Regan will also be found dead. We're working outward from the club.'

Steelie thought to herself, *go from the known to the unknown*. It was a tenet applied in forensic exhumations and it made sense here, too. The police now had a nexus between two missing persons – one found dead, the other still missing. It was an important lead.

She said, 'So what's the ask?'

West exhaled. 'Turns out that the club was never formed. It had a booth and students signed up but we don't know who they were because administration doesn't even have the Mix it Up sign-up sheet. We've only got the name of the student who sponsored it.'

'Okayyy . . .?'

'We need the sponsor to recreate the sign-up list if possible so we can go and question the other students. And . . . me and Sanchez were thinking that we could use some old Bruins here since you could talk to a student without it seeming like police questioning.'

'So, that would make me and Jayne the "old Bruins"?'

West's words tumbled out. 'I didn't mean "old" like that – I don't even know how old you are. You look about . . . what I mean is, you guys can talk to these kids in their language.'

'What is this, "their language"?'

'I just meant academic language. You guys use big words.'

'Like "anthropologist"? Should I break that down into parts for you?' Steelie started to push her new pile of weeds over toward the original pile.

'You really know how to make friends, don't you?'

'Is that what we're doing here, Detective? I thought you were asking for my professional help.'

'I am, but that doesn't mean we can't be friendly about it. You could call me Matt for a start.'

Steelie stopped playing with the weeds. 'Well, then, I suppose you can call me Steelie.'

'Thanks, I would like that. So, could you talk to this student, as, like, alumni trying to help us, semi-casual, to recreate the list or even just leads on the other students?'

'What's the security situation on campus right now?'

'Security has been increased but Officer Bryce Dodd will provide you with his direct line in case of any issues.'

'So, no hazard pay?' Steelie joked.

'Pay? We're not going to be able to pay—'

'You just wanna exploit the services of a tiny charity.' Steelie was just teasing West; she hadn't even expected that the Agency could get paid.

'If you could let me finish? I was about to say I can arrange to reimburse expenses. Mileage and parking.'

Expenses Steelie took seriously. 'Government rate or charity?'

'Government.'

'Done,' Steelie said. 'When will you need us to do this?'

'ASAP. We can make intros today by phone to the one student we know of; she's taking summer classes. Then you could go speak to her tomorrow. Would that work?'

Steelie already knew Jayne would be the one. She was the Agency's main interviewer. 'That works.'

'Great. Thank you.' West cleared his throat. 'I'll need to call you later to confirm some more details. It might be late tonight . . . is that a problem?'

'No.' Steelie had answered before she realized the question was spurious. Detective West had been fishing.

She smiled as she hung up.

Marie was standing in the doorway. 'That seemed like a very friendly conversation for you to be having with a detective.'

Steelie waved a warning finger as she stood. 'Don't you start on me. In exchange, I'll tell you if Houston's with your daughter when I call her in a second.'

Marie inclined her head in exaggerated acquiescence. 'I am nothing if not reasonable.'

Steelie looked at her sideways. 'Right.'

The doorbell rang just as Steelie was about to hit the speed dial for Jayne's cell.

'I'll get it,' Marie said.

Steelie waved her off. 'Don't be silly. It won't be for you.'

She looked through the peephole in the door and saw a pleasant-looking man in a high visibility vest and a Department of Water and Power hardhat. When she opened the door, she saw he was also holding a clipboard and some kind of specialized pen that reminded Steelie of what she used when she voted at the ballot box.

'Yes?'

He consulted the clipboard while he fumbled with the pen. 'Ms. Lander?'

'Yes.'

'I'm from the Department of Water and Power Customer Engagement and we're conducting a survey in Atwater Village to gauge interest in solar-powered streetlights. Would you be available to answer some questions, maybe about fifteen minutes in duration?'

After a quick glance back into her house, Steelie said, 'Actually, I have company right now.'

The man looked crestfallen so she added, 'Maybe another time because I'd really like to weigh in on this. I have *lots* of thoughts and not just for streetlights.'

The man had started to cap the large pen, which he stuffed into the chest pocket of his vest. 'Of course. We have survey teams rolling out over the coming weeks, so someone will be back around.'

Steelie pointed at a growing wet patch on his vest. 'I think your pen is leaking.'

He looked down in shock. 'Oh! Thank you. Appreciate it. Have a good day!'

Steelie nodded and watched him go down the steps. She didn't see any big DWP trucks on the street but someone from customer relations – or was it engagement? – was probably driving a nondescript sedan lest anyone come up to them and rant about their high summertime power bills. She closed the door and dialed Jayne.

*

Scott had been running on the boundary path around the Silver Lake Reservoir, using a system of switchbacks to keep an eye on Jayne, who was walking the same track. As he jogged up to her, he heard her cell phone ring. He watched as she answered.

She was backlit now that the sun was descending so her dark hair had a glow around it that was almost the same color as the tail feathers on a red-tailed hawk circling above. The light was strong enough to show the outline of Jayne's body through her long shirt and he traced the curves all the way down to her ankles. Her eyes were on him as she listened to her phone.

When she hung up, she said excitedly, 'So, you guys got a link between Jared Stilson and another student?'

'What link?' Scott asked.

'West just told Steelie.'

'He called her?' Scott pulled his BlackBerry from his arm pocket. 'He didn't call me.'

'Maybe it's not relevant to the Bureau?'

'It's not up to West to decide what's relevant to the Bureau.'

Jayne raised her eyebrows at his vehemence and started to walk again.

Scott fell in beside her. 'Well, what's the link? And who's the other student?'

'Her name is Regan Hart and she's missing. I guess West was saying it appears she and Jared Stilson had met in a campus club to do with being mixed-race.'

'This girl is also mixed?'

'I don't know yet.' Jayne nodded her head in greeting to a woman whose small terrier had veered toward them with enthusiasm.

The dog didn't distract Scott in the slightest. 'And why was West talking to Steelie about this?'

'Well, it's my opinion from seeing him with her that he's working himself up to asking her on a date.'

Scott threw his head back in laughter. 'Ha! So, he hasn't seen her Ban Cops T-shirt yet.'

'It's Ban *Bad* Cops.'

'Well, it doesn't look that way, which is what happens when you modify the Department of Justice COPS logo with a permanent marker. West won't think differently when he sees it. Was there anything else from him?'

'He asked if Steelie and I could help find out who else signed up to this club, which I'll do tomorrow.'

Scott rubbed his mouth. 'I don't like it. The person you saw with the binoculars could be around. Is Steelie going with you?'

'No, but campus police presence has been increased and I'll have a direct point of contact. I think the set-up is safe – it's not like they've locked campus down. Steelie also thinks it's okay and you know how skeptical she is.' Jayne pointed to an opening in the concrete barrier by the street. 'Let's cross up there.'

Scott stopped Jayne before she stepped out into the road. 'Do me a favor tomorrow? Check in with me, and if you can't get me, check in with West. And keep your eyes open.'

DAY SIX

MONDAY

14

Scott was half-asleep and on autopilot when he looked down to check the time on the clock by the bathroom sink. It wasn't there – because he wasn't in his bathroom. He looked around. Jayne's bathroom. Right. And there was a clock, just not in the same place as he kept his. He couldn't believe it was already 6:45 AM. He began shaving more rapidly than was wise for his level of wakefulness.

When he left the bathroom with a towel around his waist, Jayne was in the kitchen, yawning over her cup of coffee. He went over and put his hands on her shoulders, then pulled her into a hug. He started to let her go but found he didn't want to.

He said, 'This is crazy, right?'

She spread her fingers flat against his back. 'We spent the entire weekend together, so yes, this is crazy. But even crazier is that we both thought it was perfectly reasonable for you to get a change of clothes yesterday, precisely so you could leave from here this morning—'

'A smart move.'

Jayne kissed him, then pulled back and studied his face. 'Crazy is just one word for this.'

'But we're not going to overthink it.' He ran his hand over her hair. 'Even though I will be thinking about you today. Some very particular thoughts.'

She grinned. 'Same here.'

They kissed again before Scott went to finish getting dressed, putting on his suit from where it was hanging on the back of the bedroom door. When he'd returned from his apartment with an overnight bag on Sunday, neither of them had suggested that Jayne make space in her closet for his clothes. It was too soon for that.

He called out to her again. 'Don't you and Steelie see each other on the weekends?'

She came to the bedroom door. 'Every weekend.'

'But not this weekend. Sorry.'

'Don't be! She's the one who's been trying to get me to spend more time with other people.'

'Lucky me, counting as "other people".'

Jayne smiled. 'I think she meant I needed to physically get out more – concerts, events.'

Scott took his suit jacket from its hanger. 'If you want to go out, we can go out.'

'No, that's Steelie. *I'm* perfectly happy not going out. In fact, I prefer not to because I—'

He looked at her face but she was turning away, biting her lower lip as though to stop the words. It didn't matter. He already knew what she was going to say: that there were dangers in going out. She might end up in a crowded place that made her look for exits or might hear noises that sounded like gunshots and made her take cover no matter where she was. A film or a concert might suddenly, inexplicably, trigger a traumatic memory in a shuddering mash-up of past and present. Oh, he knew alright. But given the look on her face, Jayne didn't think he knew.

He could see her changing in front of him. The woman who had inhabited the present over the weekend was being

134

overshadowed, slowly but surely, and the shadow was coming from inside her. He knew why; Steelie had told him how Jayne had had to watch a peacekeeper bleed to death in front of her from a detonated mine. Benni, was it? It wouldn't do much for him to simply tell Jayne that it would get better, that he understood, because he had been there. Anyone still experiencing post-traumatic stress disorder had to realize 'on their own' that they had PTSD symptoms, not merely so-called inappropriate emotions they should just suppress.

He finally said, 'Should I . . . can I leave my things?'

She looked over at his toiletries bag on the bedside chair like it was a mile away and barely visible through fog and mist. When she looked back in his direction, she kept her eyes downcast so his feet were the recipients of her lopsided smile. 'Yes. Of course.'

Scott read her expression as grateful, which wasn't necessarily a good thing but it was keeping that shadow at bay right now. He leaned in to kiss her, stopping short until she closed the distance between them. It almost felt as if she was submitting to the kiss rather than participating in it, so he stopped and simply leaned his forehead against hers, thinking, *I love you, Jayne Hall, and I have for the longest time.*

*

Jayne spent the first half of the day at the Agency, aware that both Steelie and Carol would be able to tell that something was wrong. But she wasn't ready to have a discussion about why she still felt the need to hide her lack of 'normalcy' from Scott. The hiding was like a muscle that

135

was so used to flexing, it simply *flexed* without waiting for her to do it consciously. Jayne also already knew what her friends would say. Carol would tell her there was no such thing as 'normal' anyway. Steelie would tell her to just get out of her head and live.

Jayne left for UCLA with relief. Driving – moving – made her feel better and it felt good to be alone.

She navigated to the parking structure on the north side of campus and had to descend two levels before she found a space. She was reassured by how many cars were there but was then surprised to find that there weren't any people around. There was no bustle of activity, that noise of people parking or leaving. She was too nervous to take the elevator or go alone into the stairwell and instead trotted as fast she could up the ramps, looking between cars and behind her. She surfaced at the ground level of the parking structure short of breath and immediately felt annoyed for having been so spooked. The sun was shining and people were going about their business.

Jayne fell into step with a mass of humanity moving toward the center of campus. The dormitory where she was to meet the student sponsor of Mix it Up post-dated her time there as a student. From the front it looked more like a hotel, with corporate landscaping hugging glass walls that enclosed a spacious lobby. Only the bulletin boards along the walls suggested it was student housing because posters advertised used guitars for sale and roommate requests for off-campus apartments.

Inside, there was a lobby with seating flanked by common rooms and an elevator. Hearing the elevator doors behind her Jayne turned quickly but it was two young women deep in animated conversation and walking rapidly while looking at the same cell phone. They went out and the lobby reverted to silence. After a few minutes, her cell phone rang.

Steelie opened with a question. 'Have you seen anyone watching you?'

'No. It feels completely normal on campus. Did Scott ask you to call me?'

'Actually, Matt just called. He wanted me to tell you that the student you're to meet at 4PM now has to meet you at 6PM, and can you stay over there to meet her, please, pretty please with a cherry on top.'

'Those weren't his exact words, I presume,' Jayne said wryly as she left the dorm.

Steelie said, 'Look, I know it's a pain but I already told him you would. You could go into Westwood, have your favorite pastrami on rye at Jerry's.'

'Not now that I've found decent parking.' Jayne started climbing the steep stairway to main campus. 'There's a new structure over on this side. Way better than that rigmarole of finding a space on Le Conte and hiking across. And it's not a pain. It feels good to be here because I'm not looking for or *at* a dead body.'

'Good. Thanks. I told Matt he owes us one.'

'So now you call him Matt, huh?' The last word was more an exhalation than a word because Jayne was already getting winded on the steps.

'Where *are* you?'

Jayne reached the top and halted. She had to breathe before she could talk. 'I was just going uphill.'

A couple of undergraduates passed her. Not only were

they *not* out of breath, they were carrying on a conversation while they bopped along.

Jayne set off again in their wake, propping herself up with a hand on her hip. She signed off with Steelie and took in her surroundings. She was by an administration building, which gave her an idea. She walked up the path that divided the neat lawn in front of the building, which was another classic Italianate construction in terracotta and cream. A quick perusal of the directory enabled her to identify that the office she wanted was number 201. She glanced around the shiny tiled entryway and made for the staircase.

The door to 201 was closed but the posted office hours suggested someone should be there. Jayne's knock was greeted with a cheery, 'Come in.'

A woman was turning from an open filing cabinet. She looked to be in her early sixties and was wearing a blouse over a long straight skirt. Her dark hair was all gathered under one ear in a thick braid.

She smiled at Jayne. 'Can I help you?'

'Hi, I'm an alumnus and I'm trying to find out about a student club. Have I come to the right place?'

'You have but our student affairs head is out of the office at the moment. Perhaps I can help you? I'm Mrs. Thompson, the administrator here. The clubs are only open to enrolled students. Were you interested in sponsoring one as an alumnus?'

Jayne shook her head. 'Actually, I believe that the club I'm interested in was never formed but a student was trying to get signatures together for a petition about two years ago.'

'The rules are clear on minimum numbers. Any petition

138

without the minimum would have been automatically rejected so the student wouldn't have submitted it. But do you know the name of the club?'

'Yes, Mix it Up.'

Mrs. Thompson's eyebrows came together. 'I don't recall that name, which suggests to me the petition definitely wasn't submitted. May I ask why you're interested in a club that didn't get started rather than one that did? You mentioned you're one of our graduates?'

'Yes. It's more that I'm looking for some of the students involved.'

'Ah. We wouldn't be able to assist you with that, due to privacy rules.'

'Oh, right. Well, thank you for your time.'

The door behind Jayne opened just as she turned to leave. A man she placed in his forties walked in with an insulated lunch bag in one hand. He immediately used his other hand to hold the door for Jayne.

'Ah, Ken,' Mrs. Thompson said. 'Do you recall a club called Mix it Up? This young lady . . .?'

Jayne supplied, 'Jayne Hall.'

'Ms. Hall, this is Mr. Gorman. If anyone would know about it, he would.'

He smiled at Jayne in a polite fashion and, in a neat movement, replaced the hand on the door with a foot on the floor in order to shake hands with Jayne, saying, 'I'm afraid that club name doesn't ring a bell.'

Jayne was impressed. 'Wow, you know the names of clubs off of the top of your heads? Aren't there hundreds of them?'

'Well, we've both been here a long time and pride

ourselves on a good recollection of our clubs. But that's also a rather unusual name, which I think one of us would remember.'

Mrs. Thompson came over and held the door so he could cross to his desk. She pushed in a doorstop with her foot until it was in position. 'She's looking for the students who wanted to join.'

Mr. Gorman looked thoughtful while he got comfortable in his chair. 'Have you tried your search through student government? They generally have their finger on the pulse, although this is slightly more challenging because the club isn't in existence. Nevertheless . . .?'

Jayne appreciated that both administrators had genuinely tried to help her. She spoke warmly. 'Thank you for the suggestion!'

'I'm sorry I can't be of more help.'

'It's alright. I'm actually on my way to see the student who tried to start the club. She'll probably be able to give me the information I need.'

Once Jayne was on the stairs, she looked at her watch. It was almost 5PM. She had a series of realizations: (1) she shouldn't take the time to track down someone in student government because (2) she was hungry, and if she didn't eat something now, she wouldn't be able to eat dinner until around 9 given the drive home after her meeting, and (3) because she was in West LA and therefore closer to the ocean, she was going to need her cardigan, which she'd left in her pick-up. She stood in front of the administration building until she'd decided to retrieve her cardigan first and then eat, even if it meant going up and down those steps two more times. She clearly needed the exercise. She set off for the parking structure, with hunger causing her to be more preoccupied with herself than her surroundings for the first time since arriving on campus, but she was still appreciative of the large numbers of people heading to their cars.

When she left the campus café to head to her meeting later, she called Scott, respecting his request from the day before that she check in from UCLA. It seemed to her that any 'checking in' should be preceded by an explanation on her part for going silent on him that morning, but she found herself panicking when she received his voicemail, the beep coming before she was ready. Dead air was being recorded and Scott's phone would show it was her calling. She had to say something.

'Hi, Scott! I wanted to let you know things at UCLA will run a little later than expected and I won't be home until nine so I would understand if you just stayed at your place . . . okay, bye.'

She hung up. She'd said the exact opposite of what she meant.

But she had arrived at the dorm and it was time for the meeting.

15

The woman who emerged from the dormitory elevator at exactly 6PM walked briskly. Jayne could see why April Begay had been one to start a student club rather than simply join one. Everything about her suggested confidence and ambition: coordinated clothes that were the epitome of smart-casual, a rolling briefcase instead of a backpack, a print-out of her class schedule taped to the front cover of the portfolio she was carrying. Jayne was impressed, even more so when the first thing April did was apologize for changing their meeting time.

'I'm one of two teaching assistants for a class and the other TA bailed so I had to run a video tape at four o'clock, otherwise, I would have been here. Thank you for waiting. I hope it hasn't been too inconvenient.'

'Not at all. Thanks for meeting me.'

'Well, when the cops ask you to do something, you don't exactly argue with them!'

Once they'd sat down, Jayne began. 'So I was told that you were the one who tried to get Mix it Up started two years ago?'

'Yeah. I was really surprised I didn't get more interest. Sometimes you're just ahead of the curve.'

'What was the purpose of the club?'

'I was trying to make a forum where people who are

mixed-race or generally interested in racial identity could get together and talk. There wasn't any agenda; it wasn't political, although we were going to talk about race in politics – like the whole, "We can choose more than one box for race on the Census now but how are we being counted where it *counts*?" That kind of thing.'

April's delivery, as smooth as a practiced politician in a TV news clip, left Jayne just wanting to hear more of whatever she wanted to say on identity. But she channeled Detective West and mustered a question. 'Was membership only open to mixed students?'

'Oh no. It was open to anyone but I only got eight people signed up including me. I needed twelve.' April wrinkled her nose. 'Not my best showing.'

'Had you met any of them before Club Day?'

'Just two of them. The other five I didn't know, including Jared and Regan, who I know you're here to ask me about.'

'It sounds like you remember them.'

'I guess it's because I'm interested in other mixed people. Like you. You're mixed, right?'

Jayne felt surprised. Most North Americans she'd met thought she was Latina but were unaware that that could denote ethnic mixture. 'Yes, I am,' she said.

'I figured as much because of your last name. Your dad's white?'

'Yes, and American. My mother's Venezuelan and mixed herself.'

'Ah, I see,' April said. 'Do you have some African ancestry?'

Jayne nodded. 'My mom's grandmother was from

Ghana. And you?'

'My mom's white and my dad's Navajo. You seem surprised I could tell you were mixed.'

'I was, actually.'

'I clocked it the minute I saw you.'

Jayne had an instant vision of Jared Stilson's body – his hair – at the construction site. Like April 'clocking' her, Jayne had 'clocked' him. She said, 'I find I notice mixed couples, and I always look if they have a child.'

'Me too. It's like a combination of familiarity and curiosity, wanting to know if they're like me.'

'Yes! And it doesn't seem to matter what the mixture is or if I think both people in the couple are mixed themselves. It's just . . . nice to see.'

'Exactly.' April became more animated, sitting forward. 'I'm actually hoping to do a master's in sociology on this topic because I think mixed people have a dual identity, and I don't mean from each parent. There is that mixed identity but I think there's a second, umbrella-level solidarity with all mixed people that manifests itself in recognition of each other, sometimes smiling or actually stopping each other in the street and saying, "Are you mixed?" It's like an intro to strangers and I'm wondering if it could alter solidarity across borders – like, if the shared "mixed identity" is stronger than language barriers or nationality. *I* believe it is but my professors tell me I have to find the literature on this and turn my belief into a hypothesis.'

She smiled, clearly unfettered by doubt about the response from her audience, whoever they might be.

Jayne said, 'I see! So . . . Mix it Up was more than just

144

a passing fancy for you. It was tied in to your academic interests.'

'Oh, totally. Which is why it was disappointing to not get more people signed up. It was a really busy point in the quarter for me, though, and I didn't have time to do the advertising I'd hoped to do. It was all I could do to get the stand set up with the poster.'

'And it was at the stand that you met both Regan and Jared for the first time?'

'Regan arrived before Jared did. I remember because we got into this conversation about how some people don't call themselves "half" – like half-this or half-that – but "double". She liked that, "double".'

Jayne nodded. 'Did she happen to tell you what her parents' ethnicities are?'

'She said her mom's white American, and her dad's Chinese, born in China. He was adopted by an American family, though, who happened to be white.'

'Was Jared part of this conversation?'

'Yeah, and it was really interesting because Jared was saying that when he was younger, most people didn't even think he was mixed. He could tell from what they said that they thought he was white but he would just ignore that; he wasn't interested. It was only when he came to college and stopped cutting his hair that he found black folk were giving him "the nod" for the first time in his life.' April smiled. 'He said that was funny but also kind of confusing. Anyway, he and Regan were bonding over that but I had go talk to someone else who walked up to the stand.'

'Do you think Regan and Jared already knew each

other?'

April shook her head. 'I'm sure they didn't because I overheard them asking each other's names at one point and that was when I butted in and urged them to both sign the petition.'

'Which they did?'

'Yes.'

'Did you see either of them again?'

'No. We didn't live in the same dorm or anything. And because the club wasn't successful, we didn't meet again.'

'Okay.' Jayne tried to gather her thoughts.

'But I know who else signed the petition,' April said. 'Here, I'll write the names down for you.'

Jayne watched in amazement as April opened her portfolio and copied a list from one inside the folder. She ripped the sheet from the pad and handed it over.

'I'm on there for completeness,' she said, pointing with her pen. The star-shaped charm hanging from its lid spun and caught the light.

'Thanks.' Jayne felt like the interview was turning out much better than she could have expected; Detective West would be pleased. 'How did you remember all these names?'

'Oh, I didn't remember them. I made a copy of the petition before turning it in, even though you're not supposed to do that.'

'You turned it in? But you hadn't met the minimum number of signatures.'

April smiled beatifically. 'I knew that but I thought it was worth a try in case they wanted to make an exception. I turned it in with a cover letter, pleading our case.'

Jayne reflected. The two administrators she'd met had either misremembered or forgotten that Mix it Up had turned in a petition. But this had all happened a couple of years and thousands of pieces of paper ago.

16

When Jayne stepped outside of April Begay's dormitory, she rummaged in her bag for her cardigan while taking stock of the sky. Sure enough, mist from the sea was rolling in and the sun had dropped below the tops of the trees. Jayne couldn't find her cardigan and finally held her bag open. It wasn't inside. She went back to where she'd been sitting with April and found her cardigan on the floor. She shook it out and then left for the parking structure.

Once she was past the dorms, she was alone on the walkway. It was shrouded by towering pine trees on either side and all the activity of the afternoon seemed to have moved to another part of campus. Jayne found herself turning around more than once, thinking she heard something, but no one was there. She didn't think she was overreacting; she was almost positive she'd heard a noise. Then she thought of something. She pulled her keys from her bag and held them with each key sticking out from between her fingers like a knuckleduster. This made her feel better, but then she really did hear something. She whipped around, heart pounding. Nothing. She decided she couldn't take it anymore and jogged back to the dorms where there was still a steady flow of students. Once she was there, though, it was like there was an ocean between her and the truck. She wondered what she'd been thinking by coming back. She couldn't stay on campus until the next morning.

Having run out of ideas and feeling embarrassed by that, she called Officer Dodd at campus police.

'Hi, this is Jayne Hall. We met the other day—'

'I remember you.'

'Oh, great. Well, I'm still here on campus right now and I need to get to my car and I . . . well, frankly, I don't feel safe on the route I have to take—'

'You need an escort? No problem. Where are you now?'

Jayne was immediately less embarrassed. An escort. Of course campus police had a name for this; they probably did it all the time. She looked around at the dorm behind her and gave him the name.

'I'll be there in five.'

Jayne felt relieved and tried to relax but as the minutes ticked past, the numbers of people moving through the forecourt of the dorm thinned until she was the only person still standing around. It was as though she'd arrived when students were coming back for dinner and now they were all inside. Safely inside. She felt her anxiety building again. She wanted to pull out her phone to check how many minutes it had been since she'd called Officer Dodd but she didn't want to take her eyes off her surroundings long enough to look. *How long has it been?* It felt like an hour but that was impossible. She started moving toward the building but knew she wouldn't be able to get in; she didn't have a student ID to unlock the doors as the sign indicated was needed after 5PM. Feeling like a sitting duck, she again pulled her keys out and arranged them between her fingers, gripping them tightly, eyes darting this way and that, ears straining to pick up sound – not just any sound, but furtive sound, the sound of someone trying to creep up on her, the someone who killed Jared.

And then there was a sound but it wasn't furtive or even soft. It was an electric whirring noise overlaid by the crackle of walkie-talkie static and then a campus police golf cart came into view. The man driving waved to her and she recognized him as one of the officers who'd been present when Jared Stilson had been found. She dropped her keys into her pocket and waved back.

He pulled up in front her and she saw that the golf cart was the type that could fit another person next to the driver and then there was a seat on the back, facing the rear.

He said, 'Ms. Hall. Officer Dodd, at your service,' as he put a thumb over his shoulder to indicate the rear seat.

Jayne hopped up. She was actually glad to sit in this position because it meant Dodd had her back. He drove off at speed and Jayne immediately held onto both her purse and the side pillar of the cart's roof.

Dodd was in a chatty mood and they talked over the wind noise, mostly about the golf cart and other means of police transportation on campus, while Jayne sat somewhat sideways on the bench seat, which allowed her to look at Dodd while also keeping her vigilant 180-degree scan going.

Inside the parking structure, Dodd maneuvered the cart briskly around to the self-pay machines.

'You need to pay before you can exit,' he explained.

'Oh . . .' Jayne fumbled with her wallet as she felt a spike of fear at the thought of Dodd leaving her at the self-pay machines. She still had to get to the truck and hesitated on getting out of the cart.

Dodd seemed to guess what was on her mind. 'I'll drive you down to your vehicle.'

She gave him a grateful look and went to the machine. She completed the transaction without issue and requested the receipt, which, when spat out of the machine, was printed on identical cardstock as the parking ticket. At eighteen dollars, it was definitely going on the LAPD's tab.

Back on her perch on the golf cart, Jayne directed Dodd to where she'd left the truck on the lower level.

When she alighted, she spoke with feeling. 'Thank you so much.'

He dismissed this with a wave. 'It's what we're here for.'

'I guess I just picture you helping young undergrads, not someone like me.'

Dodd shook his head. 'It's normal to be nervous under the circumstances. We've got an unsolved homicide on campus, which you're more aware of than most. Even some of my guys are nervous and they weigh in at two hundred pounds before they put on their equipment belts.' He gave her a smile. 'I'll wait until I hear your truck start up. What year's your 150?'

'1984. Are you into Fords?'

Dodd was giving her F-150 an appraising look. 'I've been looking at getting one, extended back like yours, but not styleside.'

'Into flareside, huh? Well, whichever way you go, I'd definitely recommend the 4x4.'

'No doubt.'

They smiled at each other and Jayne got in the truck. When the Ford's engine roared to life, Officer Dodd made a U-turn to head up the parking ramp but then waited until

Jayne had reversed out of her parking spot. Once she was behind him, Jayne waved; Dodd waved back and drove up the ramp at speed. Jayne progressed a little slower. She felt really good, thanks to Dodd, and she was heading for home. Her positive mood was almost broken when she couldn't get the exit machine to accept her ticket. She idled there for almost a minute, rubbing the ticket on her pant leg so the magnetic stripe could be read, smoothing it out, breathing on it, but it kept getting ejected. She eventually looked more closely at it and discovered that she'd been feeding in the receipt instead of the ticket.

When Jayne finally crested the curving ramp at street level, she noticed how dark the dusk was along this part of Sunset Boulevard thanks to all the massive trees. She settled into traffic that was slow due to the volume of cars exceeding the boulevard's design. Then she put the radio on, dialed over to KROQ-FM, and cranked up the volume to symbolize her break from an afternoon that had dragged out. Before long and without trying too hard to prevent it, she was thinking about Scott.

She realized that since he'd spent the night several times, she had begun to project forward into what they would yet do together. A part of her said, 'Hold on. You can't even show all of yourself to this guy but you're planning a future?' while another part of her, a much louder and more insistent and infinitely more happy part of her, conjured up a new life with Scott, one in which she traveled again, but not for work. She would see the world like a tourist and she'd do it with someone she loved, not just a forensic team of which she'd grown fond. When home, she'd go to her mother's garden parties with a 'plus one', thereby avoiding

Marie's efforts to hook her up with any vaguely appropriate bachelor within commuting distance of the LA Basin.

But she wasn't going to say anything to her mom yet or even her dad, who was always easygoing about her erstwhile boyfriends, until things were a little further along. No point getting her parents' hopes up. But when would be the right time? How much more time would she need to spend with Scott to be confident that this was 'something'? She already knew it was 'something' – it had been 'something' since the first time they'd seen each other across the dimly lit bar at Quantico. The tug of interest had been visceral and had proven unforgettable.

She was sure that was the only explanation for why – and how – they had managed to keep up so many years of long-distance conversation and friendship. And now Jayne knew that her thoughts and dreams about Scott over the years had been paralleled in his mind. Since Wednesday, they had probably spent less time talking and more time in bed, which meant that the years leading up to this went beyond 'taking it slow'. 'Taking it glacial' was more like it. Jayne kept thinking: *We could have been doing this when we were five years younger*. Scott couldn't fail to see the stretch marks across her hips and yet—

A shattering noise accompanied by a huge inrush of cool air completely cut through Jayne's reverie. She instinctively hunched her shoulders and looked in her rearview mirror but couldn't compute: two feet were coming through a hole where the back window had been. Jayne hit the brakes as someone – a man – all but sat on top of her. She screamed as he jammed one leg under hers, lifting her foot off the brake and transferring it to the gas pedal, where he pressed

153

down hard. Jayne tried desperately to lift her foot but couldn't. She looked at the man but he brought an elbow up and pushed her face away, toward the door, holding it there as he wound the steering wheel left. It was only now that Jayne took in where she was: next to the Silver Lake Reservoir. Almost home.

But the man was steering them right for the barrier fence. The F-150's engine was roaring in response to the pressure on the gas pedal, hurtling purposefully toward the chain-link. Jayne screamed again but realized her radio was still on and the music, which she bizarrely locked on to as Maroon 5, was drowning out her voice. She tried to pull the steering wheel right, tried to get her other foot on the brake, but the man was stronger than she was and in complete control. She was jarred by bumps as the truck mounted the curb, gathered more speed and barged through the fence. She looked desperately through the darkness for a person – *Just one person!* – walking around the reservoir who would see what was happening but there was no one. In what seemed like a minute but was probably only seconds, she felt her beautiful, powerful, trusting Ford go airborne. She was so frightened that she couldn't scream. She just shut her eyes and held her breath, feeling as though she was going to her death in a cowardly, ugly way.

17

When the truck hit the water, Jayne's body jerked forward, the seatbelt pulling taut against her chest and throat, burning her skin through her shirt. Her eyes flew open and she was stunned to see that the truck was already sinking, its front end submerged in the reservoir's dark water, and *still* the intruder was trapping her legs, having used her body like a seatbelt, his arms and legs wrapped around her. Jayne craned her neck to look at him and then cried out because his face was so distorted. He elbowed her in the head again and held her face against the door.

The F-150 sank deeper with a groan. Jayne could hear water pouring into the open bed behind, weighing the back of the truck down until, inexorably, it began to sink in earnest, the water now pouring in through the smashed rear window, pushing coldly past her shoulder. Jayne took her chance to take a deep breath, expanding her lungs as much as she could within the vise she was held in, and she squeezed her eyes shut just before they went under.

The frigidity of the water was so shocking she almost exhaled. For a moment, that was all she could think of: she had never been so cold in her life. But the pressure had lifted from her foot. She frowned with her eyes shut. *He's gone?* A kick to her right shoulder made her rear back, screaming with her mouth closed, air escaping from her nose. Could he have left? *Maybe he just floated away. Maybe I will just float away*, she thought, almost giggling. *But is he here?* She began to grope with her eyes closed, afraid to expose them to the cold. But she had to. She opened them, just a little, and peered into the murky darkness. The headlights weren't on. *When did I turn them off?* She opened her eyes wider but it didn't help her to see more. She reached for her door handle. It wouldn't open. She couldn't hold her breath much longer. *Is he out there, waiting for me to emerge? But if I don't get out of here, I'm going to die anyway. Come on, Jayne. Time to go.*

With fingers that could barely function in the cold, she pressed down with both hands on the seatbelt release. It gave way with a watery click. The sound made her think of dolphins clicking and whistling in the ocean. *How do they manage, living in the cold, cold sea? Is it that they have more fat? Ha. I thought I had enough fat but I don't and – ow!* Her fingers had crashed into the metal surround of the back window but it gave her an idea of where to go to get out.

She twisted, pulling herself through the surprisingly generous opening. She felt her clothes snagging on what she assumed was jagged glass ringing the edges, then felt water pushing against her eyeballs as she kicked off the pick-up's cab. *Goodbye, truck.* She used what little energy she had left to swim in the direction she thought was up, willing her legs to keep kicking even as her lungs demanded that she do nothing but breathe. She surfaced just in time.

Taking a deep, welcome breath of fetid, blessed, watery air, Jayne threw her head back and saw the night sky through stinging eyes. Her limbs felt leaden and she was too cold to move and yet she was apparently creating a splashing sound. She didn't know how and didn't really care because now she could die looking at the sky instead of in a wet grave, like the truck. She remembered when she'd bought it, how the dealer had looked at her and said, 'Are you sure it's *this* you want? I've got lots of sporty little convertibles over here. Newer, too.' But no, she had to have the old-style truck, had to be macho and never girly, and now she wanted that, she wanted to be a girl, and now she wasn't going to be, it was all too late, too little too late, and her mother would have liked it if she'd been more of a girl but now she wouldn't get to enjoy that, and now Jayne was weeping. She could feel the tears, hot on her clammy skin, and she wondered if steam was rising from this, her last live action, this crying over herself, her life, her stubbornness, and what she had seen and known and held onto, when she should have forgotten and let go and *lived*.

The splashing was louder now. Was it her heart? Outside her chest? Beating, leaving her, swimming away from the sinking ship, her heart, the rat that it was, and then she was being grabbed – he was back to finish her off but she wasn't going to die underwater, so she screamed, or tried to, until she discerned a voice through the noise of the splashing and the chattering of her teeth and it was saying, 'Lady. Lady! Dammit, I can't help you if you keep fighting me.' It was a young voice and he sounded like he was from the Valley and Jayne decided that there was no way he was the intruder with a voice like that, and she didn't have the energy anyway, so she would let him pull her, to shore or to sea, she didn't care, and her legs floated to the surface as he dragged her by the armpits, his own breathing labored as he pulled and swore, and pulled and swore.

*

Scott had dialed Jayne's number a couple of times while he was at home eating dinner. Each time, the call had gone through to voicemail. It was after 9PM but not much after and he would have gladly driven over to Silver Lake to spend what was left of the night with her. He liked her place, but more than that, he liked waking up and seeing her, liked that they didn't need to talk in order to communicate gladness at being near each other. Most of all, he liked that she'd called in the afternoon. Given how she'd been that morning, he had worried a little. Shaking his head at the fact that he was devoting so much time to what was in someone else's head, a pastime with which he was not familiar, he went to the kitchen to deposit his plate in the dishwasher. As he cleared up, his cell rang.

He picked up when he saw who was calling. 'How ya doin', Steelie?'

'*I'm* fine, but Jayne's been in some kind of accident.'

Scott gripped the phone. 'Where is she?'

'Glendale Memorial. I'm here now and so is Marie—'

'What kind of accident?' He grabbed his keys.

'According to the cops, it was a single-vehicle accident. Scott, they pulled her out of the Silver Lake Reservoir.'

'What?' His mind reeled as he vaulted into the hallway of his condo building. 'Was she in her truck?' He hit the elevator call button repeatedly, waited for a split second more, and then ran for the stairs.

'The cops are saying she, like, drove into it purposefully.'

Steelie's voice sounded pinched. 'I don't believe it for a second, of course, but—'

'No, that's gotta be wrong.' Scott wondered if his heart was pounding from the way he was charging down the stairs or from the thought that the situation with him that morning could have made Jayne want to drive into a goddamned lake. 'Who are these cops? Which division?'

'I forgot to ask. Probably Northeast.'

'It doesn't matter. I'm on my way over. I'll talk to them.'

'What are you going to do, *tell* them Jayne wouldn't try to commit suicide? They have a witness, Scott. And she was all weird at the office this morning. Did you say something to her? You were with her over the weekend.'

'Back it up, Steelie. There's a witness saying she *purposefully* drove into the reservoir? He or she couldn't possibly know what she was doing.'

'You don't know what she was doing either.'

Scott reached the Suburban and jumped in. 'Well, I'm going to find out, if it's the last thing I do.'

'I'm sure they'll really appreciate you storming in, Houston.'

He reversed out of his space and screeched up the ramp. 'I don't give a shit about them, Steelie. I only care about one thing and you know what that is. So, I'm going to get over there and I'm going to ask some questions. And while I'm driving, I want you to tell me exactly what Jayne's condition is.'

'I don't know her *exact* condition. I'm not a goddamned doctor.'

'Give me a break here. You called me, remember?'

'Okay, okay.' Steelie sighed. 'She almost drowned, so

her lungs got strained. She's got some other problem related to, like, hypothermia and she took a knock on the head. No broken bones or anything like that but she's as fucked up as I've ever seen her and—' Steelie's voice choked and she broke off.

Scott found his own throat was constricting. He was speeding out on the street now, swerving around cars as he navigated the short stretch to the Hollywood Freeway. All he could force out was, 'Go on.'

Steelie's voice recovered slightly. 'You'll see for yourself. They've just moved her from Emergency to room 212. I'm hanging up.'

Keeping one hand on the wheel and his eyes on the curve in the 5's on-ramp – which he was taking way too fast – Scott endeavored to use speed dial to call Eric, then gave him what little information he had, asked him to contact the LAPD and accepted his partner's admonition to try to remain calm.

When Scott pulled up alongside the hospital, there was a parking space available on the street, so he took it. He ran inside, taking the stairs several at a time. The second floor was surprisingly busy, with a large crowd milling around a room some distance down the hallway. At first, Scott thought they were to do with Jayne but then he saw Steelie hovering by a door further along.

He said, 'Excuse me,' more than once but still had to push to try to get through the middle of the crowd. One thin old man wove haphazardly, deaf to Scott's exhortations. Scott had to restrain himself from bodily lifting the man to the side.

Steelie saw him coming and tried for a smile. She looked

exhausted.

He came up to her and clasped her hand. 'You okay?'

'Sorry for . . . before.' She gave his hand a squeeze.

'Forget about it.' He glanced at the woman standing behind Steelie. Jayne's mother was instantly recognizable from the photographs Jayne had on display at her apartment. She was even more stunning to look at in person – a vision in bronze and gold.

Scott put out his hand. 'Ms. Prentis? I'm Scott Houston.'

Over Steelie's apology for not introducing them, Marie gave him a dazzling smile. The worried look that had put temporary wrinkles in her forehead disappeared. She took Scott's hand in both of hers.

'Call me Marie. Please. I'm so glad to finally meet you, Scott. I've heard a lot about you.' She spoke in the somewhat British-accented voice he'd heard on the radio whenever he'd caught her show.

I'm sorry I might be the reason we're here, Scott thought. But out loud he said, 'I'm sorry we've had to meet here.' He looked through the narrow window in the door to Jayne's room. He could see a nurse inside by the bed but she was blocking his view of Jayne's face. 'Any news?'

Marie said, 'The nurse is about to let us know if we can go in to speak with her now that they've finished the tests and cleaned her up. They haven't let us in yet.'

He turned to Steelie. 'Are the cops still around?'

'No.'

'Eric will catch up with them.'

Steelie's face brightened. 'You sicced Eric on them?'

'So, you *do* like it when we go "storming in".'

Steelie grinned sheepishly.

161

The nurse came out and addressed Marie. 'You can go in now. The doctor will be here soon to let you know when she'll be ready to go home.' She gave Marie a reassuring smile.

When they entered the room, Jayne looked over. Her face crumpled when she saw her mother. Marie rushed forward and enveloped her in a hug. Jayne's arm snaked out of the hospital gown to grasp her mother's cardigan, her hand looking frail thanks to a large IV tube taped to it to keep a needle in place. Scott and Steelie waited until Marie stopped murmuring soothing noises and had wiped Jayne's face with a handkerchief.

Steelie moved in next. She leaned down and pecked Jayne on the forehead.

Jayne looked up at her. 'I lost my truck.' She looked set to cry again.

Steelie said, 'I gathered as much. But we'll get you another one.'

'I'm not getting another one. Not with that back window.' She looked away.

Steelie looked at Scott and shrugged, as if to say, *I don't know what she's talking about.* But Scott couldn't keep standing back any longer, so came around the other side of the hospital bed.

Jayne put her hand on his shirtsleeve, pulling him down toward her. He noticed welts on her face so placed a kiss carefully on her cheek.

She whispered in his ear. 'I'm sorry.'

Scott went cold. Was this an apology for trying to end her life? He didn't know what to say or how to ask what she meant. So, he just kissed her cheek one more time, then straightened up and sat on the edge of the bed.

She smiled weakly at him. 'You're here.'

'Of course I'm here.'

'I mean, I thought you might be out there, tracking him down.'

Scott shot a quick look at Steelie, who frowned back at him. He spoke gently to Jayne. 'Tracking who down?'

'The guy who forced me into the reservoir.'

Scott didn't want to be the one to break it to Jayne that she was talking nonsense. He glanced at the IV cart. What drugs had the hospital put her on that would get her hallucinating? Or was it the bump on the head?

It was Marie who stepped into the breach. 'Darling, there weren't any other cars involved in your accident.'

'He wasn't in a car. He was in my truck.' She looked at each of them. 'He got in my truck from the back – from the bed. Came in through the window and forced me into the reservoir. I told the paramedics – I told the cops. A man, I think, dressed all in black and—' She broke off, squeezing her eyes shut.

Scott was already getting up and dialing Eric. He stepped into the hallway and closed the door behind him.

18

Scott held his phone tightly to his ear as he watched Jayne from the window in her hospital room door. Marie was smoothing the hair back from Jayne's forehead as Steelie sat on the edge of the bed looking worried. He heard Eric answer.

'Eric, are you at the reservoir?'

'Yeah, just got through talking to the cops.'

'Jayne's saying there was a guy who got into her truck.'

'Yeah, they said that's what she said. But they don't believe it due to this witness.'

'Is the witness still there?'

'No, they let him get home because he's the one who pulled Jayne out of the water and the kid needed to warm up and feed his dog or something.'

'We need to talk to him.'

'I'll get his details,' Eric said.

'I thought the witness just said it was a single-car accident. Nothing about whether there was anyone in the truck.'

'No, Scott, the witness is saying she was alone.'

Scott pinched the bridge of his nose. 'That's actually just what the cops are *saying* he said.'

'Scott—'

'Wouldn't you prefer to talk to him yourself?'

'Absolutely. And we will.' Eric paused. 'How's Jayne?'

'Bruised, medicated.' Scott exhaled. 'Seems the doctor might release her soon.'

'Stay with her in case there was an assailant.'

'Yeah. I would have anyway. What else is going on at the reservoir? Have they called for the crime lab?'

'Not yet. I think that's slated for tomorrow. They've got Traffic out here checking the road where her truck veered off.'

'They find anything?'

'They're in process now. But I had a look. Saw one skid mark on the street, but early. So early, it may not be related, though it looks like fresh rubber laid down, and then no skidding after that.'

'No skid mark before the edge of the reservoir?' Scott was trying to picture Jayne just accelerating into the water that they'd been walking around the day before. It wasn't a good picture.

'Nope. That's where the suicide chatter is coming from,' Eric said.

'But Traffic knows there could be other explanations? It could be brake failure, a blown tire but not enough time to slam on the brakes, tampering—'

'We could speculate all night but they're going to raise the truck tomorrow, so let's just let them handle it.'

Scott tried to unkink his neck. 'But between now and then, LAPD will be feeling confident about a suicide attempt and discounting anything that doesn't fit.'

'Don't get distracted by what you think they're thinking. Look, they were motivated enough to send down divers tonight. There isn't anyone else down in the water or a sign that someone else was in the truck. No belongings in the truck either, from what they could see, besides what was in the glovebox, so someone needs to ask Jayne about whether she had a bag or anything that the divers should be looking for.'

Scott saw that the white-coated doctor walking down the hallway was now making for Jayne's room. He watched her go in and peered after her through the window.

He marshaled his thoughts. 'What did you give the cops as the reason for you showing up at the reservoir?'

'I explained that the subject was on LAPD business prior to the incident and our office is also involved in the case. They didn't have a problem with that. Couldn't care less, as far as I could tell.'

'Typical.' Scott paused. 'Don't call West yet.'

'I wasn't planning on it.'

Scott couldn't stop himself from trying to minimize how many people would learn that Jayne might have tried to commit suicide. 'Just because she was on his business at UCLA doesn't mean the accident is related.'

'You mean me telling that to the cops over here doesn't make it true? You slay me, Houston.'

'Yeah, yeah,' Scott said wearily. 'The doc's just left the room. Touch base later.'

'Ten-four.'

Marie and Steelie had come out into the hallway and Scott joined them.

Marie said, 'The doctor's given her the all clear. She just needs bed rest now until she feels up to moving around.'

Scott said, 'I'll take her home, if one of you has a spare key?'

'You'd have to stay with her, at least for tonight,' Steelie said.

'Of course.'

'Or I can take her back while you run to your place for some of your things?' Steelie said.

He shook his head. 'I already have—' He broke off when he saw their expressions. Marie's hand had flown to her mouth while Steelie's eyebrows had lifted almost into her hairline.

He said, 'I guess Jayne hasn't said anything.'

'Be glad,' Steele said, grinning now. 'It was for your own protection.'

'From what?'

'From me, darling,' Marie said, advancing. 'From me.'

Her arms went around his shoulders and she pulled him into a conspiratorial scrum. Their heads were that close together, he could hear the tinkling noise of her dangly earrings.

She said, 'Now, tell me. What are your intentions toward my daughter? Are you one of those modern fellows who think moving in together is simply a way of learning more about your compatibility or are you two already inseparable? How *romantic* if you are.'

Scott looked to Steelie for help but she let him squirm before coming to the rescue, calling out, 'Marie? Don't you want to help Jayne get dressed? Leave the man alone – for now, at least.'

Marie moved to hold Scott's chin in her hand. 'We will continue this conversation another time. Perhaps at my house, in the garden, when Jayne's feeling better? Of course, you're welcome any time, with or without my daughter.' She squeezed his arm before going into Jayne's room.

Scott tried to straighten himself back up to his full height.

'See?' Steelie said. 'We didn't exaggerate the Prentis-Hall effect.'

'I understand better now. Marie is . . .' He struggled to find a word that didn't sound outsized.

'A force unto herself,' Steelie finished. 'And let me tell you right now that the interrogation techniques they taught you at Quantico are no match for hers.'

'Great.'

'And if you need help, y'know, down the track . . .'

'Yes?'

'Don't call me.'

'Even better.' Tired, Scott leaned against the wall.

'All joking aside, do you want me to come back with you to Jayne's to help get her inside? She's heavier than she looks.'

Scott and Steelie supported Jayne on each side as they climbed the stairs to her apartment. She leaned on them both heavily, complaining of soreness all over despite the pain medication she'd been given. When they reached her front door, she said, 'I feel washed out,' then giggled at her own joke, but Scott and Steelie's eyes met in consternation over the top of her head. They helped her into bed, where they left her to rest.

Back in the main room, Scott watched Steelie opening the kitchen cupboards and the fridge. 'What's up?'

'Just wanted to see if I should run to the market for

Jayne but it looks like there's enough to feed an army in here. I guess the only thing left is to ask if you know where to find the guest beer? Jayne doesn't drink.'

'Bottom crisper drawer?'

Steelie nodded. She looked around. 'Well, I guess that's it.' She crossed to the front door and then returned. 'Oh, you're going to need these.'

Scott took the keys she was holding out. She gave him a hug and he hugged her back. Her back muscles were strong enough for him to feel them under his fingers but his arms could go around her twice, she was that slim. That reminded him of how small and defenseless she'd looked in the hospital bed in Atlanta earlier that summer, and the next thing he knew, he was pressing her head to his chest and holding her tight.

Steelie gave a mock death rattle. 'Houston . . . can't . . . breathe.'

He let go, ready to apologize, but she was smiling up at him and kept his hands in hers.

Then she said, 'This feels weird, leaving you here.'

'I know. I hope it's not too weird.'

'No. And I really am sorry for suggesting that you, I don't know, upset Jayne – that badly, anyway.'

'Let's not get ahead of ourselves. She could kick me out as soon as she's strong enough to do any kicking.'

Steelie gave a rueful laugh. 'And take on her mother's post-game analysis sessions? I don't think so.'

After Steelie left, Scott retrieved a Corona from the fridge. He leaned against the kitchen counter and held the bottle to his temple, then drank, draining the beer in short order. He opened another one. After the first few swallows, slower this time, he checked on Jayne. Despite his creeping into the room, she opened her eyes.

'Hey.' Her voice was soft.

'Hey, yourself.' Scott stretched out next to her, resting his head on a hand as he brushed her hair back from her forehead, trying to see those bruises even though the room was dark. 'We didn't want to wake you up.'

'Was I sleeping?'

'We thought you were.'

'Has Steelie gone home?'

'Just now.'

'Mmm.' She closed her eyes but put out an arm, pulling him closer.

He put an arm around her and rubbed her back gently. The soft cotton of her shirt caught under his fingers, putting them against her bare skin. He heard her quiet intake of breath just before she pulled his mouth to hers. After a very long kiss, Scott undressed and joined her under the covers. The night's events had banished any teasing or game-playing. Their lovemaking brought them as close as they could be and somehow closer than they'd ever been before.

When Jayne fell asleep, her head was resting on Scott's chest, so he stretched his arm out slowly to reach his BlackBerry on the bedside table. He sent a PIN-to-PIN message to Eric, telling him where he was and asking for an update. He told himself he would just confirm where things stood and then get some sleep. He could feel an epic load of fatigue coming over him after the surge of adrenaline earlier that night when Steelie had called. Eric's response came quickly:

1- Traffic prelim is acceleration + hard turn for water,

no braking. 2- PD confirms witness states clear view &
operator alone in cab. Have wit contact info - 1 mile from
yr location - rally there 0830.

Scott read the message twice before trying to put it out of his mind. He wouldn't be able to determine the witness's reliability until the next day and yet he couldn't stop thinking about it. If the guy was adamant Jayne was alone in her truck, there might be something in the suicide concern. Jayne's story about an assailant wasn't simply unsupported by evidence; it was far-fetched.

Keeping his eyes closed so he didn't lose the pull of sleep, Scott drew in a deep breath and let it out slowly. He was seriously beginning to wonder if Jayne's PTSD had triggered this reaction. After all, the reservoir accident was, at its most basic level, a traumatic incident. But could post-traumatic stress disorder actually conjure up an assailant who wasn't there? He knew PTSD was a powerful phenomenon, powerful enough to make people who'd lived through a war run for their lives in peacetime just because they heard a whistling noise: they still expected a mortar to drop on their house. Or was Jayne's bogeyman story related to the last traumatic incident in her life, during the King case? If so, he would never forgive himself, because he still felt responsible for that, despite everyone telling him that it hadn't been his fault.

PTSD and Suicide. Scott could almost see that title in his mind's eye. He felt his eyes moving behind his lids as though he was looking at it now. It was an article he'd read in the Bureau newsletter a few months back. He was trying to remember what it had said. Something like: the incidence of suicide or attempted suicide is higher among those with

PTSD symptoms than those without. He pondered this sleepily. Would Jayne's denial of her own PTSD make her go so far as to make up a bogeyman to cover up a failed suicide attempt? Oh man, that was possible. And if that was what she was doing, she could be cited for wasting police time. God, the thought of it! Suddenly, Scott felt wide awake. He wanted to get up and move around, vigorously, and now Jayne's head felt like it was weighing him down.

He extricated himself, then sat up and looked at her. She was sleeping on her side, only partly covered by the sheet. His eyes continued along her body, dropping into the deep curve of her waist, then up steeply over the side of her ribs. The desire to understand her, to help her, was strong but it couldn't override his fidelity to his job. He let his eyes take that roller coaster ride one more time and then hardened his heart. Pulling the sheet up to Jayne's shoulders, he affirmed for himself that there was no way he could be involved with someone charged with, or worse, convicted of a crime. He had a career to think about. He grabbed his clothes and his phone and left the room.

*

Junior kept the car's speed slow but steady as he cruised past the duplex. No truck. The voice in his head came quickly, jeering: *Of course there's no truck! You put it down when you put her down! What are you? Stupid?* He winced, anticipating the slap, then exhaled, trying to gain control over the voice. He pulled over to let the one car behind him pass, then he made the U-turn. Driving more slowly now, he approached the duplex again, looking upstairs. It was reassuringly dark. So, he had put her down.

He felt amazing. He'd done it, even last-minute, even without a playbook from Operation Concentration. He spoke under his breath, with quiet pride that was growing stronger. 'See! I did it! *Me!*' And then a light came on. A light turning on inside the apartment of a dead woman. He froze. Was it her? But who else could it be? The punishment for this failure would be worse than a slap. Worse than the spittle wash. It might mean the belt. Or that chalky drink. He knew the voice was coming. Where was it? He tensed, waiting. A honk rang out. A polite toot-toot but it had still startled him and he accelerated more forcefully than he meant to. His tires squealed, giving voice to his own desire to scream.

DAY SEVEN

TUESDAY

19

Jayne woke up slowly. She felt groggy, heavy-limbed, and she had a headache. As she lay still, blinking slowly, the apartment was silent around her. She sat up with effort and held her position on the edge of the bed to allow her body to get used to being upright. Feeling around with her hand, she located her nightshirt and put it on, using only one arm after her other shoulder protested in pain. She stood up. That made her see stars, so she kept a hand against the wall for good measure as she padded across the carpet in bare feet. From the bedroom doorway, she saw that Scott was sitting at the dining table, head bent over some papers and a pen in his hand.

'Hi,' she said.

He looked up with a start. 'Jayne. Should you be up?' He walked swiftly to her.

'I have to pee.' She leaned in for a hug but he held her at arm's length.

'I'll help you get to the bathroom.' He closed the bathroom door behind her. 'Call me when you want to come out.'

'It's okay,' she said. 'There's lots of stuff to hang onto in here.'

When Jayne washed her face, she looked in the mirror and did a double take at the bruises on the right side of her face. Not nice. No wonder Scott was keeping his distance.

She dutifully called to him when she opened the door. He came over and urged her to go to the couch, if not back to bed.

She looked over at the kitchen. 'But—'

He steered her to the two yellow couches that formed an L near the fireplace. 'I'll make you something to eat. You're staying off your feet today, no arguments.'

'Who's arguing?' she mumbled happily and accepted the blanket he was spreading over her.

She watched him move with confidence around her kitchen, making toast and using the microwave. She looked over at the dining table. There was a mug and plate already there, so Scott must have been up for a while. When he returned, she thought he looked preoccupied. He'd made her two pieces of toast, one spread with honey, the other with peanut butter. The mug held warm milk. Jayne found her appetite coming back as she took the first bites of toast but was somewhat unnerved by the way Scott was watching her from his perch on the edge of the coffee table.

She unstuck her tongue from the peanut butter on the roof of her mouth and took a swig of the milk. 'What?'

'Nothing.'

She took another bite of toast. Washed it down. Indicated the pile of papers on the dining table. 'What are you doing?'

'Making a to-do list.'

'For you?'

'For you, but I'll give it to Marie or whoever you want to help you cancel your credit cards, contact the DMV about salvage on your truck and so on. I presume you had your wallet with you last night?'

'Yeah, I did.' Jayne sighed, thinking about the hassle factor this was already creating. She moved on to her second slice of toast and happened to glance at Scott. He was almost frowning at her.

She stopped eating. 'Scott, what is it?'

He ran his hands back and forth through his hair and then smoothed it all down. Standing up, he said, 'Okay, here's the situation. A witness from last night told the cops that you were alone in the truck when you veered into the reservoir.'

Jayne didn't see that this was that big of a deal. 'So what? *I* know I wasn't alone.'

She took a bite of toast, looked back at Scott and read his expression. She swallowed. 'You think I was alone, don't you? You think I—' She moved to put her plate on the coffee table. The sideways stretch made her wince.

'Let me do that.'

'I'm already doing it.' But she had to let go of the plate for the pain and it slammed down onto the glass. She straightened up with difficulty, shaking off Scott's attempt to help.

Pointing at the bruises on her face, she said, 'He did this to me, with his elbow. And he crushed the shit out of my foot, okay? He came in through the back window and he made me run off the road.'

'But you don't remember anything about him?'

'He was wearing black and some kind of mask that made him look—' She almost said, *like a monster*. 'I think he was wearing some kind of mask. He was strong and he didn't say anything. Just burst in, slammed me against the side, pushed my foot down with his foot and then jerked

179

on the wheel.'

'And in the water? He just disappeared?'

'You make it sound like it's so unbelievable he could disappear! He swam away, okay? I don't know how and I don't know why, all I know is that I survived. What do you want from me?'

Now Scott's voice was raised as well. 'I need something to go on here, something to use against this witness.'

'But I can't account for the witness making a mistake. Why can't you take *my* word for it?'

'Well, how, and – and *when* did this guy get in the back of the truck?'

Jayne suddenly felt exhausted. 'I don't know.'

Scott was quieter. 'Is there a chance you thought there was someone there but there wasn't? Like, something just really scared you and you veered off the road?'

Jayne opened her mouth to rebuff this, but for an awful millisecond, she wondered if he was right. In the next millisecond, she couldn't believe she was allowing herself to be swayed like this. She knew her own mind; she knew what had happened. But it was obvious Scott wasn't sure she knew her own mind. This was it, then. They had no future. The thought of that made Jayne feel sick. She tried to get up but didn't seem to have any strength in her legs. Scott had to lift her, asking her where she wanted to go. Her mouth was salivating and she muttered, 'Bathroom,' getting there just in time to retch in the sink as Scott held her hair back. The nausea subsided but she remained hunched over, washing out her mouth.

'Please don't stay in here,' she said.

'Are you sure?' He sounded confused.

She nodded, remaining bent over until she heard the door shut. Then she reached over to the toilet, closed the lid and sank down onto it. She was tired and angry and hurt and above all – most of all – sad. But she was afraid that if she started crying, she would curl up on the floor and never get up again. She laboriously pulled off her nightshirt, the softness sliding past her skin to bring back a memory of Scott holding her in the way she wanted to be held, of them making love the night before, and now . . . now, there was this chasm between them.

She threw the shirt into the laundry hamper and turned on the shower. She stepped in and the warm spray hit her face to mimic tears as it rolled downward and dripped from her chin, and she cried after all, quietly but deeply, and for a long time, her hands flat against the tiles for support as she hung her head.

*

When Eric arrived at Jayne's apartment, Scott was ready to leave for the witness interview but Eric wanted to see Jayne if he could. He knocked on her bedroom door, which was ajar. 'Up for a visitor, Jayne?'

'Eric? Come in.'

He found her sitting on the edge of her bed wearing sweatpants and a tank top, towel-drying her hair. She gave him a wan smile and started to get up.

Eric stepped forward. 'Don't get up.' He sat down and put an arm around her. She put her head to his shoulder but just briefly. 'Doing okay?' he asked.

She nodded but didn't speak. He thought he heard her sniff and sure enough, now she was using the towel to wipe her face.

He hadn't meant to make her cry. 'I'm not going to ask you any questions. Just wanted to see you. And it's *good* to see you.' He gently hugged her again and then let go.

She pecked him on the cheek. 'Thanks, Eric.'

*

Scott asked Eric to do the driving as they went down the stairs from Jayne's apartment.

Eric nodded as they got into the Suburban. 'No problem. When's Steelie arriving?'

'She'll be here any minute. Let's go.'

'Let's wait.'

'Whatever.' Scott leaned against the headrest and closed his eyes.

When a dark green Jeep Wrangler flashed its high beams and half-turned into the driveway, Eric said, 'There she is.'

He waved to Steelie as he pulled away from the curb. Once they were underway, he said, 'What's going on?'

Scott didn't want to reply.

Eric tried again. 'Did you get any sleep?'

'Not enough.'

'That's not good. Understandable but not good.' Eric paused. 'Did Jayne remember something else about last night?'

'She said the perp was responsible for the bruises on her face, but . . .'

'But?'

'I think it could be from the door of her truck and she's just, y'know.' Scott closed his eyes again, head back on the headrest.

'It's the wrong side to be from the door of her truck, Scott.'

Scott opened his eyes and stared unseeing out the front window as he pictured this.

Eric continued, 'If she was in the driver's seat and was buckled up, the only way she's getting hit on the right side is by someone or something in the passenger seat – or in the middle.'

'You're right . . . why didn't I think of that?'

'That was going to be my next question, because it's the approach you should have been taking – if you weren't just going to take her word for it, that is.'

Scott grimaced.

Eric glanced at him. 'What's wrong with you, man? Last night at the hospital, you were sure that attempted suicide was not the right call. But now you're considering it, in spite of what Jayne says? I don't get it.'

Scott decided to drop the bombshell from the previous night. 'Look, I don't want anyone to know about this but when I arrived at the hospital, Eric . . . she apologized to me.'

'For what?'

'She didn't say.'

'So, you supplied the words instead?' Eric sounded incredulous. 'You shouldn't be allowed out alone, Houston. She could have been saying sorry for any number of things. And she was on meds, right?'

Eric looked over and caught Scott's fatigued nod. 'So, there you go. People say all kinds of stuff when they're on meds. You need to ask her what she meant when she said she was sorry. Have you ever heard of this technique?

183

Two-way communication? Way better than letting your pea-brain short out on this, especially on the back of a high-stress, low-sleep situation.'

Scott waited. 'Are you done?'

'For now.'

'Fine.'

'Good. Because we're here.'

Eric slewed the vehicle to the curb in front of a U-shaped apartment complex that housed sixteen units, all facing a bricked courtyard with a massive Ficus tree at its center. A varnished wooden bench encircled the tree's gray trunk. Its suggestion of leisure-in-the-shade initially distracted Scott's eye from the deferred maintenance on the building: peeling blue-gray paint on the window frames and faux shutters, and a few pieces of gutter hanging down. He figured the dry Los Angeles climate encouraged postponement of gutter repair while shutters were hell to paint, faux or no, so he didn't make any sweeping conclusions about the management. Then it occurred to him that was what he should have been doing with Jayne: waiting for more information before drawing conclusions, also known as taking her at her word. He caught up with Eric in front of a door with a silver-tone number 5 nailed to its panels. The door sounded hollow when Eric knocked.

It opened partway to reveal a young man with the timeless look of a surfer, down to the board shorts covered in a pattern of hibiscus flowers, a pinky-white coral necklace and an all-over tan. He kept shifting slightly to prevent a large dog from getting more than just its nose out the door.

'Derek McBride?'

'Yeah, that's me.'

Eric showed his badge. 'I'm Special Agent Ramos, FBI, and this is my partner, Agent Houston. We have a couple of questions about the automobile accident you witnessed last night.'

'FBI?' Derek looked surprised. The dog had also reacted, managing to insinuate itself further into the crack. It now had one eye on the agents, its nostrils flaring and twitching. 'It's probably easier outside. I just need to get his leash.' He closed the door.

They waited for him in the shade of the Ficus. A German shepherd led Derek via a retractable leash and promptly investigated Scott and Eric's shoes, the legs of the bench, and the few weeds shooting up between the bricks.

Eric sat down on the bench next to their witness. 'What took you to the Silver Lake Reservoir last night?'

'I was walking Cody. It's our regular walk.'

The dog looked over, possibly upon having heard the word 'walk', and then came over to settle on Derek's feet with a sigh. He put his chin down on his paws but continued to breathe noisily.

Eric said, 'And did you see the pick-up truck before it went into the water?'

Derek nodded. 'I heard it come through the fence. There was a nasty sound of metal on metal and I could see the headlights coming on an angle near the dog park. Then I saw it go all the way into the water. I couldn't believe it.'

'You were how far away at this point? Can you estimate?'

'It was dark. I have no idea. A hundred feet?'

'Even though it was dark, you say you could see inside

the truck and there was only one person inside.'

'Right, and only one person surfaced from the truck after it went in. That lady.'

Scott felt his chest tighten.

Eric said, 'You jumped in the reservoir almost immediately yourself, didn't you?'

'Totally. The second I saw it was going for the water, I was like, holy shit, and I pulled out my cell, called you guys – or 9-1-1, actually. Then we ran up to where it went in. I told Cody to stay and I jumped in.'

Eric glanced at the dog. 'I'm sorry, you told your dog to stay and he did?'

'He's a good dog. He doesn't go far. I know he barked the whole time I was in the water and probably ran around a lot but he was there when I got back with the lady. It wasn't easy getting out, let me tell you.'

'So, it sounds like there were actually a couple of moments when you looked away from the water? When you were looking down to dial 9-1-1 and when you were putting the phone away. What about your shoes? Did you take them off?'

Scott watched Derek closely and was gratified to see that Eric's careful questioning was as effective as always. This excellent witness had not, in fact, had his eyes on Jayne's truck the whole time.

Derek was looking surprised. 'Oh yeah. I forgot I did that. I figured it was going to be cold but I didn't want to get weighed down. I've got some lifeguard training so I know it's harder than it looks to rescue someone, especially if you have to dive down. Fortunately, she surfaced.'

Scott finally posed a question. 'Could you tell if the

woman you rescued was the same person who'd been driving the truck?'

'No, but it stood to reason. I was sure there wasn't anyone else in the truck before the accident because I had a good view – no glare from streetlights on the back window. I mean, there wasn't any back window at all, so it was easier to see in.'

Scott frowned at the witness, who was petting his dog between the ears. 'What do you mean, no back window?'

'The truck – an old F Series, right? – it didn't have a back window. Or the back window was down, if it had some kind of after-market thing. Which would be pretty cool,' he reflected.

Scott could feel his fingers start to tingle. 'How can you be sure there wasn't a back window?'

'There was music pouring out of the opening. It was really obvious.'

Scott was grappling with the implications of this new information: if there was no back window prior to the truck going into the water, then there was something to what Jayne had been saying about a guy breaking in that way.

Then again, the witness was still adamant there *wasn't* a second person, so that could mean the back window had been broken as Jayne had said, but not by the person she'd thought responsible. Either way, there was something off about this whole incident and no one had established that before now.

Scott made eye contact with Eric.

Eric stood up. 'Mr. McBride, thanks for your time.'

The dog got to its feet and looked back at Derek.

'My pleasure,' Derek said. 'Is that lady okay, by the

way? The cops wouldn't tell me anything last night.'

Scott said, 'She's going to be fine. Thank you for assisting her. There aren't many good Samaritans out there.'

'It was an instinctive reaction.'

Scott took the time to muster up a friendly look. 'Then you've got good instincts.'

He owed this kid big time, but right now, he needed to find who did this to Jayne and . . . hurt them. As soon as they were out of earshot, Scott said to Eric, 'We need someone to go over the Ford's back window frame with a fine-toothed comb. ASAP.'

20

Eric drove as Scott liaised with the LAPD. Jayne's truck had already been lifted and transported to the Los Angeles County Sheriff's Department crime laboratory, so Scott relayed the message that the rear window required examination and why. He then dialed Jayne before remembering that her cell phone was out of commission due to the accident. He dialed again, this time calling Steelie, who confirmed that she was still with Jayne at the apartment and Marie was there as well.

'How is Jayne?' Scott asked.

'Things are a little tense?' Steelie said.

'You're answering my question with a question?'

''Cause I got this funny feeling you know the answer to both of 'em.'

'Probably. But I'm going to make it up to her.' Scott paused. 'We're going to need to talk to her later. We should be there by 1300 hours.'

'Fine. We're not going anywhere.'

They said goodbye.

Eric said, 'So you've regained your faith in Jayne.'

'I'm already feeling bad enough over this without you doing your thing, Ramos.'

They were approaching the warehouse where Jayne's truck was being processed for evidence. Eric showed his badge to the gate guard. The tall chain-link gate started to roll back, its wheels running in a track that bisected the driveway, and the guard directed Eric to park anywhere to the left.

A woman wearing a canvas jumpsuit emblazoned with the Sheriff's Department logo met them at the door. 'Henner, Scientific Services. You're here about the one pulled from the Silver Lake Res?'

'That's right,' Eric said. 'SA Ramos, my partner SA Houston.'

'Follow me. I'm going to need you to sign in.'

She led the way down a passage to a window whose ledge was at chest height. Eric signed in on the clipboard, marking down the time of their arrival, their names and agency, and the case number they were inquiring about. For the column marked 'Appt With', Eric held the pen over the page.

The criminalist said, 'Just put my initials: AH. Okay, we're through here.'

They went through double doors that opened out into a high-ceilinged arena that could have been a hangar for small aircraft except it was divided into bays. People in garb identical to Henner's were attending to vehicles, some crushed or creased, others split open. Some vehicles were on raised pallets while others rested on tarps on the floor. The space was bright, lit by a combination of bare fluorescent strips, natural light from rudimentary skylights and spotlights set up within the bays.

Jayne's Ford was near the barn door at the far end. It was parked on a tarp. A trestle table overlapped one edge of the tarp and was covered in plastic, the surface of which was gleaming with what looked like broken window glass.

Henner halted by the truck where the rear window was bedecked with marked labels. 'This window was broken by a forward-moving force. We usually see it the other way around from when people try to kick their way out after an accident.'

'Wait, a forward-moving force? Like from the bed into the cab?' Scott showed this using his hands.

'Yes. Some kind of blunt force in this case. And I can tell you the shape of what was used to do it.' She moved toward the plastic-covered table.

Scott felt rooted to the spot. He looked at his partner, who also seemed to be suffering from a delayed reaction.

'Gentlemen?'

They joined Henner at a table that held what looked like an intricate puzzle of sea glass because the chunky shards showed deep turquoise in cross-section. The criminalist put on a surgical glove and pointed at one array.

'We didn't recover all the glass because some of it was lost when the vehicle was brought up – we did use nets up to a point and we may go back – but the initial shatter pattern is here. First, a blow to the center of the window with a circular object. Fractures radiated out to the edges, as you can see here . . . and then several more until the window lost its structural integrity.'

She moved back to the truck and the agents followed, mute.

Henner said, 'I thought you might be interested in this piece.' She brought out a small translucent plastic box marked with evidence and case numbers. She handed it to Scott.

Inside, there was another piece of what looked like sea

glass, but by turning the box around a few times, Scott could make out a dark smudge at one end. He handed the box to Eric the way a child at a science museum passes on the fossil to the next kid while waiting for the teacher to explain what's so important about it.

Eric returned the box to Henner.

She said, 'You saw the black material? I took a sample to send for analysis but the quick-and-dirty is that it's neoprene. It's not consistent with the other cotton fibers that snagged on the broken window, which, judging from the description of the driver's clothing, will turn out to be from her.'

Eric muttered an expletive.

Scott pointed at the box and then at Henner, trying to formulate his question. 'Are you saying that someone wearing a *wet*suit busted through the back window of this truck? And they used a circular object, which could include, say, a personal oxygen tank?'

'You're asking questions above my pay grade, Agent Houston. All I can tell you is that this neoprene's in the cross section of the breakage. It's an anomaly. If I was you, I'd want to explain it.'

Scott could feel his blood pressure rising. A part of him was desperate to get back to Jayne to apologize for doubting her and another part of him was responding to the fact that they now had confirmation that someone had targeted her. Someone smart, someone who believed in preparation. This wasn't a carjacker, nor was this an addict acting opportunistically. He or she was a planner and had nerve.

Scott asked, 'Was the radio on when the truck was lifted?'

Henner leaned into the cab to look. 'It's in the on position. No longer functioning.'

Scott nodded; the witness had heard the radio. 'What about the headlights?'

The criminalist didn't need to look in order to answer that one. 'They're in the off position.'

Scott thought about this. The witness, McBride, had said the truck's headlights had been on when it went into the reservoir. Turning the lights off would have made it more difficult to find it underwater. If there hadn't been a witness, no one would have even known Jayne was down there without some submerged headlights to give a clue.

The guy had been out to kill her.

Eric asked, 'Could the recovery guys have turned them off?'

Henner said, 'Not if they're bringing something to our shop. They know not to touch anything besides the ignition, and they note ignition position on recovery.'

Scott said, 'Did they recover a purse or small bag?'

'No, we've got the usual glovebox contents and, from a net pouch behind the seat: a Mylar sunshade, a pair of binoculars, a Thomas Guide, a quilted cotton blanket and a partly used tube of sun block. All sodden, of course. Keys were still in the ignition. Everything but the keys has been transferred to Property if you need to look at it before it goes back to the vic.'

Scott wanted to correct Henner; Jayne wasn't 'the vic'. 'I'm just looking for your professional opinion on whether you would have expected to recover a purse if you recovered all that other stuff.'

'Yes and no. Too many variables, between the incident and the recovery.' Henner looked at him. 'Not to mention the sticky fingers of the perp.'

21

Jayne tipped the bowl of matzo ball soup to her mouth, draining the last dregs of carrot, celery and dumpling. She burped and then wiped her mouth with the back of her hand instead of the napkin Steelie had brought to the table.

She looked at Steelie. 'Is there any more?'

Jayne noticed Steelie looking astonished.

Steelie closed her mouth. 'Uh – yes.' She began walking to the kitchen but gave Jayne a last look.

'You don't have to get it,' Jayne said, realizing that there was a thin slice of carrot that hadn't been eaten still sticking to the side of the bowl. She tried to retrieve it with her spoon.

'You need to rest,' Steelie said.

'I'm feeling better.'

'But you're acting weird. In fact, you look like shit. Did I mention that Scott's coming over to talk to you?'

Jayne missed her mouth with the spoon and had to wipe her chin.

Steelie said, 'Jesus. I say his name and what little bit of color you have left drains away. You sure you got a black granny?'

Ignoring this dose of Steelie-style humor with effort, Jayne went to the kitchen and pushed jars aside in the pantry cupboard until she found the unopened tub of chocolate icing where it was hiding behind a tin of beets.

She brought the icing back to the table.

Steelie looked at it and said, 'Oh boy.'

'It's for when I'm done with my soup.'

Steelie's voice softened. 'What happened, Jayne?'

Jayne thought about how to put it. 'I happened.'

'You're going to have to explain that.'

Jayne sat scrunching her hair, hard. In her own mind, she knew what she meant: Scott was the prize she didn't get to have because he thought she was a fantasist – and not the good kind. But to say those words aloud—

Footfalls started noisily up the outside stairs.

'That'll be him,' Steelie said.

Jayne's instinctive move to make herself presentable was quashed by the realization that it wouldn't matter anymore. She may as well pretend that she meant for her hair to sit on her head like an abandoned bird's nest.

She heard Eric ask Steelie, 'How's the patient?' but it was Scott she saw coming toward her. He looked self-conscious. That was unexpected.

Steelie said, 'Have you guys had lunch? There's more food in the kitchen.'

Eric said, 'That would be great. Are you sure there's enough?'

Scott stopped short without speaking and backtracked to the kitchen.

Steelie gave them a tour of the paper bags ranged across the counter. 'I think Marie cleaned out the deli. We've still got a pastrami on rye, a corned beef on sourdough, half an egg salad on white, a pot of borscht, two things of matzo ball soup and as many pickles as you can eat.'

Jayne sipped her soup as she watched the others jostle

at the counter, dividing sandwiches and loading up paper plates. She saw the easy way Steelie had with both men, how they laughed at her jokes and how she seemed pleased by that, the amount of swearing the three of them indulged in with each other, and how Scott looked at Steelie with real affection, even when she slapped him on the butt with some rolled-up placemats for the table. Jayne also noticed that Scott let Steelie navigate, as the one who knew the kitchen best, letting her retrieve the glass for his drink instead of telling her he already knew where to find it.

Eric carried his plate over to the table first. 'Mm-mmm,' he said, rhythmically bobbing his chin and bouncing his knees as though bopping to music.

He sat down next to Jayne. 'This looks great. Tell your mom thank you from me.'

'Easy, Tiger,' Steelie said, coming over. 'You don't want to get on Marie's radar like Houston has.'

Eric raised an eyebrow. 'Oh?'

'If she's Tom Cruise, he's the bogey at one o'clock.'

Scott took up the fourth chair. 'Are you really referencing *Top Gun*?' He handed a placemat over to Eric.

Eric took a bite of pickle. 'Having had the description of Marie from Scott, I gotta say I'm looking forward to seeing the Prentis-Hall effect in action. Sounds like they broke the mold after her.'

Where Jayne felt unable to make eye contact with Scott, she could with Eric. 'She must have been on her best behavior last night, then.'

'You don't remember how she was?'

'Not really. They put me on something. I mean, I remember her being there but I know I couldn't have reined her in.'

'Don't worry, Steelie did that,' Scott said. 'Although she could have done it faster.'

Steelie smiled. 'I did leave you hanging for a minute, sorry. It was such a nice distraction from the reason we were there.'

Her expression clouded over and her eyes flitted around the room. 'Anyhoo . . .' She filched the second pickle off of Eric's plate and chomped on it noisily.

The more they sat there not talking, the more aware Jayne became of Scott's knee just inches away from hers, visible through the glass tabletop. It was a good knee, a good shape. She knew exactly what it looked like. That depressed her. She wondered if she should just eat the chocolate icing in front of everyone. It was her apartment, after all. She put down her soup spoon.

Immediately, Scott said, 'You're finished?'

She nodded.

'Can I ask you about last night?'

'Sure.' She finally looked directly at him. 'Can I have some coffee or is this another interrogation?'

She saw Scott's mouth tighten, which made her feel bad. She fiddled with the lid on the tub of icing.

Steelie stood up. 'I'll make the coffee.'

'Could you bring me a spoon, Steelie?' Jayne said.

'Alright,' Scott said. 'Can we talk about the guy?'

Jayne looked at him. Now he was paying lip service to her account?

Scott said, 'You mentioned he came in through the back window feet-first. Was he wearing shoes?'

'Um, he hurt my foot when he pressed it down but I

didn't actually see any shoes.'

'Okay, he got his leg under yours and moved your foot from the brake to the gas. Can you think back to that, in terms of what he was wearing?'

Jayne squeezed her eyes shut. 'He was agile. He looped his legs with mine. He moved very fast and basically sat on me. I think he was wearing dark-colored gloves as well as the mask.'

'What about his hair?' Eric said.

'That was hidden by the hood.'

'The hood?' Scott said. 'You didn't mention a hood before.'

'I didn't? There was his forehead but then the border of a hood or maybe a scarf.'

'What about when he left the cab underwater? How did that work?'

'Well, I had my eyes closed. Then I got kicked in the arm and that really scared me so I opened my eyes but he was gone.'

'He went out the rear window as well?'

'I assumed so. The passenger door was still closed, I think, and I couldn't get the driver's door open. Should I come get my own spoon, Steelie?'

Eric said, 'Maybe the kick you felt was him kicking off as he went out the window?'

'Oh yeah. That makes sense.'

'And this whole time,' Scott said, 'he never spoke?'

Jayne shook her head.

'Gave you instructions, threatened you?'

'Nothing.'

'Okay.'

199

Everyone seemed to register the footsteps outside simultaneously.

Jayne looked at the wall clock, thinking that, for once, she was the most relaxed person present. 'It'll be the mail.'

'I'll get it.' Eric headed for the door.

Jayne heard the startled 'Oh!' of her regular mail carrier, who would have been expecting to leave the mail in the mailbox.

'I'll take it. Thanks,' Eric said.

A female voice said, 'Have a good day.'

Eric walked back in, envelopes aloft. 'Where do you want it?'

'Kitchen counter's fine,' Jayne said.

He looked at the topmost piece of mail as he put it down. 'Is this your middle name? Marisol? That's pretty.'

'Oh my God.'

Steelie froze in the act of putting the tray of coffee on the table. 'What, Jayne?'

Jayne tried not to stutter in her surprise. 'That's what he said. The guy last night.'

Scott leaned in. 'You said he didn't speak.'

'Dammit, Scott. I already feel like a walking contradiction, I don't need you to point it out every time.'

Scott looked crestfallen and held up a hand. 'Sorry. What did he say exactly?'

Now she felt bad about her outburst. 'It literally just came back to me.' She scooped a large dollop of icing from the tub. 'I just heard him say "Marisol" before the truck sank.'

'So . . . who knows your middle name?'

'Not that many people.'

200

Steelie said, 'Very, very few, I'd say.'

'But,' Eric said from the kitchen, 'anyone who saw some of your mail would know it.' He waved the envelope.

Jayne got up. 'Who's that even from?' She held out a hand for the envelope.

He looked at it. 'UCLA Alumni Association.'

Jayne stared at the envelope.

Scott arrived, took it from her, examined it and then slapped it lightly against his hand. 'Coincidence?'

'You tell me,' Jayne said.

Steelie twisted in her chair at the dining table to look back at all three of them. 'No freaking way is that a coincidence. Look at it: you're part of a case at UCLA involving a *murder*; the cops ask you to talk to a student, you do, and on the way home – from UCLA – someone attacks you. That's not random. My money's on one of those students or someone running them as a gang or whatever it is they're into.' She turned back around. 'Coffee's on the table, people.'

There was a thoughtful silence as they joined her.

Scott said, 'If it turns out there's a UCLA connection, I'm laying the blame on Detective West.'

'Now, hang on a minute.' Steelie lowered her cup. 'This wasn't his fault.'

'No? Jayne was only there because of him.'

'He asked us for assistance and we agreed.'

'But did he warn you it could be dangerous? Did he offer protection?'

'You should know from Atlanta that protection isn't the same as prevention,' Steelie retorted.

Scott inhaled but didn't say anything.

Steelie blew air up into her bangs. 'I'm just saying that Matt didn't need to give us, like, an OSHA warning. We know there are always risks.'

'And anyway,' Jayne added, 'I called campus police to get an escort to my truck last night. Everything was fine. Maybe this doesn't have anything to do with UCLA.'

Scott wasn't ready to let it go. 'But you were there for a murder investigation.'

Jayne said, 'All I did was speak to a student and a couple of administrators.'

'Wait,' Steelie interrupted. 'I thought Matt only set up one appointment.'

'Yeah, and I also went to see if I could find out more about who signed up to that club.'

'Well, who'd you go see?'

'Student Affairs. They couldn't help but it didn't matter in the end because the student gave me the sign-up list. I completely spaced all this. I should tell the detectives.'

Eric said, 'Where's this list now?'

'It's in my bag . . .' Jayne looked over to where she normally left it on the chair by the kitchen counter. 'Which is at the bottom of the reservoir, right? Or have the police already retrieved it from the truck?'

Scott's brow furrowed. 'No and no.'

'The divers didn't find it in or around the truck,' Eric said.

Steelie folded her arms. 'I don't like the sound of this.'

Jayne was still unperturbed. 'I'm sure they'll find it. Listen, I don't think this is about the list. If it was, someone could have just stolen my bag. They didn't need to send me into the reservoir.'

'Except the water washes away any trace evidence connected to him,' Eric said. 'It's a smart move for a perp.'

Jayne raised her eyebrows. 'True. But the list was just a copy. Why destroy it and not the original?'

Steelie said, 'The guy must not have known the list existed until you got it.'

'But how would he even know I got it? I left after the interview.'

'Maybe he saw you,' Scott said. 'Maybe he was watching you. If the perp was another student, you might not even have noticed.'

'Um, on the off chance you're right and this is all about that list, someone should check on the student who gave it to me. She's still got the original.'

Scott and Eric were up instantly, reaching for their phones.

'You call West, I'll take campus police,' Eric said.

'What's the student's name?' Scott asked Jayne as he dialed.

'Begay,' she said, eyes wide. 'April Begay.'

Jayne replaced the lid on the tub of chocolate icing. She'd lost her appetite.

22

As soon as Scott contacted Detective West about April Begay, West took over communications with UCLA campus police, telling Scott to wait. When West called back, Scott told him about Jayne's accident in the reservoir and then he did a lot of listening. At one point, Scott asked the detective to hold on and he muted his phone.

Addressing the others, he said, 'The student is fine, but there are other issues. West wants to see you, Jayne. Do you mind if they come here or would you rather meet them at their office?'

Steelie said, 'They should come here, Jayne. You're not going anywhere today.'

Jayne pointed with her thumb. 'What she said.' She looked around the apartment. It was tolerably tidy. It would probably take more energy than she had to make it look much better. But she would change out of her sweatpants before they arrived.

Later, in her bedroom, Jayne put on jeans and a clean T-shirt. She brushed her hair, put on some blush, then some bronzer, then gave up.

Scott joined her in the kitchen while she was measuring out powdered lemonade into a pitcher. He spoke *sotto voce*. 'You changed clothes.'

She nodded and doled out another heaped tablespoon. 'Was that for West?'

Jayne didn't answer because she was trying to remember how many spoonfuls she'd put in the pitcher already.

'What is it about this guy?' Scott said.

'What do you mean?' Jayne turned to get the jug of filtered water.

'Steelie likes him. You like him. I'm interested because Steelie's never liked me and, right now, I can't even tell if you do.'

Jayne used a long-handled wooden spoon to mix the lemonade. 'I don't know if it's an issue of me liking *you*.'

'Seriously?' His *sotto voce* had changed to a loud whisper.

'The way you looked at me this morning, when you thought I was making up what happened last night, you—'

'Now, hang on.' This was much louder than a whisper.

Steelie and Eric looked over and Scott took Jayne's arm lightly. 'Can we talk in the other room for a second?'

They went into the bedroom and Scott closed the door.

'Jayne . . . how can I put this?' He rubbed his palms against each other. 'I made a mistake this morning. I won't make it again.'

'The thing is, Scott, I didn't make the guy up—'

'I know.'

Jayne sat down on the end of the bed. 'What I'm trying to say is that, while I didn't make *him* up, sometimes I do make up things. I don't mean literally. It's more like, I think I heard something but there's actually nothing there. There will come another day like today, where you're looking at me sideways. And I'm not sure I want that.'

Scott looked like she'd just slapped him across the face. 'You're saying you don't want to even *try*?'

Jayne felt bleak and exhausted. This felt too hard. 'We just tried.'

'No,' his voice was thick with emotion, 'we were just getting started.'

He sat down next to her. 'Maybe there will be another day like today, and you know what? It could be me – it could be me as much as it could be you. Why can't we just give each other a break, huh? I can get better at being patient, and you can, too. And when you're ready, you go see a shrink – a good shrink. I can go with you if you want. Not into the room, obviously. I'm just saying it's not like I haven't been to a shrink before. Eventually, there won't be any more days like this. I promise you, Jayne. It will get better. I promise.'

He was beseeching her, his expression born of determination, and he moved her with his passionate hopefulness about her, about them, about a different way of living. She had finally admitted she had PTSD and Scott had taken it in his stride. Not only that, he was talking about a future with her. The enormity of the moment washed over her and she felt choked up with a curious mix of sadness and gladness.

He scrutinized her face. 'Does that little smile mean we're okay?'

She laughed a little and wiped her eyes.

'So, we're okay?' Scott repeated.

'What, I have to say it out loud for the tape?'

He smiled. 'I just want confirmation so I know what to tell your mother the next time she grills me.'

'When did she grill you?'

Voices were coming louder from outside the bedroom.

Scott cocked his head. 'Sounds like the detectives are here.'

Jayne stood up and smoothed a hand over her clothes. 'Great. This'll look good: me and you emerging from my bedroom. Very professional. Did you explain that you knew me and Steelie already?'

Scott propelled her into the front room without answering and the next thing she knew, his hand was in the small of her back. He was walking close to her, as though they were an item. Eric and Steelie grinned but the detectives were pictures of surprise.

'Ms. Hall,' West said, then cleared his throat noisily. 'We've only just heard about last night. How are you feeling?'

'I'm doing okay.'

'No thanks to you, West,' Scott said.

'Look, I didn't know you two were . . .' West used his index finger to point at Scott, then Jayne, back at Scott, and then he gave up, opening his fingers away from his palm.

Steelie snorted. 'Would that have made a difference?'

West looked uncomfortable. 'Yeah, probably.'

Steelie threw up her hands. 'Charming. Further proof of thin blue lines, double standards, maybe even chauvinism. How can you work with him, Detective?'

Sanchez smiled back at Steelie. 'You get used to it. Shall we get down to business?'

'Fine by me,' said Jayne, catching Scott's eye to telepathically ask when, exactly, he was going to remove his hand now that he'd had his fun.

He gave her an amused frown, head tilted, as though he didn't know what she meant.

Jayne allowed herself to be led to the living room and saw that Steelie had finished making the lemonade. The pitcher was on the coffee table with a bunch of glasses. Everyone found a place to sit, between the sofa, some dining room chairs, and cushions moved to the knee-height stone hearth of the corner fireplace.

West said, 'As I told Agent Houston on the phone, the student April Begay is fine, but her room was broken into about mid-morning today. Her RA reported it to campus police but it wasn't flagged for anything special because that dorm – well, all the dorms – get break-ins. Especially in the summer because, as it was explained to me, a lot of non-UCLA students are enrolled who don't have the same appreciation for security as the ones who live on campus for a couple of years. Outer doors propped open or people let someone in on their say-so.'

'Was anything taken?' Eric said.

'Fortunately, Begay had her laptop with her, so it was the usual smaller items: MP3 player, jewelry and anything good for identity theft.'

'Banking documents,' Sanchez said.

'And other documents,' West said, 'including the original of this list of student names we understand she gave you, Ms. Hall. It's missing from her organizer.'

Eric whistled.

Scott said, 'So now there's no record of who signed the petition for the club.'

'Not quite.' West sounded pleased. 'What we have here, in negative, is the list of names. April Begay pulled this off the page in her organizer that was beneath the one she gave you, Ms. Hall. Used pencil lead to bring up the impressions.'

The list was handed around.

Eric said, 'I, for one, am impressed.'

Jayne said, 'She's that type of person: resourceful, smart, motivated.'

West looked at her. 'Whoever's behind this must know that you two met and that she gave you this list – unless she told you something else important?'

Jayne shook her head. 'To be honest, things are only coming back to me in flashes. I remember wanting to tell you about the list, like that was the most important thing I'd learned.'

Steelie said, 'I guess it's a done deal that the attack on Jayne is related to your case, then?'

West said, 'Well, what these agents say happened at the reservoir last night doesn't fit the MO of a carjacking or an assault or petty theft. Not with the assailant coming in wearing a wetsuit in advance of sending the truck into the water.'

Steelie frowned. 'Wetsuit?' She looked at Eric and Scott, and then turned to Jayne. '*Hello?* Aren't you interested in what these people are talking about?'

'Hang on.' Jayne was still looking at the list in West's hand. 'Could you read those names out?' She was remembering something hazy from seeing the list the previous day. As West started reading, she closed her eyes.

'Taylor Akinwale, Daniel Chu, Brittany Miyataki, Miguel Johnson, Stephanie Hong, Regan Hart, Jared Stilson, April Begay.' West stopped.

Yes, Jayne thought. She looked around at everyone. 'What do you notice about them?'

Sanchez said, 'There are a lot of ethnic names.'

'Well, non-European ethnicities: Akinwale, Chu, Miguel, etcetera. But the two whose names don't obviously suggest a non-European ancestry are the two who went missing.'

'You're right,' Steelie said. 'Take Jared Stilson. His RA thought he was white and there's nothing about his first or last name that necessarily gives you a clue that both his parents aren't also white. And I remember Regan Hart's photo. If you knew she was mixed, that might be one thing, but otherwise you could think she's white and neither of her names suggests otherwise. If you believe in that calculus.'

'I get it,' Sanchez said.

'I do not get it,' West said.

Sanchez turned toward him. 'She's basically saying that the two students who went missing from the club are the ones whose names don't sound ethnic.'

Steelie immediately corrected her. 'Well, they sound *ethnic* but likely European.'

'Can't we just use "ethnic" the way everyone else uses it: to mean "non-white"?'

Steelie's nose tilted up and Jayne smiled to herself. She knew what was coming.

Steelie said, 'At best, that usage disenfranchises whites from their diverse ancestries. At worst, it's a linguistic extension of the hegemony of whiteness as the baseline of personhood. As an anthropologist, I actually can't use "ethnic" to mean "non-white".'

Sanchez's eyes were alight. 'But could you do it for the sake of this conversation with my partner?'

210

'Oh, for him? Sure.'

West said, 'I don't know what you guys are saying about me but I'm feeling kinda dirty here.'

Eric cut in. 'You're talking about passing, right, Jayne?'

She nodded. 'Some people call it white-presenting.'

Scott said, 'Stilson and Hart could both pass – or present – as white.'

'Even if they weren't trying to,' said Steelie.

Jayne pointed at her in agreement. 'Absolutely! This wouldn't be about them. In fact, Regan Hart told April Begay that she was exploring her mixed identity when she signed up for the club. This would be about how someone else perceived them.'

'Meaning the perp?' West picked up the list of names. 'So, you're talking about someone who's irate that some of these mixed-race kids look white?'

'No. For all I know, all of them look white. It's not just about appearance; it's about names too. At least, I think the combination of the two might be important in figuring this out. But let me caution: this is just an idea I had using that list as a filter on the disappearances.'

'But it could be useful even as a theory,' Sanchez said. 'If race is the reason these vics were targeted, we know at least one thing about the perp.'

'It would be a lead,' Eric said.

'An important one because we've ruled out the campus staff who had specific knowledge of the construction dates. They all have alibis.'

West added, 'And we still haven't found anyone in Stilson's past who'd threatened him or even argued with him.'

Scott opened his notepad to a fresh sheet. 'Let's run with this for a second. This race theory calls for a perp who had eyes on the victims but also had eyes on that list . . . or who saw the vics at the booth on Club Day.'

'And you need all the other caveats we have from earlier in the investigation, too,' said Eric. 'He needs to be able to get the drugs, needs to be able to approach the vics close enough to administer the drugs, possibly needs knowledge of the construction site and be able to access it.'

West said, 'That's a lot of knowledge and access for one person. Maybe we're dealing with several people.'

'Maybe we are,' Scott said.

Sanchez looked perturbed. 'Are we talking about hate crimes here? Because if you're talking about a group of perps making race-based targets out of UCLA students *on campus*, this isn't going to look good – for anyone: UCLA, campus police, the city. And there will be a lot of attention. I can already see headlines with KKK in them.'

Everyone fell silent.

Jayne did not like the specter of the Ku Klux Klan and didn't want to be responsible for these law enforcement officers thinking this way if it was wrong.

Eric suddenly elbowed Scott. 'We haven't circled back to the Bailey brothers either.'

Scott gave Eric a quelling look but West had already taken it up. 'The federal case with these drugs.'

Scott looked at him in surprise. 'You know about that?'

West gave him a flat look. 'You think me and Sanchez didn't look into why you muscled in on this case in the first place?'

'But how'd you find out?' Scott asked.

West waved a finger in the negative. 'You have your secrets; I have mine.'

Sanchez rolled her eyes. 'We called around the ADAs we know. They have a database of federal cases. It was, like, two keystrokes.'

West gave her a hurt look. 'Thanks a lot.'

She carried on, unapologetically. 'We know that it's the only known case of this drug combination being used outside of death row. Until now.'

Steelie was openly curious. 'Is that true, Scott?'

He nodded.

'But the case was adjudicated?' Steelie was looking between Scott and Eric for a response.

Scott cleared his throat. 'It was . . . but with the drug cocktail turning up out here, we started looking for a potential supplier or accomplice that might have been missed when the Bailey conviction came down.'

Jayne asked, 'Well, what happened in the case, if you can say?'

Scott said, 'It was Tennessee, 1980. Red Bailey was convicted of killing his brother using the death penalty cocktail followed by a shotgun blast.'

Steelie screwed up her face. 'Nasty. But there was nothing off about the conviction?'

'No. He put his hand up to killing his brother but the shotgun was never recovered and no one even asked where he sourced the drugs.'

'And you saw a little daylight in there . . .' Steelie looked thoughtful. 'As a defense lawyer, I would have exploited it. I'm surprised his attorney didn't.'

West was incredulous. 'He confessed!'

'If I'd been his attorney, I would've said that confession was coerced. Naturally.' She gave him a thin smile.

West smiled back even as he shook his head in disbelief.

Sanchez said, 'So I get it about the unique connection over these very difficult-to-access drugs. Does anything about what's been happening at UCLA seem to fit in with the Bailey case? Any of this white supremacy stuff, for example?'

Steelie raised an amused eyebrow. 'You mean, something besides white people?'

Sanchez said stiffly, 'I didn't say that.'

Eric was standing up. 'Not so far, but we've got our work cut out for us. I think it's time we merged our cases, started working together.'

Scott stood up, too, nodding his head.

'Fine by me,' West said. He looked at his partner, who gave him a nod. They both stood.

Still sitting, Jayne raised a finger but no one noticed.

As the four investigators headed for the door, West was saying, 'We can get you some space over at Robbery-Homicide.'

'If this turns out to be hate crimes, it's the Bureau's anyway,' Scott said. 'We've got a spare desk in our office.'

Sanchez jerked a thumb toward West. 'You want me to share a desk with him? He won't even let pens and pencils share the same jar.'

'Not into mixing stuff, huh?' Scott said.

West ran a finger around his collar. 'I'm not overly familiar with it.'

Still talking among themselves, the four of them left the apartment without a backwards glance. The outside stairs reverberated as they hurried down to their vehicles.

Steelie began gathering the drinking glasses. 'Well, you seem to have started something.'

Jayne said, 'And we're clearly not involved.'

Just then, someone came running back up the stairs. There was a knock at the front door. Steelie went over, checked the peephole, and then let Scott back in.

He crossed to Jayne, kissed her twice then started back to the door, saying as he went, 'Steelie, don't let her out of your sight unless someone else is taking over.'

Steelie nodded and locked the door behind him. 'I think that last part means we are still involved, Jayne.'

*

Junior waited across the street. He had no choice. The unmarked police car was blocking the driveway and the Suburban was in it, looking about six times the size of the white Subaru next to it. But he felt calm. The voice was asleep like it usually was mid-afternoon. Plus, he was fitting in with the crowd. The calisthenics routine was doing the trick. In fact, he needed to stretch. Putting the woman down in the reservoir had been more strenuous than he'd expected. He could still feel her thigh pressing into him as she tried in vain to lift his leg off hers when he'd trapped her in the truck cab. Had those strong thighs helped her get out after he'd swum away? Strong lungs were what she'd really have needed. The oxygen tank had been crucial for him. There had been altogether too much adrenaline and he'd almost used up the whole tank. It had all been too rushed. But he'd done it.

He looked around at the other runners, all mid warm-

215

up or cool-down. Beautiful people were beyond on the grass, doing tai chi, yoga, Pilates. The Good Life. Oblivious that they were sun-worshipping at the scene of a deadly accident. Or near deadly. He still didn't know which. The only sign left of the accident was caution tape and a barrier in the gap in the fence around the reservoir. That gap could be construction. Could be a space for a new gate. No one even looked curious. The Good Life.

An exodus from the duplex got his attention and he watched as he stretched his triceps behind his head. A man and a woman coming down wearing guns and badges. The same detectives from campus, going to the sedan. And now a highly muscled guy in a suit – where'd he find a blazer to go over those biceps? – was trotting down. No badge. Could maybe be some kind of personal security guard for the woman if she was in there recuperating. He had dark hair and dark skin and had just turned to look back at his fair-headed carbon copy: the man with the Suburban. They seemed to be talking. And now Carbon Copy was running back up the stairs, taking two at a time with a lively step. The cops were waiting by the sedan. No sign of the woman. *She's inside, stupid!* He pushed back against the voice. *You don't know that; she could still be dead.*

Now Carbon Copy was back, putting on sunglasses as he came down the stairs, twirling a finger in the air that apparently meant *Let's go* because they all went in a drumbeat of slamming doors. The sedan lurched into a wide U-turn to go south on Silver Lake Boulevard only to stop short and hold back traffic so that the Suburban could launch out of the driveway and take the lead, the sedan on its six. They were driving like they knew something.

216

Not good at all. He would have to move faster than them. He started his run but not around the reservoir; he went straight to his car. He dismissed the thought that other runners would notice that he'd warmed up but hadn't made the circuit. They wouldn't even remember him.

After all, they were living the Good Life.

DAY EIGHT

WEDNESDAY

23

'Are you sure you're up to being here, even for a half-day?' Carol's hands were wrapped around her cup of tea as she looked at Jayne from across the table in the Agency's small kitchen.

Jayne tested out rotating her shoulder. 'I'm still sore but work will keep my mind off things.'

Steelie was putting a leftover sandwich half into Tupperware. 'Does one of the things have green eyes and sorta dirty-blond hair?'

Jayne chuckled and then winced when that made her side hurt. 'I was referring to what happened to my truck.'

'You could find another one just like it,' Carol said. 'It might take some time, but it could be done.'

Steelie said, 'She doesn't want another truck.'

'Oh?'

Jayne said, 'I'm thinking of something more . . . enclosed.'

'Ah. I see.' Carol gave an understanding nod.

They all heard the newly installed security buzzer at the Agency's front door sing out.

Steelie frowned. 'Are we expecting anyone?'

'No,' Carol said. 'I'll see who's there.'

When she returned, she said, 'It's Regan Hart's parents. They said Jared Stilson's parents recommended they come to the Agency. Do you want them to make an

221

appointment?'

Jayne shook her head. 'No. Show them into my office.' She glanced at Steelie.

Steelie said, 'We'll have to mind our p's and q's. No mention of anything we've learned about Jared from the cops. Nuh-thing.'

'Got it.'

'Let me grab my notebook from the lab.'

They greeted the couple sitting on the couch in Jayne's office and gestured for them to keep their seats as they introduced themselves and shook hands. Jayne and Steelie sat across from them. When Jayne asked what they could do for them, Mrs. Hart spoke first. She had pale coloring: light brown hair just beginning to show strands of gray, pale eyebrows and lashes, and thin lips that shone with apricot gloss. She wore a khaki-colored belted dress that looked like what catalogs sold for easy wearing in summer.

'We're here at the suggestion of Justin and Helene Stilson, Jared's parents. We . . . you probably know that Regan Hart is our daughter. She's a student at UCLA and . . . she's been missing since December 12th, 2003.' She looked over at her husband as though for encouragement.

Mr. Hart, who'd introduced himself as Don, had a youthful look because his dark hair was gelled in a neat side-part that reminded Jayne of kids arriving at school for picture day. But lines were beginning to show around his brown eyes and there was an air of resignation about the way he sat back on the couch, arms crossed over his button-down shirt. It was as though he was leaning back from the meeting. However, he unfurled his arms and rubbed his wife on the back.

Rebecca Hart continued. 'We drove up from Irvine to see you because . . . well, we wondered if you could help us too. We've tried everything with the police and with the school. We've been told Regan ran away but we've never believed that. She isn't having issues teenagers sometimes have at college. And we don't want to think that Regan is . . . has passed away but now that Jared's been found and someone did that to him, we're worried that someone was preying on students and they might have preyed on Regan, too.'

Don added, 'And if that's the case, we want her found.'

'I understand,' said Jayne. 'There may be some avenues to pursue and we can describe for you what we do here, but could you first answer a few questions about your daughter?'

Both parents nodded and Don even sat forward, his elbows on his knees.

'Our first question is, since Jared was found, have you had contact with the detective from Missing Persons who's handling Regan's case?'

'Yes,' Rebecca said. 'We called in as soon as we heard about Jared. It turned out that the detective who used to be on the case was recently reassigned, so we spoke to a new detective. His name is Lloyd.'

'Okay, that's good. Was he able to tell you if there are any new leads in light of Jared's case?'

'No. I mean, he said that the notes on Regan's file were that she's a likely runaway and that, as of right now, there are no new leads. He did say that the investigation into Jared's death was ongoing but that's being handled by another department and there's no connection between the two cases right now.'

Steelie nodded. 'All of that is pretty standard language. The detective will be limited in what he can say, however, we could still request a status conference in light of the discovery of Jared's body.'

Don tilted his head. 'Even though they already told us they've checked for Regan in morgues and she's not there?'

'Yes, even though they've said that. One of our primary roles as an agency is to review dental records to ensure they're made part of a case and analyzed correctly. Can I ask if they gave you the form that will allow you to retrieve your daughter's dental records?'

Don nodded. 'They did. We needed it to get the records from Regan's last check-up. The ones before were while she was a child, so we already had those at home.'

Steelie nodded. 'Okay, we will want to follow up on those. We'll check to see if the records you provided were actually coded and uploaded into the missing persons database, and that they were uploaded correctly. We would actually code the records ourselves and re-submit them to the detective.'

Rebecca pulled her large purse toward her. It was a leather satchel, with four nubby brass feet on the bottom. She dug inside and pulled out a folder. 'I have the dental records here. We could leave them with you now.'

'Thank you.'

'Also, in relation to her missing person report,' Jayne said. 'Did they talk to you about Regan's ethnicity? Either how she described herself or how you described her?'

Rebecca looked at Don. He was shaking his head. 'No. I remember that someone asked us her race, just like, in a

224

list: "age, race, height", that kind of thing.'

'And how did you answer?'

He said, 'That she was mixed-race: Asian – I'm Chinese – and white. That's how she filled out her own college application.'

Jayne was aware that they wouldn't know how the missing persons detective had handled this within NCIC until they could speak to the LAPD or see the NCIC record. 'Okay, we'll want to follow up on that as well. Law enforcement databases aren't programmed well for people who don't fit into just one category, especially for race.'

'Are you saying they might have misclassified our daughter?'

'Not necessarily,' Jayne cautioned. 'But this would be an important area where our agency could ensure Regan was described accurately.'

Steelie said, 'We might need some manipulation of government databases but we're not above asking for that.'

'Speaking of government databases,' Don said. 'We asked them to do an Amber Alert for Regan as soon as we realized she was missing – she was supposed to come home on winter break but never arrived – but they told us she didn't meet some "threshold".' He spoke with disdain as he put air quotes around the word. 'We thought that meant they didn't think she was abducted and we felt they missed an important chance to find her. It's always really bothered me and I wished I'd pushed harder to get an alert put out.'

'Had Regan had her eighteenth birthday when she went missing?' Jayne asked.

'Yes, she'd just turned nineteen.'

'That was actually the reason. That's the threshold they

meant. Amber Alerts are limited by law to children under eighteen.' Jayne could see their faces fall as tension they'd held around the Amber Alert drained away.

Don wiped a hand over his face. 'I can't tell you how much sleep I've lost over that damn alert, and now it turns out they never could have used it.' He looked away.

Rebecca squeezed his knee but her husband kept his face averted, clearly trying to get his emotions under control. She said, 'No one ever explained it to us before.'

'That's why our agency is here,' Jayne said gently.

Steelie said, 'I definitely think you could benefit from a status conference with the detective in Missing Persons.'

'Is Lloyd someone that you know?' Rebecca asked.

'I don't know Lloyd personally, but we know a number of detectives there, and their lieutenant. We can set up an appointment. Our goals for the meeting would be to, number one, ensure that Regan's dental records are correctly uploaded into the state and federal law enforcement databases. Number two, that her missing person report describes her mixed-race heritage accurately.' Steelie was extending her fingers one by one as she counted off the list. 'Three, we want to convey your concern that the discovery of Jared Stilson's body might have a bearing on your daughter's disappearance, such that calling her a "runaway" is not warranted.'

Don had turned toward them again while Steelie had been talking. 'Are you saying there should be a reinvestigation from scratch?'

'It depends. A detective calling someone a runaway doesn't meant that the whole investigation hinged on that. But it's something that should be reviewed, especially now that Lloyd is on it. That's a fresh eye. We don't need to assume earlier investigations were botched in any way. We need to learn more about what they've done and we need to support them with more, and better, information about Regan than they may have gathered up to now.'

Steelie waited until the Harts nodded their understanding. 'Now, the police can't always divulge details of an investigation, even to those most concerned, like family. So, they may not be doing too much talking at the meeting but we can get some balls rolling and also set up a second status conference for a few weeks later, to get any information back about new searches for Regan in the found persons databases.'

'Found persons?' Don asked.

Jayne nodded. 'The government has a database of unidentified people – some are deceased but some are alive and in a coma, for example. Our agency thinks of all of them as people who have been found, one way or another.'

'I see. Okay.' He inhaled deeply. 'I feel a bit better about this. I feel like we're doing something.'

'You are.'

'A meeting with the police would really help us,' Rebecca said. 'Any time. We can both leave work any time.'

As they walked back into the reception area, Steelie explained that Agency 32/1 would contact the LAPD and then contact the Harts. An exchange of telephone numbers took place and then Don asked, 'How much are your services?'

'We're funded by government grants, so our services are free to you,' Jayne said.

'Free?' He looked around the reception room, no doubt

taking in the one plant and the very small sideboard with a coffee maker and fixings arranged across the top.

Steelie gave a sympathetic smile. 'As far as we're concerned, when you're dealing with a missing family member, life is already costing too much. We're going to keep our services free for as long as we can.'

Carol reached across the top of her counter, proffering a folder with an Agency 32/1 brochure clipped to the front. 'This will tell you a bit more about the Agency and how we liaise between families and law enforcement, among other things. It includes a checklist to help you keep track of what documents you've shared with us and how the Agency can use them. I've already checked off the dental records section. You can take this home with you.'

As Jayne watched the Harts leave, she felt a shift inside herself. As shaken as she'd been in recent days, she knew the role she had just played and it made her feel stronger. Grounded. Like she was looking at a map that was marked with a pin: *You are here*. She took in a deep breath and held it, giving thanks for having found her way home.

24

Eric and Scott had accommodated the LAPD detectives in the FBI office by placing them on either side of the desk that usually held the NCIC computer terminal, which had been relocated to the top of one of the low filing cabinets. Having four people in the room was tight but also provided a command center vibe, which, in turn, energized Scott.

Both of the large whiteboards on the wall were in use. One board was still dedicated to Steelie's ten-mile radius body dump map. The other had key details of Jared Stilson's disappearance and homicide. Sanchez was adding details about Regan Hart's time at UCLA and her disappearance.

West said, 'We need to get the attack on Jayne Hall up there, too.'

Scott went rigid. 'Jayne's not going on the board.'

'But . . . we're theorizing that she was attacked in relation to this case.'

'Only in connection with the list.'

West thought about that for a moment. 'Does your boss know you guys are . . .?' He hit the same blockage while trying to link his fingers.

Scott shook his head.

'Does that mean you'd be off this case if your boss found out?'

Scott didn't answer so Eric supplied, 'It's more

complicated than that.'

'And,' Scott looked pointedly at West, 'he's not going to find out from anyone in this room, so, end of discussion.'

West sighed. 'Fine. But even if Jayne Hall's name isn't on the board, we can't forget about the attack on her.'

'That seems unlikely.' Sanchez's tone made it clear she was being ironic.

'Moving on.' Scott perused the board. 'This club Mix it Up is a link between Stilson and Hart. I want to know if there's a group or another club on campus that might have had a problem with its formation.'

'I'll call my contact at UCLA.' West picked up his cell.

Scott walked up to the whiteboard and contemplated it. 'Something else. We've made an assumption on the board that Regan Hart's already deceased.'

Eric said, 'It's a safe assumption, even more so if we consider her disappearance to be connected to Stilson's.'

'But what I'm getting at is that we don't have her body. Did you bring the copy of her file from Missings?' He was addressing Sanchez.

She moved to the corner where they'd stacked the five cardboard file boxes from her office. She selected the second box in the tower and put it on the desk. Taking off the lid, she flicked folders toward her until she found the one she wanted.

'They did the usual,' she said as her eyes skimmed the pages. 'We have description of last-seen-wearing, location-last-seen, a cell phone dump, misper posters, searches of hostels, attempt to locate any romantic attachments – she didn't have any – leads from bank cards – none. All her stuff was left in her dorm room except for one of two suitcases, at the beginning of a break between quarters.'

'Based on that, they should have been looking for her remains anyway,' Eric said.

'Not necessarily; Missing Persons had a notation for likely runaway.'

'Why?' Scott said. 'Did she have history?'

'No, but the timing was right as far as Missings was concerned. Second year of college, new pressures, new influences – not all of them good. They've got thousands of mispers like Hart who turn up five years later living on the streets of Seattle or wherever. She did take a suitcase.'

'Do me a favor? Double check with them.'

Sanchez dialed Missing Persons as her partner hung up from his call.

West said, 'Check this out. The same time Mix it Up had its booth, UCLA shut down a club that was basically a white supremacy group. They fired the faculty sponsor, a guy named Patton, but the students are all still enrolled. Still on campus.' His face betrayed his excitement. 'This administrator actually feared for his safety because Patton blamed him for persecuting them, on account of the administrator being a minority, which he denies.'

'He denies being a minority?' Scott said.

'Very funny.'

'I'm being serious!'

'Well, no,' West hesitated, 'I assumed he meant that he denies persecuting them.'

'Either way,' Eric said, 'this fits with the race theory. Call campus police.'

'Already doing it.' West pointed at the phone he'd brought to his ear.

231

With both LAPD detectives on the phone, Scott and Eric were left looking at the map.

Scott said, 'Let's say both students crossed paths with these supremacists. Stilson wound up dead. Figure Hart did too. If we could get her body, we'd get two bites at the cherry. So . . .' He walked over to the map. 'Let's get her dorm on here. That's location-last-seen?'

Eric took the file from the desk in front of Sanchez and flipped to the front. 'Uh-huh. Hadley Hall. In the center, toward the top.'

Scott put a magnet on the board when he found the building. 'Okay. We know our perp likes construction sites. Was there a building under construction or due to go under construction near here when she disappeared?'

'Hang on.' Eric pulled a file. 'According to the facilities prospectus, there were four areas set aside for construction near there. I can't tell from the list if any digging had started when she went missing but here are the locations.' He read them out.

Scott put more magnets on the map. 'These are clustering in the northwest part of campus. Not far from where Stilson's body was found.'

Eric said, 'If they've done any prep for those buildings, they would've found her, just like they found Stilson.'

'Then let's find out which of these sites are untouched.'

'I'm on it.'

Sanchez and West each ended their calls at the same time.

West went first. 'This alleged white supremacy club? Campus police kicked it up the chain. Someone will call me.'

232

Sanchez said, 'Well, guess what Missings just told me? They've got a status conference with the Hart parents tomorrow thanks to Agency 32/1 pointing out the need now that Jared Stilson's body's been found. Apparently, the Harts have always maintained that their daughter was not a runaway.'

'What does Thirty-Two One want to do, scan morgues?' West said.

Sanchez made an exasperated shrug.

Scott tried for a calming tone. 'It's good if they do: then we're all on the same page. Can we get back to the map?'

But West's cell phone rang. They heard him greet his lieutenant. The conversation was short and he hung up, looking at his partner. 'I guess we're going to the Hart status conference, too. Boss's orders.'

Sanchez threw up her hands. 'Great. Like we don't have enough to do.'

Scott said, 'Let's not get distracted.' He tapped the map. 'These are possible body dump sites that are due for construction at UCLA. Eric's following up on them but is there anything else on here that looks good for a dump site?'

Heaving himself up, West went to join him. After a minute, he said, 'Anything with soil instead of concrete.'

Sanchez added, 'But someplace where no one's going to notice someone dumping a body. Or smell it.'

Scott rolled his finger over. 'So . . . earthy but isolated. That's not easy in a place wick with students and land-scapers.'

West turned his head sideways and then righted himself. 'How about here?' He touched the map.

'That's nowhere near her dorm,' Scott pointed out.

'Look at it, though. It's some kind of garden and it's on the edge of campus. There isn't even a sidewalk there, right, Chance?'

Scott said, 'Chance?'

Sanchez said, 'That's what they call me at the station – when they want something.' She walked over and said to Scott, 'You can call me Theresa.'

She traced the section on the map. 'I don't know if there's a sidewalk or not but it is a hill with vegetation all the way down to Hilgard. If I was walking there at night, I'd take the other side of the street.'

'That's where I'd dump a body,' West said. 'Let's check it out.'

'It's huge. We'd need ground penetrating radar.'

Scott said, 'Our Critical Stabilization guys have GPR gear but our SSA won't approve kit like that until we've shown probable cause.'

'UCLA's lawyers are going to want probable cause as well,' Sanchez sighed. 'Especially if this is going to involve digging.'

'Let's at least take a look at it,' West said. 'Let our noses lead us.'

Scott said, 'You think a body will still be stinking after all this time?'

'Let's hope so, right? Stilson's was.'

'Only after it was uncovered,' Sanchez countered.

Eric got off his call and came up to the board. 'Okay, there's one construction location that's still fenced off right now. Here.' He put a magnet on the map. 'It's just like where Stilson's body was found except they haven't done

234

any digging yet. It's a big area.'

'So now we've got *two* big areas,' Sanchez said. 'We could waste a lot of time on this, guys. We don't know what we're doing.'

'We'll sniff it out,' West said.

'Come on, Matt,' she said. 'Don't pretend we find bodies by doing something besides following the crime scene tape a tech put up before we got there. A buried body would make it even harder for us.'

'Then let's get Steelie Lander and Jayne Hall to help us figure out where to put the tape.' West's gaze slid over to Scott.

Scott locked eyes with him.

West said, 'Come on, Houston. I know you're tempted.'

Scott went to his desk and sat down. He hesitated and then reached for the phone. 'I'm more than tempted.'

25

When Detectives West and Sanchez contacted UCLA, the university's lawyers made it clear that the university would do anything in its power to facilitate the investigation into Regan Hart's disappearance as well as Jared Stilson's death. So, while Scott, Eric, West and Sanchez stood sentry on the other side of a tall chain-link fence, Mitch, Steelie and Jayne stood on the edge of a second construction set-aside on campus, one where the official groundbreaking had yet to take place.

Mitch was standing next to Jayne, his hands resting on the T-shaped top of a long metal rod with a pointed tip at the other end. He said, 'I guess if you're not going to tell me anything more about how you got the new bruises, we should get to work. Where do you want to start?'

Jayne put a hand on his shoulder to let him know she recognized that he was dissatisfied with the amount of personal information she was willing to share just then. 'Let's start with the depressions.'

'They look like natural ground contour, don't they?'

'Yeah, but some of them have healthy-looking weeds.'

'Healthy?'

Steelie said, 'Like they've been drinking body juice protein shakes.'

Mitch blanched. Jayne dipped her hand into his bag of aluminum spikes with fluorescent orange flags attached.

Pulling out a bunch, she gave some to Steelie. 'How about we flag the promising weeds while you start on the depressions, Mitch.'

Steelie retrieved the permanent marker that had been tucked behind her ear. 'Here, use this to mark the flags when you finish each probe. That'll help keep track of what we've covered.'

Jayne and Steelie went ahead. Mitch followed, stopping at the first depression to drive the probe into the ground with enough force to break through the top crust of dry earth. When the probe had sunk deep into the soil, Mitch pulled it out and sniffed the tip. He did this repeatedly around the first depression, while Jayne and Steelie systematically crisscrossed the weedy area, driving flags into a total of eight possible sites. Afterwards, the two women went to stand with the law enforcement officers.

Eric had begun filming with a camcorder. He took his eye off the viewfinder to tell Jayne and Steelie that he wasn't recording audio. They nodded. Mitch marked the flag at the third depression.

Detective Sanchez said, 'I heard Mitch say he didn't think these dips in the ground were suggestive. Why's that?'

Steelie looked out at the area. 'There are a number of them and they're uniform. That militates against only one of them being due to a burial. Unless, of course, they're all burials.'

'But you've got him putting the metal rod in anyway?'

'The probe? Yep.'

West said, 'Does it actually bring up the smell of a body if there's one down there?'

'It can,' Jayne said.

Mitch made his way around, using the probe, bringing it to his nose and moving on. Jayne looked out at the perimeter fence. This part of campus didn't receive much foot traffic and those who did pass didn't evince much interest in whatever Mitch was doing.

Scott said, 'This is kind of like doing surveillance.'

'Boring as hell, you mean,' Eric said.

'I think Mitch might be having some fun,' Jayne said, trying to be diplomatic.

West said, 'I think we'd all be having fun if we had something to do.'

Steelie glanced at him. 'You're bearing witness, Detective.'

Mitch finished probing the last depression. He looked up at them and shook his head.

'Bearing witness to nothing.' West sounded annoyed.

As they walked back to their vehicles, Eric said, 'We heard Regan Hart's parents came to see you. How were they?'

'Lost. Kinda angry,' Steelie said.

'And scared, I'd say, because of Jared being found dead,' Jayne added.

Sanchez said, 'They're not being told we're actively looking for their daughter's remains. You are aware of that?'

'Of course,' Steelie said. 'They don't need the details of the investigation; they just need to know there is one. A real one.'

'This is real, alright,' West said as he unlocked the sedan. 'Let's just hope we get some evidence out of it.'

They drove across campus to the arboretum, their

238

second site. West led them downhill from the road on a gravel path edged by river rock, and stopped at the first level terrace. They were under an ancient, spreading eucalyptus and the air was fragrant.

Mitch pointed up at the tree. 'At least we have a natural air freshener should we encounter . . .' He trailed off.

West said, 'I think we can ignore the entry area for now. Someone would notice a shallow grave up here.'

The trees had all been pruned to ten or twenty feet from the ground, creating an airy canopy. Along the path, occasional dwarf conifers crouched low next to labels that named their species. The slope led down to a wooden bridge spanning what could have been a creek, with taller vegetation around it.

Jayne pointed at the bridge. 'Let's try down there. It looks like it's not tended as regularly.'

West started down the path again. When the group reached the bridge, they paused to look over the side. The creek was dry and lined with river rock. West jumped down into it and examined the rocks.

'They're cemented in.'

Jayne said, 'Hmph.' She looked to the south. There were increasing numbers of trees, all encroaching on the creek. 'I'd like to check out the area with the trees down there.'

'For your next trick, you mean?' West put out a hand for someone to help him climb back up to the path even though they were all setting off after Jayne.

Steelie stepped back and gave him her hand. 'It's a process.'

Sanchez said, 'I gotta say, I wouldn't want to carry a body all the way down here.'

A few minutes later, a youngish, dark-haired woman came from their left, maneuvering a wheelbarrow onto the path ahead of them. She wore a pale green coverall with a UCLA logo on the chest, faded yellow leather gloves, a sun hat and boots. The wheelbarrow held a barrel of what could have been liquid fertilizer and a neatly folded, but worn, heavy-duty tarp that had woven handles at the corners. She gave their group an indifferent nod and continued on her way.

Jayne glanced back. The law enforcement officers had all turned to look at the retreating figure with her wheelbarrow.

Scott said, 'You could carry a body around in that wheelbarrow and no one would look twice.'

'If you worked here,' Jayne said.

'Who says she actually works here?' Scott looked behind him again.

Jayne raised her eyebrows in acknowledgment.

The stand of trees turned out to be firs planted in a triangle, the ground below them flat and covered in old pine needles.

Mitch said, 'You want me to go in there?'

Jayne shook her head. 'It's too flat.' She stepped back and looked into the distance, turning to the right, and then back the way they came.

Steelie said, 'Now that's more like it.'

Jayne followed her gaze. 'Bingo.'

To the east, various species of tall bamboo formed a living wall. It looked impenetrable. From ground level to six or more feet high, dry leaves and detritus were trapped between the trunks. They walked closer.

West said, 'I don't like anyone's chances of dragging a body through this mess.'

'We don't know what it looked like when Regan Hart went missing,' Jayne said.

Scott pulled a two-way radio from the holster on his belt. 'Let's split up and see if there's a way in. Channel two. This location will be six o'clock. Eric, take Steelie and try to come in from nine o'clock. Keep alert. Detectives, see if you can get around to one o'clock or even twelve. Mitch, come with Jayne and me. We're going to try for three o'clock. Anyone sees anything . . .' He waggled his radio.

At the three o'clock position, the bamboo was just as thick. But a little further along, there was a sense of openness – though not an actual opening – because the bamboo species planted here was somewhat less hairy. Sanchez and West continued past while Scott, Mitch and Jayne stopped.

'Why don't I go in first,' Mitch said. 'I've got the probe to push things out of our way.'

He crouched to get past the first row of bamboo trunks, which thinned and thickened but were apparently untended. Their leaves and peelings of husk formed natural mulch, making the ground soft underfoot.

They pressed forward in silence for several minutes. The bamboo increasingly muted the usual outdoor sounds. Cars, birds, flies and bees all seemed to be 'out there', Then they heard a swishing sound, as though someone was walking through a fall of leaves nearby. In a moment, Steelie's pink baseball cap was visible; she was looking at the ground as she walked. Eric was behind her and looking over his shoulder.

'Ra-mos,' Scott called out.

Eric's head snapped forward. He spotted Scott. 'Anything?'

'Nope.'

Steelie rubbed the toe of her boot across the bamboo leaves, exposing a rich soil underlay. 'Good soil for digging, if you can find a place without too many roots.'

Scott said, 'Let me find out where the detectives are.' He spoke into his radio. 'Union Tom Three, Union Tom One, what's your ten-twenty?'

West's voice came crackling through. 'Union Tom One, Union Tom Three, my twenty is one o'clock, wait one.'

Scott held his radio by his shoulder, head bowed and silent as he waited.

Then the radio came to life with West again. 'Union Tom One, Union Tom Three, ten-fifty-four-D, over.'

Scott's eyebrows shot up and he locked eyes with Eric as he depressed his radio call button. 'Say again?'

West enunciated slowly. 'Ten-fifty-four-D at one o'clock.'

'Ten-four. Hold your position. Union Tom One out.' Scott looked at Jayne and Steelie. 'You're up.'

'What?' Mitch's voice was raised. He sounded incredulous. 'That means the cops found a body? In *here*?'

'They think they have. We're gonna let you guys figure it out.' Scott started walking but Mitch was rooted to the spot. Eric prodded him between the shoulder blades with the antenna on the top of his radio.

Detective Sanchez was waiting at a point along the eastern boundary of the arboretum.

'There's some kind of depression in here,' she called

out, 'and it stinks, but for all we know it's just the smell of dead bamboo.'

As they walked with even greater haste toward the detective, Jayne felt the familiar sensation – almost one of elation – that she used to get when looking for clandestine graves with the UN. It was only when you were searching for a body that finding one was a good thing. Any other time? It was horrifying.

Steelie had been questioning Sanchez as they followed her into the bamboo grove. 'Is there a lot of dead plant matter? Like someone dug up the bamboo to make space for a body?'

'No, nothing like that. More like lots of leaves gathered in one place and they're rotting.'

The bamboo here had deep green trunks and a profusion of leaves at their topmost ends, dimming the daylight. The ground was as soft as on the other side of the grove but didn't provide the crunching sound of dry leaves breaking up underfoot. It felt more like a slightly moist carpet. They saw West on the far side of what was less a clearing than a fork between two stands of bamboo. His arms were crossed and he looked pensive.

He trained his flashlight onto the ground a short distance away. 'The depression's there.'

Steelie said, 'You may as well probe it first, Mitch.'

He stepped through the flashlight's beam toward the depression and placed the probe in the center, lining it up carefully so it was perpendicular to the surface.

'I'm going to go easy on this. It's soft,' he said.

Even with his cautious approach, the probe sank in deeply, almost rushing downward. He flinched and stopped.

243

'There is definitely an air pocket – or something,' he said. 'That was like karate-chopping through soft butter.'

He pulled out the probe slowly and was in the process of bringing it to his nose when his whole face creased and he stepped back, as though that would distance him from the probe in his hand. 'Argh. It's not an air pocket. It's something dead.'

Jayne had known before he spoke because his body language had said everything. And where he wanted to get away, she wanted to get closer. Stepping toward him with her hand extended toward the probe, she said, 'May I?'

'Be my guest.'

Jayne probed the soil around Mitch's first location. Some areas let the metal sink straight through and others felt resistant.

She said, 'The area that's been disturbed isn't big and it's not very deep – maybe three feet? Nice depression. Smell is right for something dead, as Mitch put it.' She looked up at West.

He made a phone symbol with his hand. 'Coroner's office?'

'They might rebuff you since all you've got is a stinking . . .' She gestured at the ground.

'Buncha bamboo,' Steelie completed. 'Jenny Sweetzer will slam the phone down on you.'

Sanchez muttered, 'I've told you she does that to him anyway.'

West said, 'So, what do we do, then?'

Mitch cleared his throat. 'I'm not sure this is covered by my CRM remit but . . . test pit?' He was looking at Jayne and Steelie.

The anthropologists nodded and he opened his backpack. He drew out a tape wheel, a small tarp and a folded flat-end shovel.

Jayne said, 'Eric, you should videotape this part, just in case.'

She waited for him to start the recording, and then placed a flag in the middle of the depression.

Mitch gave her the end of the measuring tape and then walked back to several of the largest bamboo trunks. He called out the distance between each trunk and the flag to Steelie, who jotted them in a notebook. He added in the GPS coordinates, reading them out from his handheld device.

Then Steelie took Polaroids as everyone held flashlights to illuminate the area. She started at a distance from the depression and went closer to the flag in the ground. She waved the photos back and forth and the little bit of wind they created was the only noise in the grove.

West was watching her. 'You don't need to do that anymore. They changed the formula years ago.'

Steelie looked at him as she doggedly continued to waft the photos. Then she checked them. She gave Mitch a thumbs-up.

First, Mitch laid the tarp out near the flag. Then he used the shovel to demarcate a square around the flag and began to dig, firmly but slowly. This measured approach allowed him to take off a couple of inches of the soil-bamboo mulch with each pass. He deposited each shovelful onto the tarp to save it, in case this did turn out to be a crime scene.

He stopped, breathing more heavily now. 'Steelie, Jayne.'

They came over. About three feet down in Mitch's test

pit, a portion of a dark fabric suitcase was visible. It bulged open along its zipper and a decaying, fleshed human elbow, partly covered by a sleeve with a frilly edge, protruded from inside the main compartment. The overwhelming smell of decomposition rose up as though liberated.

Jayne's professional excitement, that visceral thrill engendered by the hunt for a clandestine grave, left her. In its absence, she felt like a bystander observing a private horror, a horror that was going to seep out from this gravesite and end up touching all of them because it wasn't inert. It was embodied in *someone*, someone who had killed twice, buried twice – someone who wasn't done.

Steelie broke the silence. She looked over at the investigators who were shifting and making impatient noises like racehorses waiting for the gates to open. 'Actually,' she said, 'this is totally their department.' She stepped back and joined Jayne.

Eric moved forward by arcing out to the side, trying to watch where he stepped as he made the camcorder follow the area brightened by flashlight.

West only took a quick look in the pit before he stepped away and opened his phone. They heard him identify himself and ask to speak to a coroner's investigator. Sanchez took a longer look before she, too, stepped away, hitting speed dial on her phone and asking to speak to her lieutenant. Scott stayed, staring down into the pit. He muttered an expletive.

Eric cut off the video and glanced at the scientists. 'What do you think? Regan Hart?'

'Can't tell,' Steelie said. 'For now: presumptive human remains.'

Scott said, 'It's gotta be her.'

Steelie shrugged.

Scott gestured at the frilly sleeve. 'Female, though, surely. How long has it been down there, do you think? Any ideas?'

Jayne shook her head. 'Can't see enough to say. But if it was recent, someone was very good at restoring this area to something that looked untouched. Look at it.'

She turned in a circle, eyes on the ground, sending a wider beam out from the flashlight.

It was uniform; a natural-looking leafy rug, as though bamboo had just floated down when it was time and no one, human or animal, had ever tramped through it.

'Even if it wasn't recent, it's a nice job,' said Steelie. 'A smart perp.'

'Smart perp sounds like the guy we're looking for,' Scott said grimly.

West returned, phone in hand. 'Coroner's office can't send their Special Operations people until tomorrow morning—'

'No. No way,' Scott cut in, pulling out his own phone. 'I'm calling Turner. I don't care if we have to light this place up like a Christmas tree, she's coming out tonight.'

26

Under the glare of lights in the bamboo grove, four agents from the FBI's Critical Stabilization and Recovery team worked under observation. Their audience was comprised of Jayne and Steelie, Houston and Ramos, Sanchez and West, UCLA police officers Dodd and Taylor, and Lloyd, the detective at LAPD Missing Persons currently assigned to the Regan Hart case. Only Mitch Nelson had been given compassionate leave, after becoming overwhelmed with having now found the remains of two young people on campus. He'd promised to make himself available for questions.

The Critters had taken over the scene upon their arrival, as Scott had requested. Agent Tony Lee had photographed the area using a north arrow and case number on a photo board. Steve Weiss and Xavier Tollen had put up perimeter tape and, like Mitch before them, had used shovels to take off successive layers of soil in a large rectangle surrounding the test pit. They had been dropping the soil into buckets that Agent Duane Sparks then emptied into his sieve, swishing it back and forth to allow dirt to drop through the mesh while leaving any artifacts sitting on top.

Weiss and Tollen were now close to the suitcase so they switched to hand tools and asked Scott if he wanted the suitcase opened. Scott went to the edge of the excavation and assented, instructing them to photograph it first. Lee was already readying his camera but he didn't complain at being told how to do his job. Then Scott invited the others to take a look. They did so, respectful of the Critters' meticulous work as well as the fact that the pit was someone's grave.

Jayne saw that the suitcase, now open, was of the large, rolling variety with a rigid frame. The body had been flexed to fit and the frame had constrained it during decomposition, except for the left elbow. That appeared to have escaped where the zipper had given way, possibly under pressure when the body went through one of its bloating stages.

It was a female dressed in jogging pants and a shirt. The frilly edge Jayne had seen at her elbow was repeated at the neckline. The body's head was turned to its right like the rest of her, and long, dark hair obscured her face. The fact that the suitcase had been closed was key: it had prevented dirt from encrusting the flesh and had slowed down decomposition. But Jayne couldn't tell if this was Regan Hart.

Sparks brought a body bag over to the edge of the pit. 'We're going to need some space.'

Everyone else stepped back as he unzipped the bag. He opened it wide, listening intently to Weiss and Tollen who were murmuring to each other as they readied themselves for a simultaneous lift. Jayne saw Weiss grimace slightly as he came up with the body's head and shoulders resting in his hands but its arms were free and in line to impact the wall of the excavation. Tollen was leaning back, trying to make more space for the body as they sent it toward the bag, but they were too far away. Jayne figured the problem was that they couldn't step past the suitcase still at their feet.

Weiss's voice was strained. 'Sparky.'

Sparks lunged, getting a hand under the body's torso while lifting the arm closest to him, and they got the body to the bag.

They had to make some adjustments to slide one of the open flaps out from under the body's knees. When they'd done that, they took a break. Tollen leaned back against the edge of the pit, his head down. Weiss looked like he had something in his mouth that he wished he could spit out.

Lee approached the body bag with the camera to document this stage of the lift by photographing the body in the bag and then the grave with the open suitcase. Once the Critters transferred the suitcase to a second body bag, Lee took another, similar set of photos.

Weiss said, 'Let's get a soil sample before the last pass.'

Not taking his eyes off them, West asked Steelie, 'Why are they still digging?'

'Gotta sieve the soil under the suitcase for evidence as well,' she said.

Lloyd, the Missing Persons detective, faced West and Sanchez. 'Which of you wants to corroborate me on a visual?' He held up a manila envelope.

'I'll do it,' Sanchez said.

Lloyd put a piece of gum in his mouth before donning a glove on one hand. He crouched down next to the body and, using the gloved hand, moved the hair away from its face. Beetles scurried across it looking for cover. Lloyd took off his surgical glove, put it on the ground and opened his envelope. He methodically held up a series of portraits

250

of Regan Hart next to the decedent's decomposing face, keeping each one in place long enough for Sanchez to get a good look. On the last photo, he looked back at Sanchez with an interrogative expression, chewing gum placidly as he waited for her response.

She nodded.

Jayne exhaled, having not realized she'd been holding her breath. She felt Steelie's hand on her arm and she put her own hand over it.

As Lloyd got up, he pointed out his glove to Tollen for him to pick up later. He rejoined the others, straightening the photos in his hands by tapping their edges against his palm. The eyes in his dark brown face looked slightly troubled.

'I won't – and you don't –' he said, nodding at Steelie and Jayne, 'do next-of-kin notification until I get confirmation on the ID but I can say that, in addition to the visual, this body's wearing a necklace similar to what was described to us as missing from Regan Hart's dorm room. It was an eighteenth birthday gift from her parents.'

He paused and looked back at the body. 'What's happening with the autopsy? Is she staying local or are you guys taking her for some reason?'

'Coroner's office said they can do the post tomorrow,' West said, 'so she's staying here. For now.'

'You want the NOK told there's federal involvement? I know we've got that status conference tomorrow . . . unless it gets called off because of this.'

Scott shook his head. 'I don't think the family should be told that unless or until we get evidence that connects this to the Stilson homicide.'

251

West said, 'That's fine. LAPD will be letting them know the case is being handled by Homicide from this point forward. We can do that at the meeting tomorrow.'

Lloyd nodded thoughtfully. He chewed his gum and then looked at his watch. 'You can lose track of time under these lights.' He squinted out into the dark beyond the circle of brightness. 'I'm pushing my shift change, so I gotta head back to the station. Can I have a sole point of contact?'

West pulled a business card out of his wallet and wrote on the back. 'My cell number.'

Lloyd took his leave, nodding to Jayne and Steelie as he went.

West and Scott exchanged a look then a nod, and West hurried after Lloyd, whose flashlight was already disappearing as he looked for a path out of the bamboo grove.

Scott pulled Jayne and Steelie into a huddle. 'Eric will stay on with the Critters, so I'm going to escort you home. Jayne, ride with Steelie to her house and then I'll take you to yours.'

Jayne noticed that Scott pretty much herded them into Steelie's Jeep where it was parked near the entrance to the arboretum. He directed them to drive south to exit the campus and Steelie followed instructions, keeping to second gear going downhill toward Westwood. Jayne looked back. A crowd had gathered behind law enforcement perimeter tape to the north of the arboretum entrance but her view was cut off when Scott's Suburban loomed up close to the Jeep's bumper, dwarfing the Wrangler.

Jayne could tell that Scott was literally shielding the

vehicle from view for anyone in the crowd. That was a good thing but also had a counterpart: Scott thought there was a chance a murderer was standing in its midst.

*

Junior watched, rooted in a kind of fascinated horror. Jayne Hall was alive. Very much alive. And she had her own security tail – the big vehicle from her driveway with the big guy inside it. The only vehicle he hadn't seen yet was one marked, 'CORONER'. But it would be here, just a matter of time. Unless there was something else dead in the grounds of the arboretum. *What are you, thick as two planks? You funked it up!* The voice was like an explosion inside his head. His whole body reacted. And now the voice was muttering, *Just like your mother. Whore!* Junior moved to get out of the crowd that had developed, people standing on tiptoe to see what was going on, whispering questions and looking worried. He finally broke out from the back and walked briskly, as though outrunning the voice, but it was shouting from the crowd: *Man up! Finish it! Follow me like I taught you!* Junior whirled around, drawing breath to shout back before realizing that he was attracting attention. He became aware that he was sweating, chest heaving, mouth open and eyes staring into the darkness like he could see something there. He'd almost shouted aloud and that would have brought it all crashing down. It was time to end this.

*

Twenty minutes after leaving UCLA, Scott was in a small tailback of traffic stopped at a red light on Beverly

253

Boulevard. He was looking at the passenger seat of Steelie's Jeep where he could tell Jayne was gesturing as she spoke with Steelie. His cell lit up with a call from Eric and he answered.

Eric said, 'I just came up top with the Critters and the body. Campus police are holding back a decent-sized crowd. You see anyone following you?'

'I would have called you if I had.'

'Okay. Just FYI, UCLA has no records or known connection to the Bailey brothers or any of their family. No crossover at all. They were at pains to provide us with that info.'

'And did West know if any of the members of that supremacy club were there?' Scott resumed driving.

'He's got the UCLA cops on that. They say not but I bet our guy is here somewhere. West is arranging surveillance on Steelie's place.'

'Doing it himself, is he?' Scott chuckled.

'Like you, right?'

'Whoa!'

'Hey, you gotta to be able to take it if you're gonna dish it, partner. West is asking you to check Steelie's place for any problem areas. I'll call you when the dogs are on over there.'

'Copy that.'

Scott followed Steelie's Jeep into a residential street in Atwater Village. To Scott's eye, the neighborhood walked the line between urban and suburban. The houses had front yards but not large ones, and only some were laid with lawn; many had been converted to dry gardens sprouting tall grasses and succulents, including Steelie's as he saw when she pulled into a driveway.

Scott got out of his car and looked around. The street was quiet. Driveways held two cars and most of the front porches had arches lit by yellow lamplight.

Steelie and Jayne were giving each other a farewell hug. Steelie looked at him over Jayne's shoulder. 'I'm not hugging you again. I can still feel the last one.'

'I just came to see you in the door. Jayne?' He held the passenger door open for her and she got back in the Suburban.

Steelie stepped onto the porch, key in hand. 'You're making me nervous, Houston.'

'That's not my intention.' He came up next to her and dropped his voice. 'Though I would like you to be vigilant.'

'I'm always vigilant, but that one . . .' She gestured at Jayne in the Suburban and dropped her voice to a whisper as well. 'She was hyper-vigilant before you started acting like this, so I'd appreciate it if you didn't get her wound up any further.'

'I won't! Unwinding only. I promise.' He held her gaze steadily until she pushed open her door. He looked inside. 'You're not going to invite me in?'

After pretending to admire the front room, Scott went through the house without waiting for Steelie's permission. He looked in the kitchen, bedroom and the large bathroom. When he found a panel of light switches by the back door, he flipped them all and the backyard lit up. He noted that the cement block walls between Steelie's yard and those of her neighbors were low, which was good because it increased the likelihood that there would be a witness to any backyard intruders. On the other hand, low walls

255

allowed criminals to backyard-skip and thereby circumvent security measures some homeowners fitted to protect the front of their property. Unless everyone had a barrier out front, no one had a barrier.

His cell phone rang; he looked at the readout and picked up.

Eric said, 'The dogs are on. Plate is Five Charlie November Alpha Three Niner Three. It's a Crown Vic, black.'

'Ten-four.' Scott rang off and beamed at Steelie. 'Thanks. Nice place.'

'Uh-huh.' Her tone said she knew his whip around her house wasn't just for fun but also that it didn't bother her. She made a show of ushering him out, waving at Jayne over his shoulder.

Jayne waved back. 'Everything okay?' she asked when Scott got in the Suburban.

'It will be.' Scott had seen a Crown Victoria wearing the right license plate parked one house away on the opposite side of the street. The location was such that a large evergreen tree prevented the streetlight's orange haze from illuminating the car's interior.

As Scott drove with Jayne in the passenger seat, he made surreptitious extra checks of the rearview mirror, took a more circuitous route and executed a few last-minute turns. It took all his concentration to do this without Jayne noticing, so it was a silent ride. On arriving at Jayne's duplex, he reversed into the driveway so he could keep his eyes on the street. He half-expected Jayne to comment until he remembered that she'd once said she tended to park nose-out in a leftover from working for the UN in post-conflict zones. Always ready for evacuation. Sure enough, she was getting out without a comment.

Inside her apartment, Jayne went straight to the kitchen, so Scott peeled off to check the bedroom and bathroom quickly. He was over by the sliding door to the front deck, congratulating himself on the sly way he was confirming that it was locked, when Jayne called out.

'Scott, what are you doing here?'

He hesitated as he tried to place her tone. 'What do you mean?'

'You look like you're on protection detail.'

Scott opened his mouth to say, *I am*, but caught it in time. 'Uh . . . '

'I mean, I can't tell if you want to be here with me or if you're here for some operational reason, or whatever you call it.'

'Of course I want to be here with you. Especially until this case is over.'

Jayne scrunched her hair, which made her looked stressed.

'That didn't come out right.' He started toward her. 'The case, it's not more important than—'

'No, never mind. I'm just keyed up. And I'm glad you're here. Would you want some pasta?'

The swift change-up caught Scott off-guard. He'd been preparing himself for a long conversation about feelings or something. 'Yeah. Yes. Can I do anything?'

Jayne put a large pot on the stove and then drew a bag of fresh pasta out of the fridge. 'If this water comes to the boil before I get out of the shower, you could empty this into it.'

While she was in the other room, Scott stood at the

sliding door, looking across to the reservoir and thinking about Jayne being submerged in it just days ago. The fear that had assaulted him that night had been displaced by anger. *Who did this to her and why?* He thought back to what they had learned about possible racial supremacists operating at UCLA. He was sure that made more sense than a single person doing the attack. One guy to drive up to Jayne's truck when she was at a red light, one guy with scuba gear and young enough – agile enough – to overpower her, maybe another guy to pick up Scuba Guy later. *That's what? Like, three, four, maybe five guys right there*, Scott thought. *Five twenty-somethings. Assholes.*

The water on the stove was just coming to the boil as Jayne emerged. She gave him a bright smile as she turned down the flame. 'We can wait to put in the pasta.'

Scott went for his toiletries bag, but it wasn't where he'd left it on her bedroom chair. His clothes were gone, too. He quietly opened the bedroom closet door. On the floor-to-ceiling shelving, right at his eye level, were his clothes.

He found his toiletries bag in the bathroom where Jayne had left one of the cupboard doors ajar to call attention to an empty shelf. She had obviously been busy making space for him. He wondered what would be waiting for him in the shower – a note perhaps? He was almost disappointed when he stepped in and everything looked the same as before.

The instant the shower's hot water hit his shoulders, he realized how much he needed to leave the day behind him. He felt slightly guilty about leaving next-of-kin notification to the missing persons detective. Scott's excuse was that that guy was paid to do NOK visits but the truth was, he knew Regan Hart's parents would be just like Kate Alston's. Not twenty-four hours after finding Kate's body in Arizona, he'd met her parents at the coroner's. The office had felt like a coffin, with him inhaling the raw grief the Alstons were exhaling until he broke out of there, leaving them in it. He wasn't ready for a repeat of that experience with the Harts – not to mention the counseling session he'd probably need afterwards. Again. He closed his eyes and let the water pummel the top of his head before he angled the meeting place of his shoulder and neck to mercilessly expose a tight muscle to the heat.

A noise made him hastily wipe his eyes and reach for the shower door handle, but the form on the other side of the frosted glass was unmistakably Jayne. He opened the door partway. 'Everything okay?'

Her eyes dipped fleetingly down his body, then a blush came up on her cheeks. 'I just – dinner will be ready in five.'

'Five . . .' Scott's brain was stalling out because Jayne was pushing the shower door open the rest of the way. 'Minutes?'

DAY NINE

THURSDAY

27

Detectives West and Sanchez walked into Scott and Eric's office. West said, 'You heard? Coroner's office made a positive ID on Regan Hart.'

'We heard,' Scott said.

'But you didn't hear this: UCLA PD has confirmed that none of the students in the club they shut down for the white supremacy issues can possibly be on our suspect list.'

'None of them?' Scott said.

'Had 'em under surveillance or had a mole or something. They're not telling me that part. But it's gotta be that if those students are active on campus, they threaten the university's funding, so someone has to make sure they're not active. None of them are good for Stilson, Hart or the attack on Jayne Hall.'

'Well, what about the professor they fired?' Eric said.

'Confirmed teaching overseas since late September 2003. Passport hasn't come through any port – land, sea, air – since.' West leaned back in his chair only to straighten up to pull his ringing cell phone from his belt and look at the readout. 'Coroner's office,' he announced, pulling himself up to the desk to take notes.

They watched him.

When he was off the phone, West stood up and displayed his notepad. 'The pathologist has a prelim cause of death for Regan Hart as organ failure. Proximate cause may be resolved by tox tests. They had enough tissue to send off for it but we'll have to wait a day for a prelim on that. One bruise to upper left arm. No other trauma.'

He consulted his notes. 'Time since death might get narrowed by the bug experts but the MI is letting Missing Persons pencil it in at seventeen months, which takes it back to the month of disappearance. Last thing is on trace. They have a hair they weren't sure about. A section's been dispatched to your lab at Quantico.'

Scott said, 'A hair? In what way did it stand out?'

'Apparently it was consistent with her hair but was shorter. Like a lot shorter.' He shrugged, looking unconvinced. 'It could've been transferred from her to the suitcase or vice versa.'

Sanchez cut in. 'Yeah, and what about the suitcase?'

'Sorry, I forgot. I asked Lloyd to check it against the set owned by Hart. He doesn't have confirmation on that yet because all he has is a photo of the known suitcase – the one found in her room. We're going to have to ask the parents for access to the suitcase if they still have it.'

'So, the perp dragged her body around campus in her own wheelie bag.' Sanchez was shaking her head but sounded impressed. 'Who would even notice someone with a heavy wheelie bag at the end of a quarter? This also means the perp could have been in her room because how else did he or she get her suitcase? Let me answer my own question: the perp intercepts her somewhere on campus when she was already leaving. That works.'

West said, 'You know what's occurring to me? Among LAPD's best and brightest that said Hart *must* have run away because she took a suitcase, who actually established which of her clothes she packed? I mean, if *she* was in her suitcase, where was all the shit she had packed in it?'

'The perp took it?' Eric mused.

Scott said, 'We'll ask him when we haul his ass in.'

Sanchez walked over to the whiteboard. In the row labeled *HART, Regan* she rubbed out *misper* and wrote *DOA*. She removed every magnet they'd put up the day before when they were theorizing where a body might have been buried on the campus. Then she placed a magnet at the bamboo grove.

She turned around. The three men looked grim but the minute's silence was over.

Scott said, 'If we rule out the supremacy kids, we're almost back at square one.'

Eric said, 'We're a little screwed without any firm forensics on Regan Hart's body.'

'Well, what about this hair the coroner sent to our lab – did they examine it at all?'

West said, 'I presume so.'

Scott looked up the phone number and called the coroner's office, eventually getting transferred to someone named Moore. He re-identified the case and said, 'I need to talk to you about a sample you've sent out to the FBI lab. Some hair?'

'Head hair, yes.'

'Right.' Scott was reminded that these scientists made that distinction, while the rest of the population didn't feel the need to put the word 'head' in front of the word 'hair', ever.

Moore cautioned, 'This was a macroscopic look only so I won't stake my professional reputation on the one hair being from another person with the same racial background but the anomaly was enough to make me think a hairs expert should look at it under a 'scope.'

'The anomaly was that it was shorter?'

'Not just that; it was cut at both ends. Like someone had just had a haircut and this was a piece that had been trimmed again or a similar scenario.'

Scott tried to picture how Regan Hart's hair had looked when she'd been brought out of the suitcase. 'So, the hairs still on the body were, what? Not cut?'

'The decedent's hair would have been cut at some point but the distal tips were split by the time of death. Split ends, in layman's terms. Again, I caution that all the hairs could be from the same person.'

'Did you take any photos?'

'Sure we did.'

'Send them over.' Scott gave him his details and hung up. He tried to tell the others what he'd learned and in doing so, he realized he either didn't understand what Moore had said or the scientist was trying to have it both ways.

'Great.' West threw up his hands. 'That fizzing sound is the air coming out of our investigation.'

Sanchez said, 'We might get something from the coroner's report.'

'Getting cause of death out of the coroner isn't going to tell us the name of the perp.'

Eric said, 'We've still got one other report to come in besides the coroner. The neoprene.'

'From Hall's pick-up?' West shrugged. 'I'm not holding out much hope.'

'Where do you guys get lunch around here?' Sanchez

asked. She jutted her chin toward her partner. 'We should eat before we head back to Parker Center for the Hart meeting.'

Scott pointed at Eric. 'Don't get him started about his favorite food truck.'

Eric checked his watch. 'We need to hurry to get there ahead of the crowd. You want your usual, Scott?'

'Do I have a choice?'

Eric and Sanchez left with the lunch order.

West muttered something and pulled a thin, silver box out of his shirt pocket. He popped this open and drew out a cigarette. 'You realize we're up shit's creek, don't you?'

'Agreed, but you don't have to go kill yourself over it.' Scott indicated the cigarette.

'Not you, too. Sanchez is already riding me.' West crossed to the door.

Scott followed him into the hallway. 'Got another one?'

'I didn't know you smoked.'

'I don't. I just smoke a cigarette when I want to smoke a fuckin' cigarette, alright?'

West looked back at him in amusement and gave him a cigarette as they rode down in the elevator. Once outside, they stood around next to a few other smokers and lit up.

The first inhalation burned Scott's throat in a way that felt really good. Painful but familiar. It must have been longer than he thought. He held the cigarette between thumb and forefinger and looked at its smoldering end as he held the smoke deep for as long as he could.

West glanced at him. 'Does Jayne Hall know about this habit of yours?'

'I told you,' Scott exhaled, 'I don't smoke.'

'Right. So. Do you always date outside your race or is Jayne Hall an exception?'

'What kind of question is that? And why do you always use Jayne's last name? I know who you're talking about already.'

'I like the sound of her whole name. And I'm just curious about you and her. Some guys have, you know, a fetish or a *preference*, if you want to sound politically correct, for black girls.'

'Jayne's not black. And she's not a girl.'

'Woman, then. And the LAPD incident report from the reservoir has her down as black.'

Scott squinted through the smoke, then waved it away. 'She identifies as mixed.'

'Well, that wasn't going to fit on an incident report, as has been *fully* established,' West smirked. 'What's her background?'

'Like you care!'

'I'm asking!'

Scott gauged West for a moment then said, 'Her mom's Latina, from Venezuela, but the family has African as well as Venezuelan heritage. Jayne's dad is white – American – but his family was English, y'know, originally.'

West had been holding his cigarette between his pursed lips while using both hands to act like he was counting Jayne's ancestral background on his fingers and coming up with some funny numbers.

Annoyed, Scott said, 'What are you doing?'

Exceedingly pleased, West pointed at him. 'Gotcha.'

Scott rolled his eyes. 'What are you? Five?'

'It's funny, that's all. All I have to do is say, "Jayne

Hall" and you go to Defcon 3.'

Scott gave a rueful laugh. 'Good for you.'

West said, 'Look, I know my partner jokes about me not liking to mix pencils and pens but, seriously, I wouldn't want there to be any tension between you and me if I'm dating Steelie.'

'Since when is *that* going to happen?'

'She's single. I've asked around. I'm going to ask her out when I see her this afternoon.'

'Is that the best timing?'

'Why?' West flicked some ash off the end of his cigarette.

'After a status conference with a victim's parents?'

'So? That's just work. I mean, I've always got some victim's parents to deal with.' West paused. 'So does she, for that matter. I can't be waiting for retirement before I ask her out.'

Scott looked at West appraisingly – and approvingly – but changed the subject. 'So, the status conference is still happening?'

West nodded. 'Lloyd said when he notified the family, he asked if they would like to postpone the meeting but they said no. Now it's more about what me and Theresa are going to be able to share and less about what the Missing Persons Unit did or didn't do over the past couple years.'

They saw Eric and Sanchez round the corner in the distance and stubbed out their cigarettes as though by some mutual agreement.

As they walked away from the smoking area, West said, 'You know, when we were chasing down the white supremacy stuff, I asked my partner what she called herself, like, white or brown? And she goes, "Matty. I'm blue, like you.'"

Scott nodded in forceful agreement. 'She's right. That's all of us on the job.' His BlackBerry buzzed and he moved to open the email he'd just received, leaving West to go ahead.

When Scott joined the others, Eric was handing out forks. Scott said, 'I just got the photos of that hair they found on Hart's suitcase. I don't see what's so special about it.'

Eric looked up at him. 'Can we drop the case for five minutes and eat? These dishes deserve some respect. You don't talk about casework over them.'

Sanchez leaned toward West and sniffed. 'Were you smoking just now?'

West busied himself with his takeout container. 'The food looks great. What is it?'

She kept watching him as she answered. 'It's Cuban. I got you roast chicken with rice, beans and plantains. Anything you don't want, I'll eat.'

Eric spoke through a mouthful of food. 'Come on, Houston.'

Scott said, 'I'm coming. Let me just call Steelie really quick.'

28

Jayne sat in the driver's seat of the Volvo sport utility vehicle on the used car lot. She was looking through the rearview mirror to the tailgate. The passenger door opened and Steelie leaned in.

She had an encouraging look on her face. 'You like?'

'I like how far back the rear window is.'

'A little too far back, no? You could use this as a hearse in a pinch.'

'But just think of the time it would give you to get out if someone came through it.'

Steelie climbed in next to her. 'That's not going to happen again. They'll find the guy who did that. And I bet you he's one out of the box.'

Jayne let her eyes travel over the cream-tone interior, noting the airbags. She leaned on the headrest and looked to the side. There was even a side airbag. She and some Volvo designer in Sweden were totally on the same page. The Shit Happens page.

'You know, Steelie, this car is really nice. I can even afford the payments. But I'm only here because some jerk totaled my truck.'

'I don't like the look on your face.'

Jayne sighed. 'How can I put this without sounding really crappy? I'm thinking that no matter how good the Memorandum of Understanding with the FBI looks, we don't sign it.' She used the steering wheel to help her sit taller in the seat. 'I know you're going to say anyone can get targeted for crime any time and we never know what's coming and—'

'No,' Steelie interrupted, 'I was going to say, fair enough. Though I will remind you that Craig Turner specifically said he was designing the MOU to address our safety.'

'I know. That's why I feel crappy saying I'm more worried for my own – considerable – ass.'

'How about this? When he sends us the MOU, we read it with an open mind. Then we read it again with a seriously closed mind.'

'I don't know. We're not getting any younger.'

'But you were baptized only last week,' Steelie joked.

Jayne gave her a flat look as she ran her hand over some of the center console's buttons and dials, then over the leather dash. 'You think I should buy this one?'

'It's nice,' Steelie said. 'It's one of the nicest hearses I've ever seen.' She pulled her ringing cell phone from her waist and looked at the readout. 'It's your mom calling. Here.'

Jayne took the phone. 'Mom? I'm fine.'

'Of course you are, darling, but I was calling for Steelie.'

'Why?'

'So suspicious. I'm sure I didn't raise you this way. You were raised to be polite, ladylike and—'

'Okay, okay.' Jayne handed the phone back to Steelie. 'It's you she's after.'

She walked around the outside of the car and stopped by the back bumper. With the tint on the windows, she couldn't detect Steelie in the passenger seat. Jayne stepped back to get a rear three-quarter view. The car was long but

272

not longer than her old F-150. She missed her truck like someone had cut off a limb but had to admit that she could get used to the more luxurious aspects of this Volvo. Maybe it would be part of a whole new era for her. She checked her watch. She had time to take the SUV on a test drive before she and Steelie had to get to Parker Center for the status conference with Regan Hart's parents.

Steelie came up to her, holstering her phone.

'What did she want?' Jayne said.

'She just wanted to make sure I would be free tomorrow to drive you over to the radio station open house. That is, unless you're driving yourself in your *new* Volvo.'

*

Scott had re-dialed after getting Steelie's voicemail. He was in the middle of taking another mouthful of his lunch when she answered.

'Hi, Scott,' she said. 'If it's Jayne you want, she's on a test drive.'

He pushed food into his cheek. 'Who's with her?'

'One of the dealers. A lively female, before you ask.'

He started chewing again. 'Okay. Glad she's moving on to thinking about a new car, anyway. Listen, Steelie, what do you know about hair?'

'You're asking that of someone who lets her gray show? You should talk to someone like Marie – or did you mean hair in the forensic context?'

'Both, actually. How would you explain why a girl who had longish hair that hadn't been cut recently would have cut off some of her hair?' Scott took another bite of plantains moist with the juices of the roasted chicken.

273

'Did she cut herself some bangs?'

Scott chewed. 'I hadn't thought of that. I'll find out if she ever had bangs.'

'I presume we're talking about Regan Hart?'

'Mm.'

'She could have cut off a piece of her hair for someone else, to give to them as a keepsake. Though that's kind of weird as well as old-fashioned. Or someone could have cut her hair without her knowing, like those cases in England, with the women on the busses.'

'What cases?'

'I refuse to say more on the grounds that I find those cases upsetting.'

'What about: she wanted to cut something out of her hair,' Scott said, thoughtfully. 'Say she got something in her hair – chewing gum, peanut butter . . .'

'Or the perp needed to cut something out because he couldn't afford to leave it there. Something with his DNA.'

'Whatever it was, it had to be visible to the perp. Maybe some tape he'd used?' Scott put down his fork, got up and paced around.

Steelie asked, 'So, have you got some of Regan Hart's hair with natural ends and some with cut ends?'

'This isn't for public consumption but, among her hair, we've got a cut hair that's "not inconsistent" with hers, which I guess means it could be hers. The examiner thought it was from someone who was the same race as she was. Mixed white and Asian.'

'Oh. Well, if it's unknown hair, why aren't you thinking it could be the killer's hair? Suspect hair?'

'*Another* mixed Asian and white person?'

'You make them sound like a rare flower, Scott! Mixed-race people are actually the fastest-growing population in the country. Haven't you been reading the paper lately? Hang on, Jayne's coming back. You want to talk to her?'

Scott heard Steelie explaining something to Jayne. When Jayne got on the phone, she spoke quickly. 'Steelie just told me what you've been discussing around this unknown hair you found and it reminded me of something weird from when I spoke to one of the administrators at UCLA. I think his name was Gordon. From Student Affairs.'

'He's mixed?'

'I don't know but he – well, he and his colleague – denied hearing of Mix it Up but April Begay told me that she had turned in the petition for the club to Gordon's office. They might have forgotten that particular petition—'

'Or they might have lied on purpose.' Scott felt a flicker of excitement. An administrator would fit with their theories about the perpetrator. 'What's this guy's ethnicity?'

'He could be Asian-American but—'

'With a name like Gordon, he could be mixed,' Scott finished and then moved right on, his excitement taking hold. 'What about his colleague? Was she also Asian?'

'She was black, but Scott, can you just wait a minute?'

Scott didn't want to wait. 'You want me to note their behavior as possibly suspicious, not indulge in racial profiling, right?'

'Right.' Jayne sounded relieved.

He didn't take the time to say he knew that already. 'I'll be in touch.' He hung up and relayed what Jayne had said to Eric, West and Sanchez.

West said, 'His name's Gorman, not Gordon, and since

when is he Asian?'

'He is, according to Jayne,' Scott said, confident in Jayne's recollection on something like this. 'Have you met him?'

'Well, no. But I've talked to him on the phone.'

Scott shook his head in mirth. 'You think you can "tell" over the phone, Matt?'

'No! Jesus.' West looked aggrieved. 'I'm saying he isn't suspicious. He told me himself he was a minority when he gave me the lowdown on Patton and the closure of the supremacy club. I figured he was black.'

Sanchez said, 'That's because he was busy describing a bunch of white supremacists. What were you going to come away with after that, an accurate picture of him or an image of some kids wearing white sheets?'

'It'll be the sheets,' Eric said, almost ejecting food out of his mouth. He wiped his chin. 'It's always the sheets.'

Scott added, 'Even if you had asked Gord . . . Gorman his ethnicity, it wouldn't have mattered to us back then, Matt.'

West was stony-faced. He stopped eating. 'Either way, I had us chasing our tails on the supremacy club thanks to this guy.'

Seeing that West was being pummeled by the fact that he'd unwittingly treated a suspect like a witness, Scott wanted to flip him into the new reality, which was that they finally had someone to investigate and interrogate, someone to exclude or bring to his knees.

He put his hand on West's shoulder. 'Don't beat yourself up. We're looking for someone who could do that – to any of us. The situation we're faced with here is that Gorman could have the type of hair that matches hair found on the Hart suitcase, he's in a position at the university where he could meet students and they'd trust him, he's denied seeing a petition for Mix it Up that came to his office and he has access to the university database where he could easily learn Jayne's middle name.'

Eric said, 'We should find out if his access stretches to construction sites, because his name wasn't on the lists we checked.'

Sanchez said, 'I'll run a full background check.'

Eric looked at Scott. 'We should find out if he's got an alibi for the attack on Jayne. We could try for a search warrant for his home.'

Scott pointed at him. 'But we can hit his office tonight, warrantless. One call to the university legal people gives us all-campus access; at least, that's what they said. We can ensure they make good.' He looked at the two detectives. 'Can you have eyes on him while we take his office?'

'You got it,' West said.

They headed into the building, jettisoning plates and plastic into trash cans as they went.

29

Steelie and Jayne arrived early for the Hart status conference at Parker Center. West came out of the building, squinting in the sunlight, ready to escort them inside.

'Theresa and I just got here ourselves. Our lieutenant would like a word with you before the Harts get here,' he said, holding the door open for them.

'No problem,' Steelie said. 'Do you know if a car was sent for them? We requested that this morning but didn't get a confirmation.'

'Yep, Lloyd got approval. They sent an unmarked car from Anaheim Community Support. It's bringing them up from Irvine.'

'Thank you. We felt the car was safer than having them drive themselves after the news. Plus . . . how to put this . . . it could help put you on the right footing with the parents.'

'Roger that.'

Jayne said, 'Is Lloyd still going to be in this meeting or is this now just Homicide?'

'He'll be there. We need to notify the Harts that Homicide's taking over the case from Missing Persons. It's been officially assigned to me and Theresa.' He called an elevator and the three of them got on together. 'Is the family aware you were present when Regan was discovered?'

'Yes. After they got the notification call last night from

Lloyd, they called on the Agency's after-hours phone, which was routed to me at the time.'

West blew out his breath. 'You guys do an after-hours number?'

'Yeah. Our clients don't abuse it.'

The elevator doors opened into a lobby that had been upgraded from the easy-care linoleum and tile finish downstairs. This lobby had a concrete floor with reflective quartz chips strewn throughout, catching the light coming from large windows at the end of the hallway. The walls held framed aerial photographs of Los Angeles. In one corner, an American flag flanked California state and Los Angeles city flags. West led them to a closed door marked 'Conference Room A'. A slot next to it was set to show *In Use*.

The conference room was nicely proportioned to accommodate a large oval table and twenty chairs. It was on the front of the building where the windows were letting in a lot of sunlight despite being covered with vertical blinds set at an angle. Detective Lloyd stood up from where he had been sitting at the table with two people wearing dark blue suits. Jayne recognized one of them: Lieutenant Sunny Park, head of Missing Persons, who greeted her and Steelie with her usual warm smile, her dark shoulder-length hair pulled back with a clip at the neck. West made the introduction to the other, his boss, Lieutenant Charles Early, head of Homicide. Lieutenant Early's crisp demeanor, crushing handshake and specific haircut made 'Marine' a good guess for what was on his resume before the LAPD. He looked like he could still jump out of a moving helicopter if he had to. Heck, he might even do it for fun.

Once everyone was seated with Lieutenant Early at the head of the table, he said, 'Ms. Hall, Ms. Lander. I understand that the Hart parents know you were both present when their daughter's body was found.'

Jayne nodded. 'Yes, the Harts called us last night because they wanted us to know about Regan and they wanted to know what to expect today. I advised postponing this status conference since there's not much of a status on day one of a death investigation. However, they wanted to meet the detectives on the case if they could still spare the time.' She looked at West and Sanchez. 'They'll want to know something's happening.'

Lieutenant Early cleared his throat. 'I'm gratified to hear you tried to postpone this meeting, Ms. Hall. I have given my detectives very little room to talk about the case today. It's early and I don't want anything jeopardizing the investigation. Now, I know you've been involved in this case at various stages but, to be clear, information about this investigation is only going to flow one way: from us to the parents. You will not transmit anything you've learned due to your separate involvement in our case unless we've given you explicit permission to do so.'

'Understood,' Jayne and Steelie said simultaneously.

'In addition, I've been told you sometimes undertake death investigations of your own, through your own methods and channels. Now, what you do with that information is up to you. But if it would assist LAPD in its investigation, we request you update us as well as the family.'

'Chuck,' Lieutenant Park said, turning in her seat to face him. 'I've worked with Agency 32/1 on a number of cases over the past year. You can count on their discretion, and their assistance. I would say, in general, that having them in the room means more light, less heat.'

He nodded. 'Thanks for your input, Sunny. I've heard good things from my people as well.' He looked back at Jayne and Steelie. 'As long as we're clear.'

Sanchez's cell phone buzzed against the tabletop. 'The Harts are on their way up,' she said, looking at the readout.

Steelie said, 'We'll meet them in the hall.'

Jayne followed her out of the room. The elevator was disgorging a group of people. The Harts were the last to get out, led by a uniformed officer. Jayne thought Rebecca looked like she'd not only cried all night but wept the whole way up from Irvine. At this time of day, that was a good hour. Don was dry-eyed but there was something taut about him that was different from just the day before. His wife was leaning on his arm and Jayne wondered if he was simply trying to stay strong for her, physically as well as emotionally. As soon as Rebecca saw Steelie and Jayne, however, she broke away from Don and hugged both of them. Don shook their hands with a grave nod. No one spoke for a moment. Jayne had already conveyed her and Steelie's condolences the night before and had rebuffed the gratitude for finding Regan, as that had really been the work of others.

After another squeeze of Rebecca's arm, Jayne said quietly, 'Do you still feel up to the meeting, now that you're here?'

'We are,' Don said in a loud, almost combative tone as

281

though he and Rebecca were ready for the LAPD but the LAPD might not be ready for the two of them. But when his voice seemed to bounce back off the walls, he looked startled. He resumed more softly. 'We have some questions and we also want to know when we can start arrangements for a funeral.'

'Of course. You may find that some of your questions can't be answered right now, not because the police want to withhold from you but because they need to preserve information for their investigation. But you can pose the questions, and Steelie and I can clarify or probe further if needed. As for Regan's funeral, those questions need to be posed to the coroner's office, which we will help you with as well, but I can tell you right now it's going to take longer than you'd like. You may have to have a memorial first and a funeral later. What we can do today, though, is stress your family's need for a funeral as soon as possible. Okay?'

The Harts nodded.

Steelie led the way. Everyone inside had come to stand by the door as if in a receiving line, waiting to meet the honored guests. Jayne introduced each of the three detectives and then drew the Harts on to the two lieutenants. When Lieutenant Early gave the parents the official condolences on behalf of the entire department and the chief of police, who regretted he couldn't attend this meeting, the Harts looked stunned. Rebecca had even stopped using her tissue to dab her eyes, which were still red but they were dry. That made Jayne feel better.

With a nod to Jayne, Lieutenant Early took Rebecca's elbow and led her gently to two chairs near the head of the table, a spot he resumed. Jayne and Steelie sat next to the

Harts, which put Lieutenant Park and all the detectives across from them on the other side of the table. There was something vaguely adversarial in the seating arrangement but it actually afforded the best eye contact for the nature of the conversation that was about to happen. Someone had placed a box of tissues on the table where Lieutenant Early had seated the Harts, as well as bottled water and glasses. Everyone but the Harts had a notebook open in front of them.

Lieutenant Early opened the meeting. 'Mr. and Mrs. Hart, the first thing we'd like to inform you of is that the investigation into Regan's disappearance and death is now being handled by the Homicide Special Section, under the direction of Detectives West and Sanchez. Detective Lloyd from the Missing Persons Unit will continue to give assistance where needed but your point of contact will now be with my two detectives.' He gave a nod to West and Sanchez, who were each ready with a business card, which they slid across the table to the Harts.

Lieutenant Early said, 'I've instructed them to put their cell phone numbers on the backs of their cards. Don't hesitate to call them.'

Rebecca was looking at the cards. 'Homicide? Then, how did Regan die? We haven't been told anything yet.'

'I'm afraid that we don't have an answer for you yet either because the coroner's office is still running tests, however, I can tell you that we are confident that the manner of her death was homicide.'

'But . . . surely it was some kind of accident?' She sounded both confused and shocked. Jayne knew that Rebecca had just revealed her personal narrative of why

283

her daughter had disappeared, one she'd held onto despite coming to Agency 32/1 out of fear that the person who harmed Jared Stilson also harmed Regan.

After the briefest hesitation, Lieutenant Early said, 'It was not an accident. And as soon as the coroner can be conclusive about what happened, you will be the first to know.'

Rebecca turned to Don in anguish.

Don gave her a look like he had this under control. In the same forceful voice from the hallway, he said, 'I think something my wife and I would like to know is where Regan was found. We're figuring it was somewhere in LA since you all are handling it but we need to know where.'

Lieutenant Early nodded at West, giving him permission to take the question.

West said, 'Regan was found on the UCLA campus. I can't give you the exact location—'

Don interrupted. 'On *campus*? What?' He was shaking his head. 'That doesn't make sense. We were told to put up fliers, to check bus stations . . . I mean . . . did whoever did this bring our daughter *back* to UCLA? When?'

Steelie leaned in. 'Detective West, can you tell Mr. and Mrs. Hart when Regan died?'

West looked at his boss, who gave a hand movement that apparently meant the question could be answered. West said, 'We don't have the specific date Regan died as yet but we have reason to believe it was not long after she went missing.'

Now Don's demeanor matched his wife's: shocked and confused. 'She's been lying there on campus this *whole time*? This whole time, she – I can't—'

284

Rebecca grabbed for Don's arm but he was already erupting out of his chair. He stepped away with his back to the room, hands on his waist, head tilted back as though he was trying to get more air. Jayne watched Rebecca struggle up from her seat and go to him.

'Honey?'

'I just need to process this for a minute,' he said, his throat sounding tight.

She stood next to him and put a finger through one belt loop of his chinos, but she didn't try to soothe him beyond that.

Jayne turned back to the table. Everyone looked strained, West most of all, probably because he was the one who'd set Don off. West threw Steelie a look that read as, 'What the fuck?' Keeping her hands near the table, Steelie patted the air, to say, 'Just wait.'

When the Harts resumed their seats at the table, Rebecca opened her water bottle and poured some out into a glass for Don, who drank but didn't speak, his eyes on the table.

Sanchez spoke, pitching her voice levelly. 'We recognize how difficult this is for you to hear but I'm sure you can see why we are so concerned about finding the person who harmed Regan because that person may still be at large. In light of that, my partner and I would like to ask you if you have Regan's belongings from her room? Were they provided to you after she went missing?'

Rebecca said, 'Yes, we have them. We have everything.'

'We specifically need to see her luggage set. Do you have that?'

'Yes, but why? Is that important?'

'At this point, we just need to collect the suitcase to

examine them. Now to do this, we will need to send an officer to your home to pick them up. We will give you a receipt for them, so you can be sure they will be returned. We may need to take samples of your DNA in order to exclude you from our examinations. Would you both consent to that?'

'Yes,' Rebecca said faintly.

But Don's tone was different. He was still looking at the table. 'So, you're going to come to our house and take Regan's belongings and take our DNA but you're not really telling us anything or giving us anything.'

Jayne spoke before anyone else could try to reply to what was essentially a statement of emotion. Law enforcement didn't always know how to respond to people's emotions and could default to a defensiveness that helped no one. 'In relation to that, we'd like to make a request on behalf of the Hart family. While the LAPD is working on getting them the answers they need, could you take them on an escorted site visit to where their daughter's body was found?'

Don finally looked up and his eyes were on Jayne. 'Would that be possible? That would mean a lot to us.' A light appeared in his eyes and he looked over at West.

'Sir?' West was looking at his boss, along with everyone else.

Lieutenant Early thought for a moment, then said, 'That can be arranged. Lieutenant Park, can you have your detective take care of this as soon as the techs clear the site?'

Lieutenant Park nodded. 'Of course.' She addressed the Harts. 'Detective Lloyd will make the arrangements and take you at your convenience.' She and Lloyd each made notes in their pads.

'Can Jayne and Steelie be there?' Rebecca asked. 'We'd like them there as well.'

'Yes. We'll liaise with them.'

The Harts looked like the wind had gone out of their sails. They were holding hands but not looking at anyone or speaking anymore. Jayne glanced down at her notebook to check the bullet list she'd made the previous night when the Harts had peppered her with questions. The meeting had covered almost everything.

'There are just two more items for this meeting,' she said. 'Mr. and Mrs. Hart will be requesting expedited services from the coroner's office so they can prepare for a funeral. Anything you can do from this department to facilitate that would be appreciated.'

West and Sanchez made notes on their small notepads.

'And the second thing, Ms. Hall?' Lieutenant Early said.

'Another status conference in two to three weeks.'

'We can do that,' Lieutenant Early said. 'But the time frame will have to be dictated by the investigation.'

'Lieutenant,' Steelie responded, 'we're requesting that the status conference happen even if there's nothing new that can be shared from the department. The Harts may have something to share with the detectives, for example.'

After a momentary pause, Lieutenant Early said, 'Point taken. There will be a second status conference.' He made a note in his notebook.

'Thank you,' Steelie said.

Lieutenant Early looked around the table. 'Does anyone have anything else?'

No one did and everyone stood. The meeting was over.

30

UCLA police officers Dodd and Taylor were waiting for Scott and Eric outside the administration building that housed Student Affairs. It was just after 6PM and the building was locked. The officers let the agents into Gorman's office on the second floor and unlocked the filing cabinets in the room. Then they took up positions to monitor the agents' activity.

Eric had opted to look for hairs to take for comparison with the unknown hair found on Regan Hart's suitcase. The desk and chair looked clean but he started there with the tape lifts anyway.

Scott went through the filing cabinets, looking for anything to link Gorman to the club Mix it Up or the two dead students. It took him a few minutes to get through half of the first cabinet. He didn't find anything. The positive in the negative was that there should have been something on Mix it Up in the file called *Pre-registered Student Clubs & Orgs* for the year 2003. No drawer held equipment that would raise a flag in the case, such as anything to do with poisons, a shovel for digging a shallow grave, or a wetsuit.

Scott turned away. 'Anything?'

Eric placed the piece of tape he had been working with into the evidence bag. 'Can't tell if this stuff is hair or fluff or what.'

Scott went on to the second filing cabinet. His cell phone

vibrated.

'He's mobile,' West told him over the background noise of a moving car. 'No telling where he's going specifically but he's just entered the southern end of campus on foot, heading north, with a manila envelope in his hand. ETA fifteen minutes tops if he is coming to your location.'

Scott hung up and relayed this to Eric.

Eric said, 'What the hell? Coming back to campus now? He just left.'

'I don't know where he's going but we need to wrap this up in ten. I don't want to tip him off that we're looking into him.'

Eric turned on his flashlight and went on his knees under the desk.

After a minute, he said, 'I think I got something.'

Scott came over and looked. 'I don't see it.'

Eric handed him the flashlight. 'Farthest edge of the bottom drawer.'

Scott knelt down, directed the light and saw what looked like a hair trapped in the drawer's runner. 'Pull the drawer out carefully.'

Eric crouched down. 'I tried that already. I think it's going to break the hair.'

'Shit.'

'We want as much of it as we can get.'

Scott's cell vibrated again. He shimmied out from under the desk to read the text message.

Office could be his target. You have 5.

'They think he's coming here,' Scott said.

'Let's take out the top two drawers, then try to lift this one off of its runner.'

Scott nodded and they each slid out a drawer. It took a moment for each of them to master the catch that was designed to prevent a drawer from falling out all the way when rattled by an earthquake.

Eric said, 'These are going to be hell to get back in.' He tried to tilt the drawer. Nothing happened. He swore and tried again.

Scott said, 'We could cut the hair.'

'That's not ideal.'

'We're running out of time.'

'Hang on.' Eric did something.

'Stop. I think it's breaking. And I'm getting another message.'

ETA 2.

Scott came out from under the desk. 'Taylor, he's almost here.'

The thinner of the two young officers nodded. 'I'll take a position outside, sir, and notify you when he's entering the building.'

'Copy that,' Scott said. 'Ramos, you go under. Take the tape and stick it on one end of the damn thing.'

When Eric was ready, Scott turned around and slammed the heel of his shoe upwards under the drawer. It came out of its housing with a bang and Scott was aware of Eric shifting his weight away from the drawer to protect his face.

Eric rolled back. 'Got it.' He shimmied out. 'We've got a good inch.'

Scott tried to re-seat the drawer he'd just forced. It didn't want to go back. He peered at its underside. Some of the metal had bent. 'Hand me that three-hole punch from on top of the filing cabinet?'

Scott used the heavyweight metal tool to hammer the drawer's runners. That did it. 'It's not moving smoothly but he'll think it's a maintenance issue.'

Eric was struggling to get the upper drawers in. 'Well, he's not going to think someone's been in his files because we didn't take anything.'

Officer Dodd stepped into the room. 'Sir? Shall I re-lock the filing cabinets?'

Scott had forgotten all about them. 'Yes.' His phone vibrated.

'Sir, this is Taylor, sir. Subject is visible. You have thirty seconds, max.'

Scott hung up. 'We've gotta move.'

Eric managed to slam the topmost drawer home and Officer Dodd locked it. But when they went into the hallway, they could hear the front door of the building already opening.

Eric said quietly, 'We won't make it.'

'In here,' Dodd said.

He unlocked a door marked *Facilities 2-A*. Footsteps were on the stairs as they pressed themselves into what turned out to be a storage closet for cleaning equipment. The footsteps reached and passed them. They heard a door being unlocked and then opened but not closed. His back to the agents, Dodd held up a fist to indicate that they would only move on his signal. They were able to hear each other's breathing. Dodd's cell phone started to vibrate. The burring noise seemed loud in the confined space. He cut the vibration and kept his fist raised as he opened the door and looked around it. Then he raised his index finger and twirled it in a circle. Scott and Eric followed him into the hallway. They saw Taylor at the top of the stairs and nodded their thanks as they moved past quietly. Once outside and around the corner, Scott called West.

'I've got something to cheer you up after your hellish status conference: we lifted a hair from Gorman's office before he got there.'

West grunted something unintelligible. Then: 'Is it his?'

'We lifted it from under his desk. If the lab boys even think it might be a match for the hair on the suitcase, we're golden for a warrant on his house, his car and anything else he has.'

West said, 'How long is the lab going to take, though?'

'It's not a matter of how long but how fast you can get across town. Meet us at our office?'

31

Eric, Scott, Sanchez and West ascended the FBI building in an elevator and alighted at the tenth floor. There, they went into a secure laboratory where rows of aluminum tables held scientific instruments, while bookshelves supported reference texts whose wide spines proclaimed content that spanned forensic pathology, entomology, ballistics, trace evidence analysis, DNA comparison and scene searching.

A man who'd been standing by a fume hood along the back wall walked over with a regimented step. Above his black boots were deep-tone khakis and a midnight-blue T-shirt, the yellow and white FBI insignia sitting over a prominent set of pectoral muscles. His haircut's short fade style made him look like active-duty military and significant eyebrows over hazel eyes gave him an appearance of intensity. His youthful brown face was clean-shaven and he greeted Scott with a familiar handshake.

Scott said, 'Detectives, this is Agent Sparks of our Critical Stabilization and Recovery Unit. Duane's the go-to guy for hairs and fibers.'

As Sanchez shook his hand, she said, 'I think we saw you at the arboretum for the body recovery?'

'That's correct, ma'am. I understand you got an ID on the body. Congratulations.'

He turned to greet Eric, who murmured, 'How ya doin', Sparky.'

They gave each other a quick handshake that started with a regular clasp, then pulled out to a fingertip-lock before they made a fist-bump.

Sparks said, 'One of our examiners is on standby to receive images. He's in Denver to testify, so that bought us some time. If he was in Virginia, we could forget about him waiting for us.'

'Let's do this.' Scott handed over the evidence bag with the hair.

Sparks gloved up and broke the seal on the bag.

West said, 'What's happening here, exactly? Don't you have to send the hair out to Quantico?'

Scott said, 'Eventually, yes, but thanks to technology, we can get enough of what we need to submit an affidavit tomorrow instead of next week. Or next month.'

Sparks had put the tape lift onto a plain piece of white paper and was examining it under a magnifying glass. 'Okay, you've got a root bulb on the end that's adhered to the tape. I'm going to leave that intact for future testing and just cut a section from the other end. Okay with you?'

Scott said, 'Do what you need to do. You're the expert.'

Sparks reached for a camera with a digital back that was on the table. He brought over a light on a flexible gooseneck and illuminated the hair on the paper, placing a forensic ruler and a pre-prepared evidence label next to it before turning the hair over by the piece of tape to allow photographs from various angles. Then he used a scalpel to cut the hair beyond the tape and photographed it again.

He wrapped the cutting in a fold of paper and took it

over to one of the stations with a fume hood. He activated the hood, which emitted a deep hum, and put on a surgical mask. The others came over to watch as he selected a dark brown bottle with a poison warning label on it and used a dropper to put a single bead of its translucent golden liquid onto a glass slide. The bead was apparently gelatinous because it kept its shape on the slide, looking like a jewel.

Using tweezers with soft grips, Sparks placed the hair on the bead of liquid, which held it aloft. When he gingerly dropped a cover slide on top, the liquid was immediately drawn out to the edges of the slide, spreading the hair flat as it went.

Sparks left the slide under the fume hood as he sat back and pulled off the mask. 'It's not perfect.'

'What's in the bottle?' West said.

'Mounting solution. Allows me to look through the hair instead of just looking at its outer surface once it's back under the microscope.'

'And you need the vent because it's got poisonous vapors or what?' Sanchez said.

'Yep. You can get high as well as damage your brain if you're over-exposed. The solution does need a minute to cure – don't want to be looking at it under the scope only to find the cover sliding off. You can't exactly put it back on.'

West had craned his neck to look at the slide over Sparks's shoulder. 'How long's a minute?'

Sanchez punched his arm. 'You're living up to your nickname, Matty.'

Scott said, 'Oh I want to hear this.'

'Sweetzer—' Sanchez began.

West pointed at her.

Sanchez clammed up with a grin.

'It's a regular minute,' Sparks said. 'Should be ready now.'

He took the slide over to the microscope. Staying in a standing position, he bent over to look in the viewfinder while he manipulated dials on either side of the instrument.

'It is human,' he said. 'Head hair. It does have multiple racial characteristics.'

Scott said, 'What does that mean?'

'The hair is likely from a mixed-race person. I'm taking the shot now.'

Then Sparks crossed the room and tapped on a computer keyboard. The screen displayed an image of something that looked to Scott like a semi-translucent dark brown tree trunk, complete with knots and whorls down its edges and a tunnel running through its center. Sparks made a brief phone call and then addressed the others.

'Okay. I've emailed it. He'll make the comparison with the unknown hair they already have from the suitcase.'

After a moment, Eric said, 'Anyone want coffee?'

'What I need is a drink,' West said, following Eric to the door. 'But a coffee with a shitload of sugar might work.'

Sparks called out after them. 'Whatever you bring back has to stay on the table by the door.'

Scott watched Eric and West leave, and then took up a stool next to Sanchez. He propped his feet up on the bottom rung and tilted his chin up at her.

'So, Theresa, Sweetzer has a nickname for your partner?'

'Yeah.'

'Are they close?'

'No! They're, like, allergic to each other.'

'Allergic because they're actually into each other?'

'No, definitely not. Besides, I'd say the attraction for him lies elsewhere.' She gave Scott a meaningful look.

Sparks raised an eyebrow. 'He's not into Houston, is he?'

'Sparky,' Scott warned.

Sparks smiled and turned around to do something with the microscope.

Sanchez said, 'You and Matt do seem to have forged some kind of bond.'

'Not *that* kind of bond.' Scott sliced the air with his hand.

'Oh, I hope you're not *that* kind of person.'

'I'm not,' Scott said defensively. 'Can we get back to the subject of Matt and Steelie?'

Sparks swiveled around. 'Steelie Lander?'

'Yeah,' Sanchez answered.

'So, you've noticed it?' Scott said to her.

'It was obvious to me when they met. She's his type. Blonde, petite, feisty.'

'So did he ask her out when you were at Parker Center earlier?'

'No. I doubt it anyway.'

'What's he waiting for?'

She shrugged. 'He got taken for a ride by someone a year or so ago. He's been dating but he's still in that once-bitten-twice-shy mode.'

'So, he's not the love 'em and leave 'em type?'

'No way. More like the other way around.'

Scott and Sparks both winced, just as the laboratory door opened.

West called out, 'Heard anything yet?'

Sanchez shook her head. 'You bring any sugar?'

A cup in each hand, West just indicated his hip pocket.

'You wanna get those, Houston?' Sanchez said.

'Ha ha,' Scott said, standing up.

West reached the table where he could put down the cups. He threw the sugar packets onto the tabletop. 'Here. Save you two from fighting over me.'

'Yeah, no one wants to see that,' Eric said, taking a sip of his coffee.

The telephone by the computer rang. Sparks picked it up, then used a mouse to manipulate the image of the magnified hair on the screen as he listened, trading the mouse for a pen at intervals so he could take notes. He asked the caller to email something.

'Folks,' he said. 'The analyst puts the hair you just brought in as consistent with the cut hair recovered from the suitcase in color and morphology. In addition, those two hairs are somewhat more consistent with each other than they are with the decedent's hair, though all are largely consistent with each other barring the length issue. He's confident that all the hairs exhibit both Asian and European characteristics.'

The computer beeped and Sparks turned around. The screen was filling from the top down with an image of two hairs side by side as though taken by a comparison microscope. One side was marked *UNK#1* and the other *UNK#2*.

Sparks pointed at the second one.

'You'll recognize that. I had it up here earlier. The analyst compared that with the hair found on the suitcase, here on the left.'

Someone whistled in approval but Sparks said, 'Listen, if this is all you have to go on, you're gonna want to have the lab run a DNA comparison – and you need a known hair from your suspect. The sample you brought me today is only presumptively his because it didn't come from his head.'

Scott shook his head. 'Right now, we just need this to get a search warrant for his house. It'll be strong enough for that.'

West was grim. 'I can't believe I talked to that guy and missed this.'

'Well, you're gonna get another chance to talk to him, and with any luck, it'll just be the two of you, no lawyer.'

'I know Gorman's type,' Sanchez said. 'He won't want a lawyer. Thinks he can defend himself, thinks he knows how we work.'

'I think he does know how we work,' West grumbled.

'Let's prove him wrong,' Eric said. 'He doesn't know we lifted anything from his office or the suitcase. Let's get that warrant and take his house apart.'

*

Junior rewound the tape and pressed play again. That beautiful – matchless – voice came out of the speakers and he reclined the driver's seat to a restful angle, closing his eyes and letting it wash over him again. He felt like her voice could stop *his* voice from coming into his head. And he felt sure she had the power to absolve him before this last kill. There wouldn't be any more after this. There couldn't be. She would understand. She would stroke his hair, kiss his forehead, let him apologize. She would absorb and then dissipate his anger, as she always had. As her voice had always done. It was too late to talk to her tonight. Timing was everything. *Timing is everything!* He made a fist and the knife sliced his finger. He'd forgotten he was holding it. He groaned but at least he hadn't recoiled. He dug in the door pocket for a napkin and wrapped his hand. Then he sat up and twirled the volume dial, turning up the voice. He put his hand in its wrapping above his head. He didn't have any more napkins but it didn't matter if the wound bled through and stained the seat. It would just be one more forensic detail for the cops to find after he reached her and then was gone.

DAY TEN

FRIDAY

32

Scott and Eric had faxed the Gorman affidavit to Assistant United States Attorney Evelyn Edwards after Lance, their administrator, had told them she had a reputation in the Bureau's LA office for efficiency and flexibility when dealing with their kind of casework. What the Department of Justice website trumpeted about Edwards was slightly different: she was a defense lawyer turned prosecutor born and raised in Hawaii and one of the few Native Hawaiians in government office on the mainland. Scott and Eric were about to meet her for the first time, at the place of her choosing.

They were outside the entrance to the federal courthouse in Downtown, standing at the railing and watching the line file through the metal detectors: people on jury duty, security guards, lawyers pulling briefcases on wheels. Scott eventually turned his back on the building and leaned his elbows on the railing, looking beyond the roof of the County Law Library to trace the top of the *Los Angeles Times* headquarters and then left a little, trying to make out his own building, but it wasn't visible. The thought of how close he was to his apartment, and therefore a bed, almost pained him. He hadn't had much sleep due to writing and re-writing the affidavit, which had required summarizing their case so far.

He closed his eyes and let his head hang. 'Christ, I'm tired.'

Eric said, 'Did you get any sleep last night?'

'Barely.'

'I did offer to help you draft that thing.'

'I know.'

'I'll do the driving.'

'You're going to have to.'

'Here she is.' Eric was nodding at someone.

Scott turned to look. Edwards was carrying the jacket of her gunmetal-gray suit, revealing a white tuxedo shirt above a belt made up of interlinking silver hoops, its understated brilliance played up by its proximity to the utilitarian ID badge of the US Attorney's office suspended from a lanyard around her neck. Tan nylons on her legs disappeared into black high-heeled shoes, which clacked on the concrete as she approached, a letter-sized envelope in one hand and her other hand on her shoulder, stabilizing the strap of her black leather expandable briefcase. It must have been heavy because she was leaning slightly to the opposite side. Her dark hair was upswept on its way to a bun and her face showed laughter lines when she was closer, but she wasn't smiling.

'Gentlemen. There's your search warrant. It's for the Gorman condominium unit, its associated storage area, designated parking space if there is one and his car.' She spoke rapidly, her words clipped.

'Thank you,' Scott said, taking the envelope.

She drew a business card from the outer pocket of her briefcase. 'I'll expect to hear from you later today.'

He demurred. 'We don't usually—'

'This isn't Atlanta, SA Houston, and although I share a first name with AUSA Trent out there, we're not the same

304

person. This is the way we do it out here.' She smiled. 'You'll get used to it.'

Turning on her heel, she waved a hand in farewell as she walked away.

Eric gave a low whistle. 'Nothing like beginning as you mean to continue.'

Scott huffed and they began to walk in the same direction as Edwards.

'Of course,' Eric said, considering the prosecutor from a distance, 'she's begun by doing all the talking.'

'I noticed you didn't say anything either.'

'She wasn't talking to me.'

'She will be when you give her the update later.' Scott tried to slap Edwards' business card into his partner's hand.

Eric sidestepped deftly, hands raised. 'You can't pull that one on me.'

They climbed into the Suburban, which Eric had left parked in a space reserved for the LAPD.

Scott buckled up and held the prosecutor's card out. 'I'll owe you one.'

'You already owe me, like, five.' Eric pulled out from the curb, accelerated into the left lane, only to have to stop short at a red light. 'Get Gorman's address up on the GPS, would you?'

They weren't far from UCLA when Eric parked the Suburban across the street from Gorman's condominium. Scott took in the building. It was a three-story, peach-colored behemoth whose landscaping was dominated by tree ferns growing out from a carpet of impatiens. A wide driveway swooped down to subterranean parking. West and Sanchez's sedan sat at the curb nearby.

When the detectives emerged and unlocked the back, West made a fatigued gesture toward a cardboard box that held scene gear. Everyone selected a Tyvek jumpsuit, surgical gloves and booties, then Sanchez filled a single, larger evidence bag with a handful of smaller ones, and they moved toward the building.

Eric said, 'Campus police will let us know if the subject goes mobile?'

West finished a yawn. 'They've got me on speed dial.'

'Good. We don't want any surprises.'

They reached a pair of glass entry doors. The foyer beyond was all peachy-red Saltillo tiles and potted palms, the brass-fronted mailboxes for the units gleaming out from a white-washed stucco wall. Scott pressed the bell marked *Manager*. A voice came through the intercom.

'Yes?'

'Please come to the door. This is the FBI. We have a warrant.'

A man's face peeked out from behind one of the palms in the foyer. He came toward the door cautiously, walking almost sideways in his indecision, until he stopped completely. Scott and Eric held up their badges. The man opened the door a crack.

'I'm Special Agent Houston. This is Special Agent Ramos. We're here to search number 7. You need to unlock the door.'

'But it's Mr. Gorman's,' the manager said.

Eric waved the warrant. 'This is a search warrant, sir, and you will unlock the door of number 7. If you do not unlock it, we will break it down.'

'Oh, goodness,' he said, in the manner of someone who didn't make a habit of cursing.

Scott pushed past him and the others followed, leaving the manager to catch up with them as they headed for the door to the stairwell and started climbing.

Scott called back over his shoulder, 'Is it the second floor?'

'Yes, second floor, down the hallway. Oh, dear.' The manager continued to make small noises of concern but brought out his keys.

The second-floor hallway was lengthy and dark, the only light coming from a window set into the front of the building. There were four doors, two on each side. Scott and the others halted at number 7. The manager opened the door and daylight spilled out from within. The law enforcement officers put on their protective gear and Scott told the manager to wait.

They stepped into Gorman's unit. The entry gave way to a large open-plan space with wooden floorboards. The kitchen was to the left, the dining area straight ahead, and the living room to the right. The far wall held a row of large, southwest-facing windows and a glass sliding door. Sunlight was streaming into the unit on an angle from between rows and rows of potted plants, flowering vines, even some small trees.

The dining table was glass and four clear Lucite chairs were pulled up neatly against its reflective aluminum pedestal. In the living room area, the bookcases were designed to lean at an angle from floor to wall with space behind, and the stereo components were spread out on different shelves, not stacked atop one another. The kitchen had clearly been remodeled recently with freestanding industrial units that left every dish, pot, cup and can visible.

West whistled. 'This is not a guy who's into hiding things.'

Sanchez called out, 'This might be where he does some hiding.'

They joined her at a doorway down a hallway. The small room stood in stark contrast to the rest of the condo. Its walls were clad in 1960s-era wood paneling and the carpet was deep-pile and burnt orange. A child's rocking chair was on the floor among a scatter of aging, misshapen cardboard boxes spilling out their contents: old 45 records, black-and-white photographs with scalloped edges, pulp paperbacks with vivid covers.

'What is all this crap?' West said, stepping around the obstacles to get to the lone window. He pulled aside the black sheet tacked up over it. 'And what does he sleep on?' He instinctively waved his hand in front of his face when a shaft of light illuminated the dust disturbed when he had moved the makeshift curtain.

Sanchez was down on one knee, reaching into the first box. 'This isn't his bedroom. And some of the stuff in this box is from before Gorman's time.'

'Could belong to his parents,' Eric said.

'Alright,' Scott said. 'West, take the bedroom. Eric, take the bathroom and I'll do the kitchen.'

Fifteen minutes later, Scott was done. He'd searched inside the fridge, behind it, checked every cupboard, looked in the oven, been through the trash and dismantled the U-pipe under the kitchen sink. There was nothing there to link Gorman with poisonings, burials or students – nothing other than the benign leavings of a man with an interest in cooking from scratch.

He walked over to the sliding glass door and stepped onto the balcony. It was clean. Spotlessly clean despite having potted plants all the way around the perimeter. Scott had been expecting – hoping for – something that held a cache of poison. He was coming back over the threshold when Eric walked in shaking his head.

'I've bagged some hairs but the bathroom looks clean to me,' Eric said.

'That figures. Let's get down to the storage unit.'

The building manager led Scott and Eric to the underground car park where several cars occupied spaces against a wall fronted by large built-in cupboards, each door numbered. He pointed toward the cupboards like they had radioactive waste inside.

'Mr. Gorman's is number 4 but I don't have the key!'

Scott held his arm out to stop the manager from leaving. 'What's your name?'

'Phil. Phillip. Antonini.'

'Okay, Mr. Antonini. You can relax.'

Scott waited until Eric had the camcorder rolling, then he broke through the lock on number 4 with a bolt cutter. He held the lock, which was jacketed in fluorescent green rubber, and opened the door.

The storage area was about four feet deep, two feet wide and seven feet high. It held three gallon-sized jugs of windshield wiper fluid and a used piece of chamois, all of which were on the floor. Scott unscrewed the lid on each jug to ascertain that the safety foil was still in place. It was.

He met Eric's eyes and Eric turned off the camera.

Scott murmured, 'Call up to West. See if they got anything.'

He knew West would have already called them if they had found something.

He was just stalling, unwilling to walk away, unwilling to believe this was over. He stepped into the garage and surveyed the wall of storage units. All of their doors were locked with padlocks. Most of the locks were brass or stainless steel but two had a rubberized finish, one black, and one bright green. Scott looked down at Gorman's lock, still in his hand, then back to the green one.

They were identical.

33

When Steelie pulled her Wrangler up to the curb next to the UCLA arboretum, Detective Lloyd was already there with Don and Rebecca Hart, the three of them standing alongside Lloyd's unmarked car.

Jayne and Steelie had told the Harts to wear shoes appropriate for walking through dirt or mud. The couple had followed those instructions and dressed in jeans as well. Once Jayne and Steelie had greeted them, Lloyd led the way down the concrete path under the eucalyptus canopy, following it around to the right past the marked specimens of specialty succulents. It should have been a beautiful stroll but it didn't feel like that. When the path curved into the bottom of the U, they could see the stand of bamboo and Officer Dodd from campus police, who was waiting for them.

Lloyd introduced the Harts to Dodd and then the young man led the way off the concrete path, skirting the stand of bamboo until he reached the opening Detectives Sanchez and West had originally used when they found Regan's grave.

'Watch your step through here,' Dodd said.

The Harts walked behind him, with Lloyd, Steelie and Jayne following. As before, the warmth and noise of the afternoon all but disappeared as they went further into the bamboo grove. The effect of cool, cushioned silence was

311

complete by the time they entered the clearing where the grave had been. Detective Lloyd quietly informed the Harts that they were welcome to approach the hole, if they felt able. Everyone else stayed back as Don and Rebecca took tentative steps up to the edge, their arms around each other for support.

Once at the edge of the hole, Rebecca turned around to face them. 'It was kind of you to bring a wreath.'

Lloyd gave Jayne and Steelie a strained look, like, *Why d'ya have to go make my job even harder?*

Steelie looked right back at Lloyd. '*We* didn't bring anything.'

Lloyd's demeanor changed immediately and he launched forward, Jayne and Steelie on his heels.

Nestled in the space where Regan's body had lain there was a circular wreath made up of star jasmine in bloom twined among willow stems.

Lloyd pulled his cell phone from his waist while saying, 'I need everyone to move back from the edge. Try to step where you stepped coming in if at all possible.'

He used his phone to take a photograph of the wreath in situ. The faux camera shutter sound was audible, then the sound of a text being sent. Lloyd put his phone to his ear after that.

Rebecca hadn't moved an inch. She looked at Steelie, eyes wide. 'What does this mean? Is this . . . did someone leave this here for us to see?'

Steelie held her hands out, palms up. 'No one knew you were going to be here to see it.' Then she gestured for them to step back with her and Jayne.

They retreated to the edge of the clearing but everyone

312

could still hear Lloyd clearly as he reported new evidence at the site, first to his superior, then to Scientific Services as he requested a crime scene examiner be dispatched. He carefully stepped over to them when he was off the phone.

'I'm sorry, Mr. and Mrs. Hart. I'll have to ask you to leave at this time. The area needs to be cordoned off again.'

Don wasn't ready to go. 'Was the wreath from the university? Perhaps from the president? Some kind of acknowledgment of . . .' He trailed off.

Lloyd took a moment to choose his words. 'The wreath is not an official mark of condolence, no.'

Everyone heard Rebecca's sharp intake of breath. 'I thought . . . I was happy because it was something nice but it wasn't—' She made an anguished noise.

Don put his arm around her. 'So, the person who took Regan left this here.' He sounded like he was trying to get the whole situation under control again. 'That person has been here in the past few days? Is that what you're telling us?'

Lloyd's eyes looked pained. 'That is a possibility, but at this time, I do not know how that got there or who left it. We need to get the whole area examined. I'm going to have to ask that you keep this information to yourselves for now. The detectives in charge of the investigation haven't released any of this.' He regarded them. 'Do you both feel able to walk back up to the street level?'

The Harts nodded mutely but Lloyd apparently ignored that and addressed Officer Dodd. 'Officer, get transport to meet the family on the path right around front. You and I are going to stay to secure the scene.'

Dodd already had his walkie-talkie in his hand. 'Yes,

sir.'

Lloyd addressed Jayne and Steelie under his breath. 'Can you get mom and dad out to the main path or do you need a guide?'

'We can do that,' Jayne said. She and Steelie shook hands with him, then guided the Harts, who were completely silent but for a quiet whimpering sound that was escaping from Rebecca, through the path in the bamboo, then the path along the edge of the arboretum, and back around to the concrete walking path where a golf cart was parked with campus police officer Taylor at the wheel. An ambulance was also approaching, driving slowly, partly on the path and partly on the soft verge. It pulled up behind the golf cart and two EMTs emerged.

Officer Taylor walked up to the Harts. 'Mr. and Mrs. Hart, I'm Officer Taylor from campus police. I'll be giving you a ride back up to the vehicles but I've brought a couple of paramedics if you feel in need of medical attention before we go up.'

The Harts looked bewildered. Rebecca was taking very short, shallow breaths and Don had that taut look again.

Steelie suggested that they sit on the bench seat on the back of the cart, which faced outward, and let the EMTs check them over. They assented to this but didn't say more.

Steelie, Jayne and Taylor stood back to give them some privacy. They watched one paramedic have Rebecca lean down with her head between her knees. The other paramedic fitted an oxygen mask on Don after taking his blood pressure.

Taylor glanced at Jayne and Steelie. 'I forgot to ask if either of you need medical attention?'

'I'm okay, thanks,' Jayne said. 'It was worse for them, for all kinds of reasons.'

'My primary need,' Steelie said, 'is to get out of here.' She gestured at the beautiful surroundings. 'I've had enough of this quiet oasis in the city. I'm craving blazing sunlight, hot concrete, and a Krispy Kreme. Failing the donut, I'll take something really processed and life affirming, like a Twinkie.'

Taylor smiled. 'I hear you.' Then he responded to the EMTs, who were waving him over.

*

Scott was looking at the bright green lock hanging on the door of storage unit number 9 in Gorman's underground parking area. He turned around. Eric shook his head as he hung up from his call to West and Sanchez.

'Mr. Antonini,' Scott said. 'Whose storage unit is this?'

The manager stuttered, 'Th-th-that would belong to unit 2. Every unit just gets one storage locker.'

'I need you to check your records on that.'

Eric escorted Antonini upstairs and then returned with him to the garage. Eric reactivated the camcorder. 'Turns out that one belongs to Gorman as well. Got it as part of a deal years ago.'

'It was before I worked here,' Antonini volunteered. 'I didn't even know about it! Sometimes people get a deal so they get more storage space. Personally, I haven't made any such deals since I started working here.'

Scott ignored him, watching for the thumbs-up from Eric, whose eye was already focused on the camera's viewfinder. He hefted the bolt cutter and broke the lock, then opened the door and peered into the darkened room. He tensed.

Someone was hanging from the ceiling.

Scott tried to keep his flashlight on the body as he felt blindly along the wall for a light switch. The bare light bulb came on with a *ting*. Now he could see that it wasn't a body. It was a wetsuit whose bulbous shape looked exactly like a body. But Scott's heart started thumping even more painfully in his chest. Could this be *the* wetsuit? Worn by the man who tried to kill Jayne? Did it have a tiny bite taken out of it by the window of Jayne's truck? It took effort to not pull the suit down right then and inspect it himself.

He looked at the rest of the room. A metal shelving unit at the back bore what looked like empty jars. A basket on the floor held what looked like cuttings from the same flowering vine Scott had seen on Gorman's balcony. Leaning against the left-hand wall were several clean gardening tools, including shovels. It was time to call in the criminalists.

Scott and Eric sealed the storage unit door, made the necessary calls, and went upstairs. They found both detectives on their knees in the room with the burnt orange carpet, which was now covered in Gorman's belongings.

Scott said, 'We've got enough from downstairs to pick this guy up. The techs can do the rest of the search.'

West and Sanchez stopped to listen to hear Scott's recap but Eric crouched down and ran a hand over some photographs that had fallen out of a box. He spread them like a deck of cards, and then stood up, holding one of them.

'Scott, look at this.'

It was a faded color snapshot of two men standing

lakeside, each holding up a fish and fishing rod, their smiles and physical proximity suggesting familiarity with each other.

'What the hell?' Scott said. 'Is that Treat Bailey?'

'Looks like him to me,' Eric said with excitement.

'As in *the* Bailey brothers?' West said. 'The ones you were talking about?' Vinyl records snapped into pieces as he crossed the room without looking where he put his feet.

'But how did Gorman get a photo of Treat Bailey?' Scott asked. 'And who's the other guy?'

Sanchez put her hand out for the photo and examined it. She said, 'Judging from what I've seen, the other guy is Gorman Senior.'

She turned around to a pile of papers behind her and brought up a photo album. Opening it to the first page, she held it up, the clear plastic covering crackling with age at the spine.

'Look at this family photo.'

Scott said, 'That is definitely the guy who's standing next to Bailey with the fish.'

Eric said to him, 'For all we know, Bailey is extended family.'

'But the name Gorman never came up in the Bailey file.'

'Screw the file,' West cut in. 'I'm calling campus police. They can pull him right now.' He stepped away as he dialed his phone.

Scott asked Sanchez, 'Is Gorman the father's name or is our guy using his mother's maiden name?'

Sanchez shook her head. 'No, mother is Thi Le.'

'T-e-e-l-a-h?'

'No, first name is T-h-i; surname is L-e. And I did check

317

on Gorman Senior – he is Senior, by the way. Our Gorman at UCLA is Kenneth Gorman Junior. Father has no AKAs, no record. Died of a stroke in 2001.'

Scott pointed at the photo in the album. 'Okay, bag that. We can use it on interview while we're waiting for results on the evidence downstairs. Wait.'

Sanchez paused in the act of putting the album in the bag.

Scott opened it to the same photograph. 'This woman in the background. Do we think that's Thi Le?'

Eric took the photograph. 'She's almost not in the shot. Like she's just there to cook the fish.'

Sanchez rolled her eyes. 'Then it's probably her, having to be the good little woman.'

'She's not smiling like the men.'

'What's to smile at?' she said.

West was off the phone. 'Gorman's in the wind.'

Everyone talked at once but Scott was loudest. 'Weren't they watching him?'

West answered while dialing his phone again. 'They were watching the entrance to the building where his office is and they don't even know how long he's been gone. His car's gone and someone in his building is claiming he has a suitcase. Coworker said he was leaving as they were arriving for work and muttering something like, *I have to see her*—'

'I'll get a BOLO out,' Eric interjected.

'I'm already doing it,' West said, angling his phone closer to his mouth. 'Hey, Cindy, I need an immediate Be on the Lookout. You ready for the readout?'

He opened his hand to Sanchez, who whipped out her

notebook and placed it in his palm, indicating it was open to the necessary page. He walked off into the hallway, reciting Gorman's license plate number and physical description.

Scott said, 'If Gorman snuck out of his office, he probably knows we're onto him.'

'Could the manager here have warned him?' Sanchez asked.

Eric said, 'No, I confiscated his cell and locked him out of his office.'

Scott thumped his fist into his hand. 'We need to think about where he'd go. Who was it he wanted to see?'

They went out of the apartment and sealed the door. West wasn't in the hallway.

Sanchez suddenly blurted out, 'He said "her". That's gotta be his mother, right? She's the only family he has according to the background check I ran.'

'Where does she live?' Eric said.

'Koreatown.'

Scott said, 'She's in *LA*?'

'Well . . . yeah.'

Scott increased his pace down the stairs. They found West outside, directing an LAPD patrol car to pull up and block the driveway.

Scott stopped abruptly and put a hand on Sanchez's arm. 'Why'd Gorman take a suitcase if he's only going across town?'

'Maybe his mother is his next victim.' Sanchez's eyes widened as though she hadn't realized that until she heard herself say it.

'But why would he go after his own mother?'

'The fuck if I know,' Sanchez said hotly. 'I'll radio for the nearest car to get over to her location.'

West finished arranging for the uniforms to guard the evidence they'd just found, then he told the others that it appeared Gorman had left a memento at the Hart gravesite. He started to describe the wreath.

Scott interrupted. 'Tiny white flowers, you said? There's a vine like that on his balcony and a bunch of cuttings in his storage unit downstairs.'

'We'll have the crime lab match 'em to the wreath.'

Eric said, 'What's up with the wreath? Is he apologetic? Gloating?'

West was dismissive. 'Who cares? Especially now that the Hart parents saw the wreath when Thirty-Two One took them for the site visit.'

'Shit!' Sanchez was vehement. 'Those people have been through enough.'

'Let's get this guy,' West said.

The four of them pulled out of West Los Angeles, piercing the air with the cacophony of tandem two-tones and screeching tires as the detectives' sedan made a U-turn and fishtailed momentarily just ahead of the Suburban's front bumper.

34

Steelie had suggested 'retail therapy' as a way to offset the depression brought on by the arboretum site visit with Don and Rebecca. Jayne wasn't sure if looking for a replacement cell phone could count as therapeutic when none of the models mounted along the wall in the cell phone store resembled her beloved old flip phone, now resting at the bottom of the Silver Lake Reservoir.

'How about that one?' Steelie pointed at something large sitting on its own pedestal.

'What is it and why is it so big?'

'It's a BlackBerry. Used by Scott and Eric – and every post-9/11 Fibbie.'

'Why would I want that?'

A store employee who had been circulating stopped next to them. 'That's a very popular smartphone. It has a fantastic organizer, a calendar, a QWERTY keypad and full internet access.'

'Internet?' Jayne echoed.

'Yes, the phone comes with a data package.'

'Cool,' Steelie said enthusiastically. 'How much does a data package cost?'

'It depends on how much data you use. Many of our customers spend about $150.'

Steelie casually picked up the phone, whose retractable

elastic security cord extended toward her. 'And that's per year, as long as you sign another contract?'

'No . . . that's per month.'

Steelie let the phone go as though it had burst into flames. It snapped back to the pedestal, which rocked on its axis.

The employee steadied the display unit. 'The data package is on top of the usual monthly fees. It's very competitively priced.'

Steelie gave him a withering look and he melted away. She hissed at Jayne, 'Is he trying to tell us that Scott and Eric are spending upwards of, what, $200 a month just on their *phones*?'

'I'm sure they're not paying. The government will be.'

'That's worse. That means *we're* paying.'

Jayne looked around the shop, trailed by Steelie who was calculating how many taxpayer dollars it was taking to keep FBI agents in BlackBerrys with '*full* internet access' when most of their 'fat asses' were usually seated behind desks whose computers 'already *have* full internet access'.

In the time it took Steelie to blow a few more gaskets, Jayne chose a basic phone. Bright pink was the only color in stock but she signed another two-year contract and received a new SIM card programmed to her old number. She drew Steelie outside.

Steelie promptly stopped on the sidewalk. 'I've worked it out: a bazillion dollars. That's what we're paying to keep them in BlackBerrys.'

'Are you sure it's not a gazillion? A bazillion sounds a little low.'

'You can joke all you want, Jayne, but I'm going to be

doing some letter writing tonight.' She hopped into her Jeep.

Jayne sat in the passenger seat as Steelie drove east through Glassell Park. She tried to navigate around her new phone. It wasn't easy because the buttons were flatter than she was used to. The phone was sleek but not user-friendly. That was her review so far. She thought about paying yet more money for some kind of cover that could tone down the pink, and then she moved on to opening the large manila envelope that had come in the Agency mail they'd picked up from Carol earlier. The return address was the FBI building on Wilshire. The specific sender's name hadn't been added.

Raising her voice over the noise that accompanied the open-topped Jeep entering the 110 Freeway North, Jayne said, 'I think it's the MOU.'

Steelie gave the envelope a quick glance. 'Did Scott give you a heads-up it was coming?'

Jayne shook her head and pulled the contents partway out of the envelope, aware that the wind might whip away any loose sheets of paper. She peeked behind a cover letter from Supervisory Special Agent Turner and drew out a stapled document.

'Wow, Craig Turner's not messing around. He proposes compensating us beyond expenses . . . and he's included time at the DOJ's contractor rate plus travel coverage.'

'Interesting,' Steelie said.

'There's a whole section here on security that includes, believe it or not, a BlackBerry phone that we would use while on their business. Apparently, it would have a GPS tracker fitted in it so they could find us in an emergency.'

'Like the Fibbies need a tracker to find people.' Steelie changed lanes to let another car onto the freeway and accelerated. 'It's Big Brother. They're not even trying to hide it. And *we're* the ones actually paying for that BlackBerry. Does Turner take that into account in the rates?'

Jayne was reading the next page. 'How do you like the sound of this? Quote, casework that results in international travel will be compensated by per diem at the government rate for contractors in addition to standard compensation, end quote.'

'International travel? Let me see that.' Steelie put out a hand.

Jayne exclaimed, 'You're driving!'

Steelie returned her hand to the gearshift with a grin. 'Are they really thinking about using us overseas?'

Jayne put the document back in the envelope. 'I think Turner's just covering all the bases. But that's kind of an exciting thought, isn't it? Not having to do family interviews by phone just because the families are over a border?'

Steelie exited from the freeway and decelerated in short order for the first stop sign. The noise in the cabin dropped.

'Except it won't be our clients, Jayne, it'll be some government case.'

'Maybe that doesn't make any difference. We'd still be helping people.' Jayne looked contentedly at their surroundings. She liked Pasadena's freeway off-ramps. They were leafy and the pink geraniums seemed to bloom year-round.

Steelie put the car into first gear and turned the corner.

'Just yesterday, you were saying you didn't want to help people if it put your ass in danger. Has your ass heard it's on the line again?'

'I think Turner noticed that I wrote down the word "safeguards" when he said it in our meeting.'

'He did. In fact, I noted him noting you noting it.'

Jayne smiled. 'And speaking of asses, are you sure you won't risk yours and come with me to my mom's shindig?'

Steelie downshifted for the next stop sign. 'Let me put it this way. We're not even at the radio station yet and I'm already experiencing shortness of breath.'

'My mom won't do what she did last year.'

'You mean another episode of *Jayne Goes Speed Dating*, the hit show set, incongruously, in a public radio station.'

'She won't now that she's met Scott.'

'That's why *I* can't go in. I'm her next contestant.'

'She wouldn't try to hook you up. She knows you won't wear the obligatory dress, for one thing.'

'She'll try! I saw her sizing me up for one as soon as she found out Scott had left an overnight bag at your place.'

Jayne laughed.

'You don't have to sound so smug,' Steelie said, halting the Jeep at a safe distance from a pair of descending railway barriers. 'I can't believe you're finally off the hook, anyway.'

'There's nothing final about me and Scott,' Jayne said. 'But why don't you stop pretending to hate cops and try dating Detective West?'

'Matt?'

'Ask him to join you at bowling tonight.'

325

'He's too – I couldn't.' Steelie sighed noisily and slumped in her seat.

'You just hate getting down off your high horse. Admit it.'

Steelie checked her mirror, looked over her shoulder, and made a sharp right turn, putting them on a side street parallel to the tracks so they could continue moving.

She accelerated. 'For that little dig, my friend, I'm taking you on the shortcut to the station. You go deal with your mother.'

35

Scott was driving hard on the detectives' back bumper as they traveled west on 3rd Street, lights and sirens going on both vehicles. When Sanchez cut her sirens and put on her indicator to go south on Kenmore, Scott followed suit. Tall, wrought-iron fences uniformly enclosed the yards along a street where huge, old houses appeared to have been divided into multiple units. Partway down, two LAPD cruisers blocked the road. A couple of officers were standing around and Sanchez went to speak to them.

She returned to the others. 'Uniform has cleared the house and grounds. Gorman's not here, if he ever was. No one's questioned Thi Le, though. I think we should see if she can help us find her son.'

Scott said, 'I want to show her the photo of Treat Bailey. See what she can tell us.'

'Are you wanting to take the lead on this?'

'No. I'll only step in if I need to.'

They went through the gate to follow a packed earth path through lush vegetation where the air temperature felt cooler. They stooped to get past the low-hanging boughs of a loquat tree where a basket on the ground had been half-filled with the pale-yellow fruit, and then they skirted a frangipani. Scott recognized some of the same plants as those on Gorman's balcony. A whirring noise accompanied something swooping past their heads. Sanchez ducked, batting at the air.

'Chance,' West said from behind her, 'it's just a hummingbird.'

'Well, it should watch where it's going.'

A stucco two-story house painted a deep pinky-orange became visible. Standing on the front steps was a petite woman wearing a white T-shirt and beige three-quarter trousers. She was wearing rubber flip-flops and looked about fifty, though they knew Thi Le was in her sixties. Her dark hair stopped just below her ears. Her expression was open but worried.

Sanchez introduced herself and referred to the others as her 'colleagues'.

Thi gripped the handrail. 'My son is alright?'

Sanchez said, 'As far as we know, he is, but we do need to locate him as a matter of urgency. Do you have any idea where he might be?'

'He works at UCLA.'

'Ms. Le, your son's not at work and he's not at home.'

'I don't know where he lives.'

'You've never visited your son at his home?'

She shook her head in the negative.

'When was the last time you saw him?'

'I saw Kenny last in 1985. Since then, we only talked on the phone.'

'Was that when you and your husband divorced?'

She gave a knowing smile and waved a finger. 'No divorce. My husband pushed me into mailbox. I had to leave.'

'He pushed you . . .?'

'He said he was sending me back to Vietnam the same way I came to America, but I was not a mail-order bride. He only called me that. We married in Vietnam.'

'And your son stayed with his father after you separated?'

'Ken kept Kenny. Always.'

Sanchez glanced at Scott, who handed up the photograph of Ken Gorman Sr. with Treat Bailey.

'Ms. Le,' Scott said, 'Do you recognize the men in this photograph?'

Thi nodded. 'Yes, that's my husband and his friend from the Army. They saw each other when Kenny was small. After that . . .' She turned the photo over and returned it. 'After they saw each other, I didn't know what was in the food or even drink my husband made. For many years, I ate only from cans. I keep my food separate today even. My friends, they laugh at me.' She smiled up at the house.

Scott shifted. 'And why did you eat only from cans?'

'Ken said his friend gave him poison.'

'Do you know what kind of poison?'

'He said it was for killing animals.' She switched her gaze back to Sanchez. 'He said I was the "animal" in his house.'

Scott thought about how one of the drugs in the death penalty cocktail was what veterinarians used to put people's pets to sleep.

'Did your husband ever use the poison?' he asked.

'I never knew. I told him many times to throw it away, to not be stupid, but he said no. He told me I was the stupid one. *Stupid, stupid!*' She uttered the two words in a loud, American-accented sneer.

Scott was startled and momentarily lost his train of thought.

'That's how he talked,' Thi explained with a shrug.

Scott recovered. 'Would your son have kept the poison after your husband died?'

Thi shook her head. 'I asked Kenny one time. He told me he buried it because it is dangerous to put in the drain. It can kill fish if it goes to the sea.'

'When did he say he buried it?'

'Maybe two years ago. We spoke on his birthday. He said I didn't need to worry. He said he grew up and buried the poison. I was glad.'

Scott said, 'Thank you for your help, Ms. Le.'

But Thi wasn't finished. 'When you find Kenny, I want to see him. He's not a bad boy, just sad.'

'If you can wait inside, please.' Scott drew the others away and said, 'They're clearly estranged; she can't lead us to him but we'll want a written statement from her about the drugs.'

Sanchez said, 'I'll arrange a patrol car to take her to our station if you're good with that?'

Scott nodded and they started back down the path. He glanced back over his shoulder to West. 'Did the BOLOs go out beyond the airports? Train stations, bus stations?'

'Of course. We haven't had any hits yet.'

Eric said, 'What I don't like is the suitcase. Gorman has form with suitcases.'

Out on the street again, Scott rubbed his mouth. 'I don't like what his coworkers said. Gorman wanted to see "her". If it's not his mother . . . '

'It could be anyone,' West said.

Scott looked at him. 'It could be Jayne. Or Steelie. We need to notify them.'

Eric said, 'Tell them that Gorman is our prime suspect? We can't. Not Jayne, anyway – she's a witness. It would prejudice her for the trial.'

Scott's eyes flashed. 'There's not going to be any trial if Jayne's not around to testify.' He pulled out his phone.

'Choose your words carefully, Scott,' Eric cautioned. 'AUSA Edwards isn't going to thank you if you screw up her case.'

'Look, Jayne's met Gorman, which means that if he were to turn up at the Agency or just in front of her on the sidewalk, she's not going to treat him like a stranger, which'll buy him time. I want to buy her some time.' He hit a button on his phone. 'She was getting a new phone. Let's see if it's up and running.'

36

Jayne was about to go into the building that housed the KDIG radio station when her new phone rang. She put the hot pink contraption to her ear.

'Jayne, you got a phone. Good. Where are you?' Scott sounded somewhat breathless.

'About to walk into KDIG, why?'

'Is Steelie with you?'

'She just dropped me off. What's up?'

'We don't have eyes on those administrators you spoke to at UCLA. I want you to be vigilant.'

Jayne agreed to this and signed off with Scott, but she felt on a different wavelength as she took in the gorgeous Southern California sky and felt a breeze that was the same temperature as her skin. She wasn't prepared for the crush of people in the radio station's lobby, however. The noise level was considerable and she couldn't see her mother. She was about to step outside to text Marie when someone called her name.

Her mother's producer, Art, was squeezing past some people to reach her. He looked excited, his cheeks almost as rosy as his red KDIG T-shirt.

'Look at this turnout, Jayne! Can ya dig it?'

Jayne smiled. Art was like an uncle to her after the many weekends of her childhood spent at the station while

Marie was working there. She hugged him. 'You'll take any chance to use your slogan, won't you?'

He looked back at the room. 'It's Marie who's responsible for this. The draw for last quarter's fundraiser was tickets to the Hollywood Bowl. Not quite the same turnout, not quite same crowd. Of course, with this one, we added your mother's portrait to the flier.'

'Is she still using her photo from ten years ago?'

'Of course.' Art smiled. 'But no one notices the difference when they meet her in person.'

'She claims to have stopped time by drinking Noni juice. I've even had people ask me if I'm *her* mother.'

He looked shocked.

She patted his arm. 'I'm joking. It hasn't happened yet but it will soon. Where is the garden goddess, anyway?'

Art used Jayne's shoulder as a balancing post as he went up on tiptoe to scan the room.

'Oh, she's with that guy again. This one listener has buttonholed her twice. Every time I go to see if her drink needs a top up, she says, "Don't worry, darling, Ken's already taken care of me" and flashes me a smile. You know how she is. Come on, let's split them up.'

He took Jayne's hand and started to make his way through the crowd, calling out, 'Excuse me, comin' through,' as he went. When they came up against the outer limits of a particularly tight-knit bunch of people, they couldn't get further. Jayne peered over their heads and saw Marie listening to someone, then throw her head back as she laughed. Jayne smiled involuntarily, her mother's expression infectious even at a distance.

Art gained a few inches. Jayne leaned to the side and caught a glimpse of who was making her mother laugh so heartily.

She went cold, then hot in sickening succession. It was Gordon. From UCLA.

She clutched wordlessly at Art's arm.

He looked back at her. 'Heavens, Jayne. You look awful. Let me get you out of this crowd.'

'No! Art, get Marie away from the man she's with. Don't tell her I'm here. Just get her away from him.'

She sent him back toward Marie and then pushed right, trying to get a vantage point on Gordon as she fumbled with her phone. Her call went straight to Scott's voicemail. She re-dialed, and this time, Scott picked up. Hearing his voice made her throat close.

'Jayne? I can't hear you.'

She got some words out. 'He's here. Gordon's *here*.'

'Gorman?'

'What*ever*!'

'Are you hurt?'

'He's got my mother!'

'Is he armed?'

Jayne went on her toes but she still couldn't see anything besides the tops of people's heads. 'I don't know! Could he be armed? He's been getting her drinks!'

Scott's voice was muffled. 'Code Three, Pasadena, the radio station, KDIG, Kilo Delta India Golf . . . copy that, raise West, wait one. Jayne.' He was talking to her again. 'Listen to me. Stay calm. We're on our way. Do not, I repeat, do not let Gorman see you. Get out of the building.'

'I can't *leave*!'

'Yes, you can. We're three minutes from you. An ambulance is coming for Marie. Get outside and get somewhere safe away from the entrance. Keep your phone on you. Are you hearing me?'

Jayne shoved past people who looked startled by her aggressiveness and burst out the front doors, only to be enveloped by quiet and warmth. It was like a time warp from when she'd walked into the station, feeling that all was right with the world. Her head was pounding.

Somewhere safe, Scott had said. She ran around the corner of the building, put her back to the wall and sank to the ground. Within seconds, though, she knew she couldn't comply with Scott's orders. Her mother was in danger, like she herself had been at the reservoir.

With trembling fingers, Jayne dialed Marie's cell. No answer. She dialed Art's cell. Same thing. *Oh, God, he's killed them both.* She hurriedly pecked out a text message, focusing on the unfamiliar keypad, and then checked the screen. It read, *Fime pir gekby rmyesbew BOQ.*

'Stupid idiot!' she shouted.

She forced herself to slow down and re-do the text. *Come out front entrance NOW.*

She sent it to Marie and Art simultaneously, then put the phone in her lap so she could rub her hands together in an effort to stop them shaking.

After a minute or two, the noise of the open house reached her. Someone must have opened the front doors to the station. Jayne sprang up just as she remembered the phone but it was too late. She heard the unmistakable smash and clatter of a cell phone hitting concrete but she didn't look back. Cornering the building, she saw Art first.

He looked disheveled but he'd brought her mother, *thank Christ*. Then Jayne saw Gorman.

He was very close to Marie, his face obscured where he was leaning into her. Jayne stopped. *Something's wrong.* She strained her eyes, desperately looking for the weapon he must have been holding on Marie, then felt utter terror. Her mother had her mouth open and was wailing horribly. But it was becoming inhumanly loud. Only then did Jayne turn and see that emergency vehicles were streaming into the parking lot, their sirens blaring. Deafened, Jayne covered her ears and began turning back to her mother.

In a moment she would always remember in slow motion, she was ninety degrees through her one-eighty when someone with very strong arms stopped her cold.

37

Scott kept his gun trained on the target until West had pulled Jayne to safety. The last siren behind him was abruptly silenced. Scott shouted anyway.

'Mr. Gorman, move away – slowly. Keep your hands where I can see them.'

Gorman didn't move.

Marie was the agitated one. She was shouting, 'You don't understand.'

'Ms. Prentis, I need you to go to your right.'

She didn't go right. If anything, she and Gorman moved closer together as he spoke to her. Scott couldn't tell what Gorman was saying. He checked for Eric but his partner still wasn't close enough to tackle Gorman from behind, not without taking down Marie as well.

Scott briefly made eye contact with the older man standing to Marie's right like a deer in headlights.

'Man in the red shirt. Yes, you, sir. Move away. Get behind the fire trucks.'

At least Red Shirt Man followed his orders.

Scott said, 'Ms. Prentis, listen to me carefully. Is this man restraining you?'

'No,' she called out. 'That's what I've been trying to tell you!'

Gorman started to step forward. 'Let me—'

Then he stopped, apparently to unlink his arm from Marie's.

Eric pounced from behind. 'On your knees, Gorman! Get on your knees!'

Gorman went down as Marie exclaimed, grabbing for him, but Sanchez was already running in and she pulled Marie away. Gorman was wriggling and crying out, his face against the concrete. Eric put a knee in his back.

Covering Eric, Scott approached until he was above Gorman. He stared at the man's profile, picturing him in a wetsuit trying to end Jayne's life, trying to make a lie out of her, and out of him. To have that face in the same plane as the barrel of his Glock, just inches away . . .

Scott felt like a charge was about to ignite inside him, but now West was in the frame and that confused Scott. He didn't want to shoot West. Then he heard the Miranda warning as though from behind a waterfall and began to realize that West was handcuffing and arresting the man.

Scott was vaguely aware of West lifting Gorman to his feet and examining his ripped clothing and cuts.

'Houston.' Eric was watching him.

The noise in Scott's head subsided. He nodded at Eric, who acknowledged his nod with a furrowed brow.

Scott intended to put the safety back on his gun and put it away but his elbow wouldn't unlock. Then he caught sight of his knuckles. They were white around the grip of the Glock. He looked for Jayne. She was okay – more than okay: she was arguing with her mother while a couple of paramedics tried to examine Marie. But something else was happening. A woman had just pushed past Jayne. Jayne was turning and shouting but the woman was running at full tilt, her purse flying behind her. Now a man was running after her as though to stop her but the woman was screaming like a harpy, her target becoming obvious: Gorman. Gorman, with his hands cuffed behind his back. Scott found himself instinctively moving to protect Gorman, getting between him and the woman, who was now upon them. Scott tackled her at the waist but that didn't stop her arms from flying forward, her purse extending her reach. The purse hit Gorman on his averted cheek, its contents raining down his shirt front even as Eric tried to pull him out of the way. Scott had been forced back against West, who pushed him forward like a counterweight, which enabled Scott to plant his feet and wrestle the woman into submission only to find that she was now collapsing against him in tears.

And just then the man who had been running behind her arrived. 'You!' he shouted at Gorman, his face reddened, veins standing out on his temples and neck. 'You!!' And then he spat at Gorman's feet, hitting everyone else's shoes in the process.

'Ramos, get him out of here,' Scott commanded, his legs trapped by the woman half-draped on his feet.

'I'm trying,' Eric said.

West moved to help Eric and they dragged Gorman away.

Sanchez and Scott were left looking down at the two people now huddled on the ground.

Sanchez looked frustrated. 'Regan Hart's parents,' she said quietly to Scott by way of explanation.

'I got that,' he said. He gestured at a paramedic to come over. 'Bring a gurney,' he called out.

Jayne came up with the paramedic, waiting until the

EMT had taken Rebecca Hart's vitals and got her to sit on the stretcher that had been lowered to the ground.

Jayne put a hand on Don Hart's arm. 'Don. What were you doing here?'

He wiped his face but still looked about to burst into tears. 'We were—' His voice wavered. 'We were coming for a radio interview because we announced earlier today that we intend to sue the LAPD.'

'Oh.'

Sanchez said, 'But how did you know what was going on here when you arrived?'

Don looked embarrassed. 'We saw you and the other detective and we saw Jayne and we just knew. You had a guy in handcuffs. Who else would he be besides the man who ki . . . who killed our daugh—' He covered his mouth like he was going to be sick, then sank down onto the stretcher next to his wife.

The paramedic whistled loudly to get a colleague's attention.

Rebecca put her hand on her husband's leg. 'I got him, honey. I looked him in the eye and I got him with my purse. And you know how heavy that is.' Her lips twitched with the effort of smiling between tears.

He nodded but his eyes were filling too much. He covered his face and began sobbing. The sobs sounded like they had been building up for much too long. Rebecca put her arms around him until the paramedic gently moved her aside to get a blood pressure cuff on Don's arm.

Sanchez started to pick up Mrs. Hart's scattered belongings and put them back in her bag. Scott guided

Jayne back over to where Marie was being checked out.

Marie broke away from the paramedic. 'Scott. That young man didn't hurt me in the slightest. I don't understand why Jayne was castigating me for helping him. And why did that woman attack him? Will someone please tell me what is going on here?'

'Ms. Prentis – Marie. I'm sure you recognize that we need to satisfy ourselves that you're unhurt. Please let these folks do their job.'

She tilted her chin up. 'I see I have no choice. But I will need to speak with you when they're finished.' She allowed the paramedics to help her into the ambulance.

Scott took in Jayne's expression and body language. He could see that the adrenaline that must have kicked in when she thought she was going to have to single-handedly rescue her mother was receding. He guessed that what was left would be mixing with the raw devastation on show from Regan Hart's parents – a devastation that he was himself trying to push out of his mind because it had veered dangerously close to bringing him back to Kate Alston's parents. He knew he needed to consciously ground himself. Suddenly, he knew he would do that by taking care of Jayne. He was going to let her know she wasn't alone.

He squeezed her hand. 'Are you alright?'

She looked tearful but nodded and squeezed back. 'How did you get here so fast after I called you?'

'I was already on my way.'

'But why?'

'To check on you.' He watched her face.

That brought on a flicker of a smile. 'You brought three

fire trucks and four ambulances for that?'

'Actually, West brought those. Wanted to impress Steelie.'

And there it was. A genuine smile. A break from the sadness. She said, 'She's not here; it's her bowling night. But I need to call her. Can I tell her what happened here?'

'Yeah. Of course. In fact, can you ask her to come down to Parker Center? You haven't said anything to your mother about Gorman, have you?'

Jayne shook her head, patting first the pockets of her pants, then her shirt.

Scott leaned in. 'Anything I can help with?'

Now Jayne's face took on his favorite expression. It was a knowing and surprised smile, her eyes wide before she looked down with a blush. He felt he could spend the rest of his life just trying to make her smile like that.

'My phone,' she said. 'It's around the side of the building.'

'I'll get it.'

'It'll be in pieces.'

He looked at her face, then to the beauty mark on her throat, before whispering in her ear, 'I'm just glad you're not.'

Scott found the phone without difficulty. Among ferns and mulch, hot pink stood out. While the phone was nice, the color was loud and, frankly, girly. He wondered if Jayne had chosen it or if it had been the last one in the store. Then he smiled, liking the idea that, one day, he might find out.

He put the phone back together as he walked, threading

his way through the crowd that had spilled out from the open house. Local police were starting to take statements.

Eric intercepted him. 'Gorman's complaining of injuries from when I dropped him.'

'Figures.'

'We've got an officer doing photos now, then we can take him Downtown. He's not claiming injuries from Mrs. Hart's attack. He knew exactly who she was; doesn't want to press charges. It's a good thing she didn't have a weapon – like you did.'

Scott squinted. 'Her purse could give my Glock a run for its money.'

'All I know, partner, is that you and she both wanted to kill him. You're going to have to deal with this, you realize that, don't you?'

'Can we do this later? Or never?'

Eric held up his hands in surrender. 'I've spoken to the paramedics. Jayne's mother is good to go but she's reading like an uncooperative witness right now. What about the Harts? What do we want to do with them?'

'Uniform can stay to make sure they're uninjured. Then cut 'em loose.' Scott turned on Jayne's phone. It made a pulsating noise like a nightclub caught in a tin can.

'Whose monstrosity is that?' Eric said.

'Jayne's.'

'Really?'

The phone rang. Scott recognized the number so answered.

Steelie's voice came through loud and clear. 'Why are you on Jayne's phone?'

'Hello to you, too. Jayne was about to call you. Can

343

you get down to Parker Center in a couple of hours and pick up Marie?'

'Marie?'

'Long story, everyone's fine.'

'If everyone's fine, then why do I hear firetruck noise through the phone? I distinctly hear diesel engines. Are you at KDIG? What's going on?'

Scott exhaled. 'I am at KDIG. There was an incident here but we've apprehended our UCLA suspect.'

'Holy shit! Wow. I didn't realize how relieved I'd feel to hear that! But wait, what's up with Marie?'

'She needs to give a statement.'

'Oh no, I'm coming down to give her advice.'

'She's just a witness, Steelie. And Jayne's with her so all I'm asking you to do is take Marie home.'

'But is Jayne okay?'

'Yes. Trust me.'

Steelie still sounded doubtful. 'Well, who's taking her home?'

'Steelie . . .?'

'Yes?'

'Thank you.' Scott hung up before she could talk again. He rotated the phone in his hand as he looked over to where Jayne was being examined by a paramedic.

'What's up?' Eric said.

'Steelie just asked me who'll be taking Jayne home.'

'And . . .? Oh. It hit you like a thunderbolt that you're gonna take her – to your place.'

'It'll be fine.' Scott started walking.

'Houston, this is where you always get into trouble. You move too fast.'

Scott stopped. He stared his partner down. 'Not with Jayne.'

After a moment, Eric shrugged. 'Well, at least her initials won't change.'

'What?'

'When you get married. She'll still be JMH.'

Scott frowned. 'I'm not going to make her take my name. Not if she doesn't want to.'

'So, you've thought about it already.' Eric grinned, pleased that he'd caught Scott out.

38

An hour and a half later, Scott and Eric were waiting in the hallway outside the conference room at Parker Center where they'd first met West and Sanchez. West walked in through the doors at the end. He was carrying Styrofoam cups of coffee with two packets of sugar balanced on each lid.

He handed one cup to Scott. 'Sanchez is booking Gorman in. He said he doesn't want a lawyer so I'll pick up a waiver form for when we talk to him.'

'Like you don't already have one on you,' Scott said.

Eric's hand was on the conference room door. 'In the meantime, let's see if we can get Ms. Prentis to come to the party.'

Marie sat at the far end of the table. She looked cool and composed.

Scott said, 'Thanks for waiting, Marie. This is my partner, Special Agent Eric Ramos, and this is Detective Matthew West of the Los Angeles Police Department.'

West took a cup of coffee over to her. 'I know you said you don't take sugar, Ms. Prentis, but this stuff can be hard to take without it.'

She tasted the coffee while she held the sugar packets. 'Dear me, that is dreadful.' She placed the cup carefully some distance from her, looked at Eric and West, and said,

346

'I'm glad to meet you. I did see you both at the radio station and as I told you at the time, Scott, I was not harmed by that lovely young man.'

'Marie, we've been investigating Mr. Gorman in relation to a number of incidents and—'

'Yes, he told me you'd say that.'

Scott cocked his head to the side with interest. 'Okay. Tell me more about what he said.'

'After my producer insisted I leave the building, Ken told me that the police were after him because he had done something bad, as he put it. So, I insisted he come outside with me. It was too noisy to talk inside and I wanted to encourage him to turn himself in for whatever it was. I was not expecting to see the parking lot filled with police.'

'I see. You called him "Ken" just now. Did you know him before today?'

'No. Well, only slightly. We've emailed.'

West shifted in his seat.

'Regarding . . .?' Scott said.

'Regarding my upcoming special. I'll be recording a few episodes of *Weekends with Prentis* in Venezuela and yesterday we started asking KDIG listeners to send in their requests for what they'd like to hear about while I'm there. Ken wrote in and I responded, then I met him today for the first time.'

'I'm not following you, Marie.'

'And I can't see how this is relevant.' She regarded him levelly.

Scott knew he needed to try another tack. He couldn't make sense of Gorman's focus on Marie. Did he just target her because she was easy access at a public event? Was Marie a stand-in for Jayne in some plan Gorman had? 'Is he aware that you're Jayne's mother?'

'Jayne? No, I don't believe so. Why?'

'What was the nature of his email?'

'He said he'd like to hear more about me personally, how I felt about my identity in relation to my grandparents. I imagine Jayne has told you about them?'

Scott began to discern a thread that linked to Regan Hart and Jared Stilson. 'Go on.'

'Well, my grandfather was a Spanish Venezuelan. He grew up in a family that held enslaved people, only to marry my grandmother, who was the daughter of two Ghanaians who'd been enslaved. They'd been sent from Ghana to Barbados before being freed in Venezuela in an exchange. This is hardly a secret now that it's on the station's homepage to promote the transmissions. We put it up yesterday.'

Scott felt sure about the link now. Something had triggered Gorman in relation to ethnicity or race – or mixed heritage. Something was here. 'And what did Gorman talk about today?'

'That he felt we had something in common because of our family background but he thought I experienced the world differently. He wanted to know how to be comfortable in his own skin, as though there was some formula. Let me think . . . he told me about his mother, who is by no means enslaved, but that his father treats her as though she is and . . . treats Ken the same way.'

Scott's ears pricked up. 'He spoke about his father in the present tense?' If he did, that would speak very directly to a mental health issue beyond the homicidal intent issue. It would probably affect the prosecution. He watched Marie closely.

Marie had leaned slightly forward. 'Yes? Has something happened to Ken's father? I wondered if that was what he was trying to tell me. He harbors terrible resentment of him, seems to blame him for his lack of self-esteem as a person of mixed heritage.'

West's phone made a noise on the tabletop as it vibrated. He read a message, and then nodded at Scott.

Scott said, 'Marie, thank you for your cooperation. Can we get you something else to drink?'

'No, but thank you. Will you tell me what's going on?'

Scott stood up. 'I will, as soon as I can.' He followed Eric and West out of the room.

West pointed down the hallway and started walking. 'Forensics has promised my partner a report on the wetsuit from Gorman's storage unit within the hour. They've processed it, just checking it against the neoprene from Jayne's truck.'

West held a door open for Eric and Scott and they entered another hallway. He showed them into the room that had two-way glass onto the interview room where Kenneth Gorman Jr. was being held.

Looking at Gorman through the glass, Scott said, 'Who's taking lead?'

'I'm so touched you're asking,' West said. 'Because, of the three of us in this room, I'm the only one who actually works here.'

Scott rolled his eyes.

Eric chuckled. 'I'll observe from here; get any updates from Theresa.'

Scott and West then went in to sit across from the suspect.

West took his time filling out a basic detainee form. Gorman watched this, which gave Scott a chance to study him. Barring the bored expression on his face and the scrapes on his cheek, he was a nice-looking guy. His straight hair was dark brown with a lighter, chestnut color on the crown and his face had some plumpness. Scott thought it was Gorman's hair in combination with his eyes, or maybe it was his high cheekbones, that could allow someone to place his ethnicity as Asian. Then Scott wondered how much meeting Thi Le was playing a role; he saw the family resemblance between mother and son. The red hair on Gorman's chest – evident due to the Tyvek suit he had been made to wear when his clothes were taken for evidence – said 'white guy' in Scott's mind, however. He scanned Gorman's arms, visible where his hands were shackled to the table. The hair there was also red.

West stopped writing and looked up. 'Mr. Gorman, I understand you've said you don't want a lawyer.'

'I want to confess.'

'Hang on. You do have the right to a lawyer, Mr. Gorman.'

'I don't need a lawyer.'

'You're facing serious charges. Most people need a lawyer at this stage.'

'I'm not most people.' Gorman looked at each of them. 'I've looked this part up. You give me some kind of form and I can sign it. I'll need a free hand, though.' He jerked a hand up and the shackle banged against the table.

Scott moved his feet inside his shoes, readying his legs

for movement. While the sight of the suspect no longer made him sick with anger, he hadn't forgotten what Gorman was capable of, plus, he'd seen Gorman's build earlier: like a runner, lanky but surprisingly muscular.

West lined up the paper with a pen in front of the suspect, explaining that he was waiving his right to an attorney, and freed one of his hands. The second Gorman's signature was on the line, West shackled him again.

The detective said, 'Now, Kenneth, what exactly do you want to confess to?'

'I killed two students at my university. I also caused the car accident of an alumnus.'

'I need names.'

Gorman gave a deep sigh. 'Regan Wei – that's W-e-i – Hart and Jared Alun – with a u – Stilson. Those are the students.'

'And the car accident?'

'That was a Jayne – with a y and an e – Marisol – no e – Hall, Class of 1992. I forced her into the Silver Lake Reservoir. I suppose I stalked her, too, if you want to get into details.'

Scott had been irritated by Gorman's pedantic spelling of Jayne's name, like he knew her and they didn't. He jumped in with a question. 'Did you intend to kill Ms. Hall?'

Gorman gave Scott a curious smile. 'Did you intend to kill me earlier? She's your girlfriend, isn't she?'

Scott's leg twitched under the table but he managed to keep his face blank. 'I repeat, did you intend to kill Ms. Hall when you forced her into the reservoir?'

Gorman looked around the room as though searching the sky. 'Well, let me see . . . I guess the best way to answer that question is, who knows what we intend versus what the universe intends for us?' He brought his eyes to Scott's. Then he laughed, the shackles on his wrists banging against the table as he endeavored to clap his hands together.

Scott was almost sure that a psych eval was going to be needed but he persisted. He needed to know. 'Why did you do it?'

Gorman's laugh tapered off and he became serious. 'Well, the alumnus, your *girl*friend, she came to my office. I'd seen her from a distance when the Stilson corpse was found and I recognized her and the other one with her right away, Lander, because they were featured in the university magazine a couple of months ago. I remembered what I'd read about their backgrounds, their drive to uncover hidden crimes, help grieving families – all of that stuff. If anyone was going to make a link between Jared and me, it would be those two.'

Jesus Christ, Scott thought. *Jayne and Steelie's unique skills made them targets – again? This was Atlanta all over again?* And if this really was just 'different shit, same smell', then he was going to make Gorman draw him a picture. 'Why just Ms. Hall and Ms. Lander?'

'Well, the only link between me and the students I killed was the club Mix it Up. I'd nixed the club – buried it. So, to get to me, you'd first have to figure out that the students' race was what got them killed – and still find out about the club. I wasn't scared of campus police, the LAPD, or hell, even you FB-fuckin'-I agents on that front. But based on what I'd read about those two Bruins . . . they were a problem. And then the alumnus was in my office way sooner than I'd expected. I thought I would have a few

352

more days. I had to get rid of her and I had to do it right away before she had a chance to give any information on that club to you. It was hasty.'

He looked preoccupied and then stared up at Scott. 'I didn't enjoy it! It wasn't *fun* to get her into the reservoir but I'd run out of the drugs because of the . . . accident I had at the Lander residence.'

Scott sensed West tensing and tried to head him off without conveying to Gorman that he didn't know what the hell he was talking about. 'Ms. Lander's house.'

But Gorman was in his own world and hadn't seemed to notice West getting twitchy. 'I spilled too much of it when I went to put her down. I would have still had some, but before I'd used it on the two Dilutes, I'd practiced on some stray cats. It's best to practice and do research for important things in life.' He nodded to himself as though to confirm he'd repeated a phrase correctly.

West exhaled audibly before he spoke. 'Dilutes?'

'Yes, Dilutes. My father has taught me all about how dangerous they are.'

'Can you elaborate on that?'

Gorman sat up straighter in his chair and took on a professorial tone. 'Dilutes are people that look white and have white names but are the product of race mixture between white people and anyone else. They're not like me. White people can tell I'm not full white. But Dilutes are dangerous because they can infiltrate white society and take it apart from within. They can influence other white people to do things not in the interest of their race.'

'Like . . .' West opened his palm upward. 'What things?'

'Well, *you* should know! Have liberal attitudes, *be*

liberal, be vegetarian – even vote for a black man if he ran for president! My father says Dilutes can't be allowed to live because bit by bit, drop by drop, they will dilute the white race. He learned all this from his Army sergeant, Staff Sergeant Bailey. Mr. Treat Bailey. This was their mission ever since they came back from 'Nam. They planned all this out there, sitting in the foxholes, because of Loving. He told me Loving was the trigger. All kinds of people were going to start marrying across color lines. Having kids. They knew it was the beginning of the end for white people. Dilution would begin. The only antidote to dilution is concentration.' Gorman paused, apparently thinking over what he'd just said. Then he nodded and started again.

'Mr Treat's the one who got the poison, well, it's really a concentration solution. He gave it to my dad years ago but Father needs my help to do his part. His diabetes makes it hard for him to walk. That's why he's taught me everything, showing me how to find Dilutes and use the concentration solution. He's made sure I know how to do injections; I help him with his.'

West had been scribbling notes and now waited to ensure Gorman was done. Then he said, 'So, your father identified Regan Hart and Jared Stilson as targets?'

'No! Argh! *I* chose them based on Father's Operation Concentration chart. He had it in his command center. He had added people to the chart but they were Hollywood celebrities. We couldn't get close to them. But in my job, I could access student profiles. Find the Dilutes by seeing their parentage, seeing their race choices. It was still a long time before anyone came to UCLA who fit the specifications. I spent so long going through student profiles before they enrolled. And then I got two. I was lucky. Very lucky in fact, because some student wanted to start a club that attracted Dilutes like flies to a sticky strip. Saved me a lot of work.'

West nodded like that made sense. 'How did you administer the poison to Stilson and Hart?'

'You don't know?' Gorman looked pleased. 'It's amazing what you can get away with on campus if you've got identification. It doesn't even have to be a real ID. The kids are so trusting. If you can get in the front door of the dorm, you're safe . . . that's all I had to do, was get in the front door. I told Stilson that he'd been chosen to feature on a Student Affairs magazine cover. Him and others. I had him meet me at the patch of land for the photo session, early morning for the best light, and I injected him there. Right over the hole in the ground. Hart, now . . . that was a different story. She was wary. I had to tell her that we'd had a complaint about broken furniture in her dorm room and that her parents would be charged if we couldn't resolve it. She was . . .' he laughed softly at the recollection, 'mortified. She let me in . . . I injected her there but couldn't leave her in the building. Her suitcase was handy. I took her clothes out, put 'em in a donation bin, then left the building with her body right in the suitcase. Stashed her in the arboretum. Probably passed about a hundred people with her inside. See? Lucky.'

Gorman suddenly looked into the distance. 'Until . . .' He went silent.

'Until?' West prompted.

Gorman eventually spoke but his voice had lost some of the forcefulness. 'After I put those two Dilutes down,

355

I knew Father approved. But then I heard Ms. Prentis yesterday – I listen to *Weekends with Prentis* without fail, she's amazing, I have a radio on my balcony and I listen to her while I work on my plants. I record the show and listen again, through the week. I go to sleep to her voice . . .' He closed his eyes for a moment and then opened them.

'Anyway, she said some things . . . I mean, I always thought she was a Latin American of the purest background, Spanish I thought. But then she said she had a grandmother from Africa. I was so shocked. *Africa?* Of all places.' His eyes glistened.

'She said it was the jewel in her crown. Those were her very words.' A tear overflowed and tracked down his cheek.

When he spoke again, it was a whisper. 'It wasn't a stain, like Father said came from my mom and her people. And . . . that made me think maybe Father's wrong about everything . . . or some things, and maybe I shouldn't have killed those Dilutes like that . . . so, I made the wreath for the girl and that felt right. Then I started worrying that Father won't love me anymore, right when I finally got his approval . . .' The tears were flowing freely now and Gorman was looking at West and Scott to see if they understood.

Scott was trying not to look at West. He said, 'Kenneth . . . your father is dead.'

Gorman's face contorted further. He tried to point at his chest with his shackled hands. 'Not in here.' He leaned down so he could point at the top of his head. 'Or in here. Or here.' He was pointing into his open mouth.

He started to make an odd noise, his head now on the table, the fingers of one hand in his mouth.

It was a moment before Scott realized the man might be gagging himself. He was about to get up to check when the door burst open and Evelyn Edwards walked in, her face stern.

West immediately held the waiver up.

She took it and peered at Gorman, who had sat up, his face streaked with mucus and tears, his mouth red at the corners where it had been stretched wide by his hand, now dripping with saliva.

She said, 'Mr. Gorman, I'm Assistant United States Attorney Evelyn Edwards. We're arranging to get you some dinner; you can get cleaned up and then we'll resume this interview.'

She gestured to someone outside. A uniformed officer came in and took up a monitoring position by the door. Eric emerged from the viewing room as Scott and West followed the attorney into the hallway.

Edwards held up the waiver and looked at each of them. 'Is this on the up-and-up?'

West raised his hands. 'We didn't beat him up, honest.'

She looked at him. 'Detective West, I presume?'

He nodded.

'I understand Mr. Gorman's complaining of injuries,' she said.

Eric said, 'Those are from when I cuffed him in the parking lot. We've got photos. You'll see there are no new injuries since then.'

'I want those photos but I would still prefer to see him with a lawyer in there,' Edwards said, relenting a little. 'His mother's in the lobby. Someone needs to see her. I'll rustle up a PD for him.' She took off down the hallway.

West stared after her. 'She's getting *him* a public defender? Did I miss something? She *is* a prosecutor, isn't she?'

Scott sighed. 'She wants some physical evidence in case Gorman's intending to flip, plead not guilty and have his brief file a motion to suppress the confession he just gave us on a platter. Or worse, go with an insanity defense.'

Eric's face fell. 'You just seriously killed the mood.'

Scott started walking. 'Let's get those photos for Edwards. Try and get in her good books.'

39

Scott, Eric and West could see something had developed the minute they walked into Robbery-Homicide. Sanchez was on the phone, her feet up on her desk. She smiled. She waved.

West hovered over her until she hung up the phone. 'Chance. What's happening?'

She put her feet on the floor. 'Crime lab came back to us with a prelim on the evidence at Gorman's condo. They've found trace in Gorman's wetsuit that could only have come from the Silver Lake Reservoir, from some treatment chemicals the city tried out there the week before Jayne Hall's truck went in. And they've got trace of one of the target drugs inside the seal on a jar in the storage unit.'

'Does Edwards know?'

'That was her on the phone, thanking you guys for the photos of Gorman from the arrest. That'll kill the police brutality claim. Gorman's brief – yes, he has a lawyer now, Matty, don't interrupt me – has just said he'll take a deal if the US Attorney's office wants to offer one. And that's on three charges, two of murder and one of attempt. There's nothing doing with Ms. Prentis from the radio station incident, though. This guy didn't touch her drink, claims he doesn't have anything left of the poison.'

'That's what he claimed on interview,' West said.

Eric said, 'Why was he running around with a suitcase then?'

Sanchez glanced at her notebook. 'Doing just that: running. Suitcase held his life savings in cash. He was going to disappear in Mexico after getting what he called "absolution" from Ms. Prentis. Had no idea she was Jayne's mother.'

'Bullshit,' Scott said.

Sanchez shrugged. 'If you go on the KDIG website or anywhere else, she's Ms. Prentis not Mrs. Hall. She doesn't use her married name as her professional name.'

'I still think it's bullshit.'

'You can question him to your heart's content tomorrow. And Agency 32/1 had a report as well: the Harts asked them to convey that they have decided against suing the department over the investigation into Regan's disappearance. The parents are focused on Gorman now. Lieutenant Early is *very* happy.'

Scott asked, 'Where are Jayne and Steelie, anyway?'

Sanchez pointed at the papers on her desk. 'I got Ms. Hall's written statement, so when Ms. Lander arrived, I sent them to the conference room with an escort.'

Scott was about to say something but stopped because West made a sudden about-face and headed for the door.

*

Jayne thought 'loitering' was the best way to describe what Detective West was doing in the hallway. He dismissed their escort, nodded at Jayne and then addressed Steelie in an unnecessarily loud voice, given that he was standing inches from her.

'Could I take you to dinner some time?'

Steelie regarded him levelly. 'Twenty dollars says it'll end in tears.'

'Make it forty – and bring your money. I'm going to enjoy winning this one.'

Feeling like she was at a tennis match, Jayne looked from West back over to Steelie and couldn't believe her eyes. Steelie Lander, who always had something to say about everything, was speechless.

West made a little snort of satisfaction and headed off down the hallway, breezing without a word past Scott, who had just walked in.

Scott turned to look at him, walking backwards for a moment before facing the two women again. 'Steelie, thanks for coming to get Marie. She's just in here.'

He opened a door and sent Steelie ahead while stopping Jayne. When he'd closed the door again, he said, 'Jayne, my apartment is about five minutes from here and I haven't slept in the past twenty hours.'

Jayne tried not to show the huge wave of disappointment she felt at the thought of parting from Scott even though she understood. She tried for a bright tone. 'That's fine. Go home. I'll get a ride with Steelie.'

'No. What I'm trying to ask, if I can just get the words out, is: would you come home with me?'

'Oh! Um, yes.'

It warmed her that he looked suddenly relieved.

Steelie emerged from the conference room with Marie in tow. Scott took Marie by the elbow and steered her to walk with him.

'Marie, I owe you an answer to your question from

361

earlier. We believe Kenneth Gorman was the person who forced Jayne into the reservoir.'

Marie's hand flew to her chest. 'Good *Lord*. Are you sure? I can't believe it. Do you have evidence?'

Behind them, Steelie murmured, 'I've trained her well, haven't I?'

Jayne whispered back, 'She does sound like a lawyer.'

'I can imagine her new show: *Gardening . . . on the Inside*.'

'Prison gardening, Steelie? Do not even joke about that, you know how she is.'

Scott had kept Marie moving through the door at the end of the hallway, on to the stairwell, and up and out of the building. By the time he was handing her into Steelie's Jeep, Marie was smiling. She kissed Jayne's cheek so hard that she left a depression in it. Then she rubbed the spot to remove her lipstick stain. Jayne wasn't sure what this was about until her mother spoke.

She tilted Jayne's chin up with her hand, to match the tilt of her own. 'I, Marie Valencia Prentis Hall, proud Venezuelan woman, am going to call your father.'

Jayne hated it when her mother used all the names. This wasn't about the case: it was about her daughter going home with a man, especially on a Friday. Jayne's only defense was exaggeration.

'No, Mom. It's the middle of the night in Caracas; Dad will think someone died.'

'It is not the middle of the night there and Elliott doesn't have to teach tomorrow morning, so he'll be awake. Sorry, darling, this is my news now.'

Steelie revved the Jeep's engine, cutting off further

conversation, and Jayne watched them depart. Scott held open the door of the Suburban for Jayne. After driving for a bit, the automatic door locks retracted with a *thunk*. Jayne began to notice how comfortable and solid the car felt. She looked around at its appointments but then just looked at Scott.

She said, 'I obviously heard what you said to my mom about Gorman being the one who forced me into the reservoir.'

Without taking his eyes off the road, he reached for her hand. 'I just wanted to stop her talking about him like he was a good guy. For your sake.'

Jayne let him hold her hand in his on top of the center console. 'I know. But you didn't say anything about Jared and Regan.'

'Well, I couldn't. Not to your mother.'

'But you do have reason to believe Gorman was the person who killed both of them?'

He squeezed her hand. 'We do. You sound worried. What's worrying you?'

Jayne looked out the window. 'I'm aware you can't talk about this in any detail but . . . was he working alone?'

'Yes. Jayne, you have nothing to fear. It's over.' He kissed the back of her hand. 'Now. What did Steelie say to West?'

Jayne's surprised laugh broke through her tension. 'Oh, you know all about this now, do you? You claimed to be clueless the other day!'

'I know a little more than I did then. Did he ask her out?'

'Yeah, and she said yes.' Jayne thought back to Steelie in the hallway of Parker Center. Her speechlessness. 'Actually,

I think he just beat her at her own game.'

Scott pressed the remote to open the gate to his building's underground parking. 'I hope they get past the first date. Matt's a good guy.'

When they got upstairs, Scott only turned on a few lamps, allowing a magnificent night view of Downtown and the classic white neon sign of the *Times* headquarters.

Jayne took in the huge windows that soared from knee-height practically to the ceiling, their windowpanes delineated by metal mullions. The wall was unpainted brick while the ceiling was a mix of exposed ductwork and crossbeams, except for the kitchen, which had a dropped ceiling and was separated from the living room by a long counter.

Scott opened a closet near his front door. 'Let me take your jacket.'

Jayne shrugged out of it and walked in further, glancing at the well-appointed kitchen as she went past. 'This is really nice, Scott. Is it completely open?'

'The only concession to the traditional idea of rooms is this wall. The bedroom is on the other side.'

As Jayne entered the living room, she saw how the furniture floated in the center of the space. It looked inviting: comfortable chairs and a couch situated over a large rug, flanked by lamps that must have been plugged into outlets in the floor. It was a plush oasis in the polished concrete space. The far end of the room appeared to be on its way to becoming a study. There was a desk, low bookcases not even half-filled, and a lot of filing boxes stacked up next to cardboard boxes that had been emptied and flattened.

Scott came to stand next to her. 'It's still a bit of a mess.'

'It's not. How did you choose this building?'

'It was the option closest to your place.' He walked back toward the front closet.

Jayne sank down into a chair. This seemed like a really big deal and she needed to make sense of it in light of everything she knew, or thought she knew, about Scott's feelings for her.

He returned, holding what looked like a toothbrush still in a packet. 'This is for you and I've got fresh towels as well.' He paused when he saw her face. 'What?'

'Scott! I have, like, a *hundred* questions about this. About you! What's in your head!'

'Well, all hundred of them are gonna have to wait till morning.'

He put his hand out to her and she stood. Pulling her close, he murmured, 'And when I say "morning", that doesn't have to mean tomorrow morning.'

Jayne couldn't stop smiling, even as he kissed her. When she started laughing, Scott gave up and kissed her neck, right in the center of her throat, and she promised herself that she would ask him – some morning – what he found so fascinating there.

Acknowledgements

Fulsome thanks to Anna Soler-Pont and Carla Briner, my fantastic literary and film agents, and all at Pontas Agency. This is happening because of you.

Amy Baxter and Helen Huthwaite, my editor and publisher, have a clarity of purpose and a professional approach that has enlivened me as a writer and storyteller. Thank you to Amy and Helen and the whole HarperCollins Avon team, on both sides of the Atlantic.

I have set parts of this book at the University of California, Los Angeles because my own summer sessions at that campus and the stunning Mathias Botanical Garden together set my imagination alight.

Credit for the phrase, "like karate-chopping through soft butter," goes to Alex Clain of The Maret School who spoke those words in class over thirty years ago; while credit for "more light, less heat," goes to the attorney Mike Gennaco who used the phrase in conversation not quite so long ago.

Lieutenant Tom Prevo of the Nebraska State Patrol gave generously of his time to educate me about NCIC files when I was a graduate student. I have attempted to honor him by using his name in this book but there the resemblance ends.

I am so grateful to Stephen Mwinyipembe, Bob Koff, Jacob Koff, Silva Masrelian, the late Amy Uyematsu, Jan Sidebotham, Peter "Stick" Sturtevant, Jr., and Kevin Sairafian.

My nearest and dearest listen to it all and read it all. Special thanks to my little one for enthusiastically asking me if Jayne and Steelie are "real". To Msindo, Kimera, Jon, Sam, Anne – and David, from your perch on my shoulder: *Thank you*.

Jayne and Steelie
will return